Praise for Michael Frost Beckner & SPY GAME

"Pass the popcorn!"
—*Amazon Editors' Pick*, Vanessa Cronin, Sr. Editor

"Brilliantly executed...First-class spy novels with a smart, gritty atmosphere."
—Charles Cumming, *New York Times & Sunday Times Best-selling Author of KENNEDY 35* and *BOX 88*

"A thinking man's thriller... A real adrenaline blast... I loved it!"
—Robert Redford

"There's nobody quite like Beckner. Cerebral and unvarnished...with dialogue so sharp it's like dancing on hot coals. You'll swallow this book whole."
—I.S. Berry, *Edgar winning Author of THE PEACOCK AND THE SPARROW, A New Yorker & NPR Best Book of the Year*

"Michael Frost Beckner serves up a judicious blend of showy action, political

intrigue, ticking-clock suspense, and CIA one-upmanship for mainstream entertainment."
—*Variety*

"There is nothing like *The Aiken Trilogy...* Laced with absurdity & stylistically daring ... Beckner [is] a razzle-dazzle showman at the top of the thriller heap."
—Editor's Pick, *Publishers Weekly*

"Beckner is one of the most unabashedly duplicitous writers I've ever encountered ... Brilliant work."
—Stephen England, *Best-selling Author of the SHADOW WARRIOR Series*

"Michael Frost Beckner is the rarest of spy novelists, a beautiful and compelling writer who also has a mastery of tradecraft and a deep understanding of how espionage really works."
—Joe Weisberg, *former CIA Officer and EMMY Award-winning creator of The Americans*

ALSO BY MICHAEL FROST BECKNER

HITLER'S LOKI

Berlin Mesa

SPY GAME

The Aiken Trilogy

Muir's Gambit

Bishop's Endgame

Aiken in Check

KALEIDOSCOPE: A SPY GAME SERIAL

4th of July

Birthday

Halloween

Thanksgiving

Christmas Eve

A NATION DIVIDED

Volume I: From West Point to the Seven Days Battles

Volume II: From the Battle of Second Manassas to Chattanooga

Volume III: From the Battle of The Wilderness to Appomattox

Kaleidoscope

A Spy Game Serial

Part 5:

Christmas Eve

Michael Frost Beckner

MONTROSE STATION PRESS

Las Vegas
2025

Published in the United States Montrose Station Press LLC, Los Angeles.

ISBN 9798992993226 ((paperback)
ISBN 9798992993219 (ebook)

Printed in the United States of America

Jacket design by Andrew Frost Beckner

For Daisy

KALEIDOSCOPE:
CHRISTMAS EVE

"Love is a trick played on us by the forces of evolution... Only Might is Right."

—T. H. White, *The Once and Future King*

Prologue

SILAS KINGSTON SLEPT WELL. Rarely a sleepless night. But while his body—and presumably his mind—gained the rest good health required, rarer than sleeplessness was the experience of sleep at all. Each night, sleep met Silas Kingston like death meets the atheist. Instant, absolute, existent nil. Silas couldn't remember when he last encountered the letting-go descent to slumber. A stranger to the pleasurable surrender into relaxation/revitalization, sleep functioned in Silas like an electrical circuit. A power switch.

On, Silas lay down.

Silas shut his eyes. *Off.*

Silas opened them—*on*—and it was morning.

If he awoke in the night from discomfort/discomfiture, awoke to an intrusive sound—

Doris's voice across the Foxtail Farm chimney top

—his mind light-bulbed. Silas dealt. Silas shut eyes. Opened eyes. Met the morning head-on.

For many years, had anyone asked—casual, polite, curious, or concerned— *"How did you sleep?"* His response came curt. *"No idea. Don't care."*

No one asked Silas anymore.

Silas Kingston's unusual condition first presented itself as a creeping absence sensed in the blur of his thirties, followed by a bleak realization in his forties: sleep had become nothing. Doris insisted he see a doctor. And then another. And then another. And those he half-listened to all agreed on one useless diagnosis: his condition was rare enough not to have a name.

No, it wasn't the *paradoxical insomnia* a couple bright-boys tried to push on him; Silas never felt he *hadn't* slept—and, since it didn't bother Silas (because the true name of his disorder was a name none of them would ever clear for), no one got around to inventing an alias, and Silas gave up on it all.

By then the doctors belonged to Doris and Doris belonged to the cancer.

Bed. Lights out. Repose. Eyes shut. Nothing.

Or *mostly* nothing. A ninety-nine percent of the time atheistic null-state-nothing with a one percent epiphanic kicker.

A soul hiccup.

Rarest of all but exact and exacting in recurrence. Once, twice, some years a dozen times: the dream. Silas's dream. The it/that/*this dream—hiccup-hiccup-hiccup*—without variation.

A block of cheese pressed in a Soviet's hands.

A block of cheese. Width of an unwritten book. Pressed to that man's eye.

A block of cheese peered into/peered through.

James Jesus Angleton off to the side—

(though also at my ear)

—movie director jodhpurs. "Action!"

Internal gears unwind a spring; staccato sprocket; ticka-ticka *tickle of light and shadow store upon celluloid inside.*

A block of cheese. Almost rectangular. Two shaved corners uneven to the other. An irregular hexagon. Tawny white, soft-textured—a big ol' Monterey Jack of how's-that-do-it-for-ya?*—and somehow cheese-but-not: a kind-of (but not) faux-leather pebbled texture covers it as a groovy decorative outer shell.*

Or does memory just fill in a useless blank?

Get my mind's eye looking the other way. Looking away.

(Never was a cheese at all.)

The white instead of the red.

The white instead of the pink.

The cheese instead of the camera instead of the meat instead of the texture of the splattered gray matter on the asphalt caulked cobbles, gun smoke wafting from my fist, up my nostrils, stinging my eyes.

A look at the useless.

Stop fooling yourself, Silas. Look at the useless: the head you splattered.

A bizarre and immutable script. The dream/vision/nightmare commands and Silas always looks.

Such effort; such violence. Such too clever-for-no-good gamesmanship.

Such a fucking waste. Evander Lott and half-a-head, and a face I've dum-dum'd into a red/pink dandelion puff exploded and gone.

In another Soviet's hands—the pearly gates blaze wide—a light bar/winged reflectors held aloft.

Say cheese.

Silas came to know this other guy, the Sov with the quartz-halogen bulb-bar. His handler. His case officer. His Pinwheel.

Alley steam forms genies from drainage grates. Whirling/grasping will-o'-the-wisps from wall piping. Fairy's breath from the Volga's tailpipe.

"Leave it running. This shouldn't take long. Mr. Kingston, you know what is required."

Jump cut/reset.

With the shouting. With the heaving. The breath-catching heart-hammer mimics the sprocket spool. Ticka-ticka ticka-ticka ticka-ticka—

Silas's heart: troublesome/woeful bad; and Lott's apportionment of that bad? Worse for his heart's about to stop.

Scrabble of leather soles on cruddy Soviet asphalt. Poorly spread. Raggedly rolled over pre-Revolution cobbles. Alley rats scurry ahead, feet rattling/scattering broken glass. They stop. Turn. Watch. Eyes neither fervent nor cruel. Just rats.

Angleton inside my ear. "'I think we are in rats' alley...'"

A muffled, almost silent pop—

(maybe imagined, these forty long years)

—of wrenched limbs, joint-separating beneath the heavy coat, the heavy thump of struggle. Zipper-like tear of fabric. Knee-crack on exposed domes of black-buried gray cobbles.

"'...where the dead men lost their bones.'" Angleton blinks, eyes always keen, always curious, always reach-out-and-slash-you but for the owlish glasses that keep them caged.

"Stay fucking still!"

"Fuck you! Pigfuckers-wanna-whack me—? 'Specially you, ya bloody Yank-fuck! I'm not afraid!" Wild-terror-eyes.

From the placid distance of time, Silas remembered. The anger and the exceptional terror that held no fear.

Like the MI6 agent, I am terrorized, and I am unafraid. I accept the pistol, grip first, from Kalaydoskop.

Maybe the color of the camera's casing—the cheese of it all—dominated Silas's memory of that night, of that alley, of that murder committed, because, as his own final reckoning neared, it was the only incongruity left. The rest of the chaos ordered by the passage of his life.

But why its texture? Why do I linger on faux-pebbling I never saw? Imagine the texture on my fingertips? To what purpose do I invent/invest false memory?

(Fools first fool themselves.)

Never saw it again; only the film it shot.

(The man I shot.)

Never held, ever saw, another camera like it.

Then, as now, its specular black lens. Its high-gloss metal barrel, silver ridges round. The camera lens appeared out of proportion—a large photo loupe shoved into the side of a groovy white faux-leather Isabelle Huppert-on-holiday block of cheese. The whole ugly thing mounted on a handle engineered by some jackass who'd gotten the wrong set of designs. Or had a goof for 1930s comic books. Every KGB/GRU/Soviet handheld movie/surveillance camera Silas studied at The Farm, encountered during his Agency Cold War career, had been compact. Box-shaped black. Lens flush, buried inside the casing for concealment. Some had a strap.

None had the home-movie/Buck Rogers raygun handle like this one.

Silas (omniscient observer): *No business like show business.* Silent in his head.

Silas (first-person executioner): *Render unto Satan...* Silent in his head.

"Pigfucker." Bang! *exploding the head.*

A Soviet, Super 8, *Svema* color snuff film.

Silent. Immutable. Irredeemable. An irrevocable act for CIA/MI6 viewing pleasure— *"the first occasion you displease me."* Kalaydoskop.

Wife saved. Son saved.

Country betrayed.

Future saved and eternity mocked.

"What if we never get what we deserve?" Silas.

Doris. "We give thanks—" Beaumont squiggles from her arms. Bounces around their feet— "for all the grace we do find, and hold, and keep."

He crushes himself to his wife, to his future. Whispers, "Our tornado balances inside a kaleidoscope."

A kaleidoscope turn. Doris, the dog, our Foxtail Farm scatters and shatters and falls to a central image that becomes my vision through the camera lens. Through the cheese block. I see: me/Silas standing, pistol aimed at Lott's head; I see Lott's head briefly/minutely turn. Straight look into Kolya's eyes.

Kolya's eyes flicker a silent exchange. Fatalistic. Familiar. Cruelty.

It's all cruelty and where shadow meets the steam, the alley rats gather, cluster, shoulders rubbing, on the edge of light.

Ticka-ticka ticka-ticka—*and a voice takes its mechanical tempo. Disembodied. Feminine. From the vortex of the steam devils' swirl: "We're more than what we survive."*

I flinch. The gun goes Bang! *And James Jesus Angleton yells what he always yells; what I have always heard: "Cut!"*

But tonight he pronounces it "Bait."

Kolya looks into my camera's lens: "Cheese, pretty please?"

Silas's eyes opened. Mind: *Why the hell "Bait?"* Voice: "All rat trap bait. Each of us to the other and the whole damn shame of it all."

He'd slept in his chair. Pulled from his map table. Close to the tall, shallow Rumford fireplace with its cast iron facing, the logs furred with thick white ash, hatched with black seams and faint orange dying smolder-veins inside. The windowpanes and swing-pane glass door glistened wet in the moonlight; blown over the river bay, the narrow, remnant Thanksgiving rain-clouds unfurled and whipped across its setting face, war-torn pennants galloped from the battle.

The Soviet radio hummed. On Silas's computer screen, Fergus Lott—Evander's living ghost. Slumped. Passed out drunk. His surveillance equipment inside Garde-Joyeuse. A gross and awful man.

A better man than his older brother.

Silas collected Doris's copy of *The Once and Future King*. The code key. Tucked his encoded confession to Fergus's queen inside its cover. Placed the book and the letter in his standing safe in the corner. Left the steel door open for his radio, his laptop. Glanced at the letter Harker thrust upon him over last week's lunch.

Still inside its envelope.

Still upon the table.

Added the equipment inside the safe. Shut the safe's door. Twisted the handle. Engaged the lock. Yawned.

The letter.

Harker.

He opened the envelope, but his mind drifted back to his phantasma.

Lott's head briefly/minutely turns. Kolya's eyes flicker a silent exchange.

Explode blood. Explode brain and face.

Letter read, he descended to the second floor. His bedroom. Laid out clothes, his thoughts already dressed-and-arrived at the Old Herbert C. Hoover Building—OTRAC/KALEIDOSCOPE headquarters—preparing instructions for Meryl Hofmyer; much to do before Harker's December first deadline. Beginning of the end of KALEIDOSCOPE.

Note: add Baku, December 26. Add Brits...? Meryl dig/Meryl ping. Meryl: Lott/link/Kolya(?) Business to settle. Find Jilly Bregado.

He settled, shoulders slumped; bullet-head bore the full flood of his Savoy showerhead. Gruff sigh. "Hhuuh, Michael. Lynn. God, you two..." into the spray, into the steam. Into the downpour of all the tears unshed and forsaken.

Unnecessary. Weak. Squeezed his eyes. Face-upped the water. Stilled. Drifted. Began a prayer that got no further than *Oh, God...*

"Do you love me?"

"You know I do, Silas."

The Silvanus Bench. Doris beside me. Untouched for months. Untouching now.

*"I'm not with you to betray you. To spy. Michael's birth—*that *way—was not my choice. Kolya poisoned me. That's how much* he *loves me. Loves Michael."*

"Never was a Doris DeGrange," I hold her gaze, deep cerulean blue.

"The real Doris died in that tornado."

"If the tornado never happened?"

"Kolya would have dropped me into another disaster to walk from, blank-slate to you. As far as he's concerned, I'm here only to keep you in place. A harness."

"Your name would be something else."

Doris smiles. Doris loves. "The only real name I've ever had is Kingston. Doris Kingston is everything who I am."

Silas faced the shower wall. He switched the taps. Braced himself against the tiles. Against the flood of icy water.

"Make a wish!"

Doris glows, ecstatic in the flicker of birthday candles. The faces of our three children encircle her. I watch. I wait. I wonder.

"Make a wish!" Michael. Lynn. Hal. Children glorious.

"Oh, you guys know all my wishes came true in you and your daddy."

Memory phantasma.

Boone Kelso finishes hanging Doris in her red dress. Hung in her gilded frame. He steps back between me and Doris on the landing, admiring our portrait.

I speak. "Sublime. Let's go upstairs."

Boone Kelso speaks: "We've business to settle, you and me." We march. Up. Past the railing. Doris's gallows.

Peering in the night: Melody: her child-face: envisioned by me outside the birthday candle flicker that highlights my born children's faces. Little-girl-Melody, I imagine her peering from the shadows. Dull fear. All the terror of a child's broken universe.

Melody. Child-face. Horror behind the window of Roberta Kelso's car.

Roberta never looks. I never see her face until I see it in the newspaper. The ashes of their poor cottage house. Arson. Murder. Unknown assailant. Father, Boone, wanted for questioning. Daughter, Melody, missing. And the factual truth—as God knows it—I cursed the child; I was there. The ghost who pulled the trigger. I shot her mother dead.

Dressed, Silas put Harker's letter inside his breast pocket. Found his Cadillac keys. Found his way outside. A glance across the "tournament" field in shifting cloud-stroked moonlight. Wet and bent beach grass. The silhouette of the unsafe stairs.

Ought to fix those.

Silhouette of Hal. As he sat through the fall, drifting away on pipe smoke.

Drexler. Houton. Iraq.

My son drifting to CINDER CROWN. Drifting to Iran—Ahvaz? Bushehr? Abadan? Sacrificial ignition?

Silas watched the wiper blades slash Thanksgiving rainwater from his windshield. Engaged the transmission. Eased through Foxtail Farm's heavy gates.

"Doris, you're mine. Not his."

"Of my own free will. He never counted on that. I've told you. So many times. I was a very little girl when my mother gave me to him. He was barely a man."

"He passed you to the State."

"He was the State. The Soviet was all he ever knew. Better than an orphanage. We wouldn't have each other had he done that."

Silas drove out of Hollywood, Maryland.

"Kolya didn't abandon me. He looked out for me. Understand, his was the only love I ever knew. But it isn't true love—man-wife love, father-mother love. The love that takes my breath, that pounds my heart to know I'm yours and have you know you're mine."

"He infected your blood."

"Shhh. Silas. Please? You have better things to fight over. I'm yours. Not his."

She lifts her hand. Like a vow. Our palms touch. "Faithful and forever," she responds.

We make love. Warm together on the unfeeling stone of the Silvanus Bench. One night, beneath a winter moon; the first time in our new life, three years after Moscow.

Once more true man and loyal wife, the Kingstons would add a daughter the following year. They would name her Lynn.

Silas drove into D.C. He wondered about that daughter. Wondered about the Christmas calendar he'd had distributed at her tennis club.

Dawn, two hours yet away, he pulled up in darkness to the yellow-striped drop arm. Waited at the unassuming guard shack for the red light on the post to flash green with the electronic reading of his license plate. Waited for the night guard's visual recognition of his identity. The drop arm lifted like a portcullis and Silas drove through the limestone arch, a tunnel hollowed through the ground floor of a great building, to arrive at the courtyard space reserved for the Administrative Secretary of the Office of Treaty Regulation and Administrative Compliance. The long forgotten OTRAC, KALEIDOSCOPE hidden within.

If Lynn's following Op Sec, she'll have found it/seen it first. Know her cover blown and is somewhere nursing a bottle nursing her wounds. If not...that calendar embarrassment will have met her last night at the Azerbaijani embassy. Girl's own damn fault. But out of Kolya's reach...

...which could reach inside that embassy more easily than Silas. Whatever trouble Lynn got herself into, Silas never lacked confidence she wouldn't always get herself out of it. He dismissed the girl from his thoughts. Entered the dark and slumbering building.

Christmas Eve – 1972

1.

THEY WOULD ERECT THE nation's Department of Commerce, a modern castle, upon the dry bed of a ghost river. A tributary of the Potomac once navigated by pirates. It was 1928 and Edward York, the building's architect, had returned to New York City from Washington impressed and invigorated by his inspection of the steel framework, an eight-acre skeleton for the largest American government building yet conceived. Yet constructed. In his York & Sawyer Manhattan offices penthouse: champagne. He laughs off abdominal cramping as "—a tickle in my bellybutton. Youthful excitement. I tellya, at sixty-three I'm as slaphappy as a five-year-old with his first red balloon." In the ambulance to New York's Presbyterian Hospital, his pain intensifies. Migrates to the lower right of his abdomen. Through pain, he regales the attendant that his Commerce Building will last one thousand years. A monument to order. To financial stability. His fever spikes as his appendix ruptures. Through pain— "An imperial palace based on world trade instead of world war."

Designed by rival architects Allen & Collens, New York's Presbyterian Hospital—where surgeons open and operate on Edward York—shuns the fortress qualities of American empire; their hospital evokes in spires and arches the spirit of man, medicine, of a moral authority that stretches beyond a mere one thousand years to recognize (a last quick glimmer of Edward's eye) eternity. Under anesthesia, Edward York dies in a temple of healing.

"Unlike York, the building he left behind needed no surgery. The stock market crash, the Depression—running dogs for a more significant World War, and the rise of our Military-Industrial Complex, this—" James Jesus Angleton gestures, his gangly arm describing a carnival barker's flourish— "with its eight miles of corridors and staircases and hallways: it was already a mausoleum when it opened its doors for business."

Silas Kingston jog-steps to keep pace with his mentor's wide, stooped gait. The nation still reels from the "energy crunch"; heat is off, the corridor unlit. Their breath puffs. Fifteen minutes from the closest stairs (closer than the closest elevator), they arrive at an old oak door. A faded sign reads: Office of Treaty Regulation and Administrative Compliance.

"Is this an Agency annex? Separate counterintelligence offices?"

Angleton works the double locks. "A much more dangerous building than Langley." The first lock: CLICK. "In the 1930s, when the Chicago Zoo chose not to accept them—" The second lock: CLICK. "Three full-grown alligators—Pay Cut, Furlough, and Dismissal—enjoyed free run of the basement. Terrorized archivists and the secretaries sent down."

"You're kidding me."

"I kid you not. They were here for years. Ferocious, but no one got et*—" door pushed open, gestures Silas inside— "that anyone noticed..."*

Silas notices, as he steps inside, large marble slabs—already ancient when installed—replace the high-polished limestone of the corridor floor. Scrubbed for decades but left unpolished, never buffed, their surface is hazy. Rough. As though he's stepped onto the bottom of the silent sea; a floor washed by sandy waves unceasing from the dawn of time. The door they've stepped through, now locked behind them—standard office height and width—leaves Silas catching his breath at the scope of the room (vapor gone/heat running) wide before him.

Like a station terminal.

A cathedral.

Divided into seven work areas. Two are desk clusters, six to a pod—each desk old-world wooden and heavy. Two sections contain periodical-style workstations—high titled lectern easels, racks of wooden newspaper sticks, and magazines. Three rows of library-style desks fill two more sections—each with a long top shelf stacked with books and files; a series of desk lamps spaced along its edge illuminate individual workstations. Ten to a table. Every available surface covered with books: stacked; typewriters: paper-spindled; intelligence files: opened, analysis pages folded back on staples, on clips. File carts, untended, jam foot-traffic lanes and every ribbed-back, cushioned-seated banker's swivel chair—half-turned from sudden departure—revealed empty in a circle of lamplight.

Silas determines nothing that happens here happens fast...except for the disappearance of employees that presaged his arrival.

"Santa's workshop lose its elves?"

Angleton ignores. Angleton leads.

They stand at the room's geometric center. An empty traffic hub for the two main interior doors (where the elves—Silas determines—must now hide, peer, twitter).

"OTRAC was fortunate to receive this hall. Its suite of offices. It exemplifies the Beaux-Arts Classical Revival style. A government-empire aesthetic Edward York chose to project permanence, secrecy, and power. Look up, Silas. What do you see?"

A barreled ceiling with a center skylight. The gray sheen of cold day befits the season.

"It's oval-shaped—the window—what you're asking I look at, right? That makes it unique." A curt Angleton nod. "It has the stained-glass and that curlicue framing you find in those rose windows they put behind church altars. Those are always circular."

Another nod. Sage.

"I'd say, they don't put oval windows in domes. Not like this. Not that I've seen anywhere. The ceiling structure—it's called a false dome, right?" Silas knows it is; is probing Angleton's objective. "Each other section has electric lights—the brightness and the shadows, in fact, enhance the false dome illusion."

A wry smile stretches the older spy's thin mouth.

"Look again, Silas. You see it—the color?"

"Not much color today. Winter light, sir." A sidelong glance. Angleton expects him to continue. "But I can see some. Color. It bounces down the walls, breaks across

the arching fans. 'Fan vaults' or don't tell me—" wry right back at him—"'flared pilasters', eh?"

"You are *clever, Silas. Now, I want you to imagine something. Are you ready?"*

"So very."

"Look up and imagine that false dome flooded with light. Breaking apart. Bouncing about. Tell me the first word that comes to mind. Do it."

"Kaleidoscope."

"Marvelous. That's where you are. What this place is."

"A kaleidoscope?"

"Operation KALEIDOSCOPE."

"So this is *Agency."*

"The furthest thing from it. KALEIDOSCOPE is how I found Doris. 'Indiana's Easter Miracle'. The girl who walked from the tornado. Why I eased you two into proximity and hoped you would find each other. Why you stand in the middle of it now—and if Colby and Nixon have their way, which I am afraid they shall—why you will replace me at its center."

"I am not stupid, sir. You're making no sense."

"CIA—for men like me and men like you—is our job. Our career. KALEIDOSCOPE is a calling beyond."

POETRY, ORCHIDS, AND MOTTOS. Silas's recruitment into KALEIDOSCOPE that Yuletide of 1972, wasn't so much a revelation of OTRAC followed by a secure-room debriefing, it instead unfolded as a series of wintry trudges along capital streets. Wet snow, wind-iced and stinging

Silas's cheeks, his feet soddened in slushy piles and puddles along the lanes and alleyways, where Silas struggled to divine kernels of truth, practical meanings from lines of Eliot and Angleton's greenhouse allusions. The old Ghost needled-and-threaded these like popcorn garlands along the footpaths of Georgetown, leading Silas from how he'd set him up in Moscow to take the fall with Kolya, to be a mole-in-place for the Soviet where Angleton would run the feedback loop, and how from their perch in counterintelligence he'd ask Silas to see that "every business, including the espionage business, is in the business of staying in business—each side baiting the other, propping them up—sometimes—just long enough to cry 'Wolf!' while we secretly breed our wolves with their wolves to make scarier wolves."

"I see, Jim. I see it." Silas didn't see it at all.

Angleton winked. "'Oh, keep the Dog far hence, that's friend to men—'" He whispered, rubbing his black-gloved hands within a flurry of sleet. "'Or with his nails he'll dig it up again.'"

"What's the dog digging for?"

"The truth." A pointed look through steamed owl lenses. "Or the false evidence of such. Same difference in our line. Or don't you think?"

Though at least two inches taller than Silas's six feet, Angleton's stooped shoulders and huddled frame, the snug black homburg set not jauntily, no, but skewed—confused the true line of the man like a reflection in the time-bent glass of a Christmas window. Vividly observed in Langley corridors, whispered in dim D.C. bars where spooks from all the intelligence haunts warmed dry lips on whiskey and burned cigarettes and rumors: Angleton was a man shouldering a career-on-a-crutch; hunched under its weight, he was an undertaker trying to fool the tape soon to be pulled to last measure.

Stopped along the towpath, Angleton clunked the bowl of his Charatan briar on the edge of the black iron railing. Scattered ash and poured dottle into the icy water of the C & O Canal. "The two competing philosophies sum up like so. KALEIDOSCOPE: 'Hegemony Through Energy'. The Agency: 'Kinetic Pax Americana'. With one: lasting world peace; the KALEIDOSCOPE brand of dominance cannot/will-not be attained through counterrevolution, regime change, shadow governance, or lethal backstopped blackmail. It's more primal—primary—and, in that, peaceful. Drawn from the earth to satisfy humankind's most basic need. Oil. It's gas. It is pipeline diplomacy that dictates 'He who controls the power switch controls the polity.'"

The pair of them walked side-by-side, up Thomas Jefferson Street, Silas just a step reserved to allow for Angleton's lead. To catch his sardonic mutter between the jingle-belled shop doors and store-piped *Rudolph* and *Wenceslas*— "CIA sows entropy. KALEIDOSCOPE cultivates order; be it from a garden we aspire or the ash heap we may just deserve."

Among lunch-break Christmas shoppers, colorful scarfs and cozy caps, with bright red mittens, red-button noses, they ambled across M Street. Another row of modern shops plugged into old brick facades. Angleton stopped again. Made a sudden ninety-degree turn. Inquisitive. As if answering a call from over the picket fence of an incongruous country yard. Dead leaves. Dirt and dirty snow beneath barren branches of a sentinel elm. Silas's eyes followed Angleton's point of view. An odd colonial cottage, tucked between high walls of new stores. The Old Stone House.

"'Down the passage which we did not take / Towards the door we never opened / Into the rose-garden. My words echo / Thus, in your mind.' This way, Silas."

He unlatched the short white gate. Left the sidewalk. Approached the front windows of the Old Stone House. Angleton continued with his Eliot. "'But to what purpose / Disturbing the dust on a bowl of rose-leaves / I do not know.'"

"Sure is something I want to know. Jim."

Angleton's hand already cupped over his brow, beneath the rim of his hat, peeking between leaded panes into the front window where a Christmas candle burned; Angleton faced Silas as though in salute. A pleasant smile—long, tapered lips. Bemused. "That is?"

"Why you for this? You're foundational to the principles of the Agency. How can you be both 'entropy' and the other. 'Refraction.'"

"Astute and excellent," he said, but didn't answer. "You must look inside. Here." He tapped the pane of the second window beside the one he peered.

A holly wreath in this window, Silas peeped through its center. The interior construction preserved, the furniture preserved. A large plank table with plenty of antique empty chairs, decorated for an authentic Colonial Christmas dinner preserved.

"This is the oldest surviving structure in D.C. The what-once-was illuminated to inspire all our tomorrows. Set only for phantoms. The souls of institutions—as long-lasting as the walls we build to contain them, the walls we conserve and maintain—keep their symbols and dazzle and didact, long after they're spiritually vacant."

Angleton pressed two gloved fingertips to the glass, testing whether warmth remained. None did.

"'Footfalls echo in the memory / Down the passage we did not take / Towards the door we never opened.'" Exhausted of faith. "Institutions ossify even as we pace their corridors, man their ramparts, boil the oil to spill onto the upturned faces of our enemies who seek nothing more than what we ourselves set out to seek."

Silas said nothing, yet something inside him understood. Agreed. In agreement, it gave consent.

They lunched beneath old-time baseball photographs. Rich seafood chowder. Hot. Creamy. Oyster crackers sunk with the backs of their spoons into the broth. The far/last high-backed wooden booth at Martin's Tavern on Wisconsin Avenue.

"Structures remain even after the spirit rots out. I saw that early. Someone saw that in me as I see it in you."

Angleton was the second AdSec of OTRAC/KALEIDOSCOPE. He traded his pipe for a pack of Chesterfields he unwrapped and worked through at a steady pace. Silas burned Luckys. They finished a bottle of premier cru Chablis with their chowder. Moved on to Godfathers. Gin, vermouth, cherry liqueur. Stirred and strained over ice.

Useless to ask questions, Silas waited. Saw in Angleton—his confident detachment, his willful philosophical detachment from the rigors of time, his measured/cool compassion, the father figure Doris saw and had wished into being her own.

Conjured from the smoke in a thin and reedy growl, Angleton drew Silas back to Ypres. To the Argonne Forest. To the whistles, the shouts, the screams. Boots on ladders. Boots in porridge mud. The rip of machine gun. The roll of mustard gas. Blood and fear and then he sang. "'*Lord God of love, let us have peace / From war's vain sacrifice give us release—*'" Softhearted. Brittle. Recitative. "'*Grant peace that victories war cannot know / God of the Ages / Thy mercy show.*'" Hit his cigarette, drew smoke through his nose. Said, "Hmm?"

"'Let Us Have Peace.' On Grant's tomb in Riverside Park. I didn't know it was from a hymn."

"He didn't either. Couldn't. It is a First World War protest song, not a Civil War hymn."

Silas had only sipped his cocktail when Angleton twirled his finger for more. Smoked. Movements deliberate. Hypnotic. He owl-eyed Silas until the two fresh drinks arrived. Were poured. Angleton swallowed his own. Pulled in Silas's second before Silas finished his first. Blew a sudden gale of smoky words. "The war to end all wars. You think this protest against Vietnam displays outrage? Entry into World War One—? Vastly more unpopular in America. Three hundred thousand casualties in one hundred and fifty days, mothers, fathers, sisters, brothers, cousins-aunts-and-uncles, the grands and the great-grands—the babies if they could—weren't singing *Johnny Get Your Gun*, they were full-throated crying *I Didn't Raise My Boy to Be a Soldier*, and the pocket-watch men who returned from Versailles, saw regular folks in the streets and parks and stadiums singing *Let Us Have Peace*—more than we have in the mall shaking tambourines and thrumming guitars and bleating through their noses little Johnny Lennon's *Imagine*, from among those pocket-watch men, a quiet group emerged and said—" voice a shudder— "'We. Damn. Well. Better. *Do* something about this.'"

He ripped the cellophane zipper from his second Chesterfield soft-pack. Went on. "Two types of men came out of that war happy." He lit his tobacco. He hit his tobacco. He waited on St. Nicotine's arrival.

Silas. "The arms manufacturers."

"That's one. The other—? Oil. Profit from arms was ancient. It would always fit the same pattern, always thrive on human beings' worst inclination to power through violence. But petroleum as a need-all? *Heh-heh.* That was new. And there were visionaries who saw its future—and by that, I mean oil's greatest economic potential is in *peace*." He signaled their waiter. "Please remove these. Too sweet now." To Silas: "A whiskey okay with you?"

"Please." Silas nudged away his undrunk Godfather. Fingered a fresh Lucky Strike out of its box. Angleton slid his lighter across the table like a chess piece; as Silas lit, Angleton said, "Cigarettes in soft packs are all a millimeter longer. Better value."

"I'll remember that."

The waiter cleared glasses. Angleton bright-eyed. "Two Ancient Age. Neat." A cheery smile. "Happy Yuletide. Keep them coming, my friend." Hushed for the waiter's walk-away. To Silas: "'Peace through unseen dominion.' The original KALEIDOSCOPE came together under the shadow presidency of Edith Wilson. Peace was easy—humanity believed they'd cold-turkey'd off the alternative; oil, plentiful, oil-diplomacy cheap, and easy too, and KALEIDOSCOPE did little but make wealthy men more wealth. In 1925, Do-Nothing Coolidge did something we can be thankful for. Shuffled KALEIDOSCOPE over to the Department of Commerce.

"Out of sight, out of mind, pretty much out of business, and the old pocket-watch men cared little about that except their aging bones were headed one way and their souls—they hoped they had them—needed the insurance policy. A legacy. A 'we done good' entry in their spiritual ledger. And they remembered one too young—" he flung a long arm/large hand up/back/over his head without looking. Knuckled the 1920s baseball players black-and-whiting in their knickers on their dugout bench behind his head. "Too young to have made the first-round KALEIDOSCOPE roster. A smart mouth at Versailles. Carried one of their briefcases. Switched—upon reshoring to America—to a carrying a bible and joined the Fundamentalist movement sweeping the country. Until Standard Oil swept the impertinent, mad-eyed lad off to the oil fields of Mesopotamia. Hayward Lockhart. Now KALEIDOSCOPE went looking. Dug Lockhart up leading a cult of disillusioned Moravian Christians in Bethlehem awaiting the second coming. They sighed." He mimicked, reaching into a vest pocket. "Pulled their watches and watched their springs wind down."

Angleton poked holes in the smoke between them. The red eye of his burning stick mesmerized. Penetrated. "Lockhart consolidated KALEIDSCOPE. Eliminated the seven-man board. Installed a three-monkey, blind-deaf-and-dumb honorific set of mucky-muck emeritus directors (I reduced that to one when I leaned out and pulled the ring), and he made himself the first AdSec. Hayward Lockhart's great success/greater-still-failures that saw us through the Second World War are why I came aboard and why I'm asking you to succeed me."

"You want to give me the brass ring?"

"And the grenade; my hands shake too much these days to put the pin back in. And my lobbing arm, just don't lob that far, no-more, no more."

ENOUGH. NO MORE. They made for the door. Silas helped Angleton into his coat. An old cashmere surtout. Caped like Holmes, tight-waisted like Micawber, near-bald at the collar from the friction of a lifetime glancing over his shoulder. Silas guided him into the cold. It was not yet five, but nighttime gloom had rushed away the day.

Heavy snow. The wind blew bitter raw, intent upon its purpose. It swirled in lamplight like ash failing to rise and falling back into the fire. Thickened Georgetown gutters.

"'The chill ascends from feet to knees…'" Angleton thumbed his coat buttons into their proper holes. "And

'The wind shall say: here were decent godless people.' This way."

The spycatcher left the curb, his steps ginger but deliberate, the old fox knowing not to trust the silver crust of an iced-over field. Across the street, a shiny black Lincoln Continental puffed pale smoke. Eyed them malevolently with its diagonally canted headlights.

"Never traded up. Have you." Silas.

"I know all the wires in this one."

"Afraid the Sovs are listening?"

Angleton didn't answer but his expression read it wasn't the Soviets who worried him.

His hip-holster driver opened the passenger door.

Angleton nodded Silas inside. "The Lincoln brand died for me in November. Twenty-two/sixty-three. This still has the most room to stretch out. And the ashtrays are larger."

They rode downtown in silence. Passed glowing shop windows. Mannequins grinned under stringed lights and plastic holly garlands, frozen in gestures of happiness they could never feel. And the shoppers buying in the stores behind them didn't notice at all.

2.

"TRAIN *84, SILVER METEOR to Miami, boarding Track 16...*" A static voice from overhead.

The whirring clatter of the Arrival/Departure board as the split flaps updated schedules. In disrepair like most of Union Station, more than a few changes stuck halfway and, motor-jammed, they buzzed. Others jumbled letters. *On Time/Delayed/Cancelled* flashed in mechanical indecision; falling/failing patterns fragmenting into abstraction.

"Eventually, the gears strip. Eventually, no matter what the board says, these people will discover their train's already gone."

Silas stood with Angleton in the decayed grandeur of the concourse. The hall teemed with humanity. Under paint-peeling wreath-ringed arches, a frantic to and fro of last-minute holiday travelers. Harried parents hurried starry-eyed children. Soldiers in fatigues, home from Southeast Asia, looked for stars to follow with vacant eyes. Expectant-eyed college students in clusters of friends or delivering themselves reluctant into the clutches of waiting families, each expectant as a star in their own pageant yet unproduced. Candy-cane hair ribbons. Moist green scarves, and red. White ribbons and paper stars hung on the great winking Christmas tree in the hall's center. Everyone pushed and elbowed, *excuse-me's/pardon me's,* or just huffed at each other to get around and get on with Christmas.

"Are we here to meet someone?"

"Just killing time before we must."

Marble muddied. Luggage lost and piled. A lost present trampled. Angleton shepherded Silas into the rows of heavy oak benches beneath the Liberty Bell replica. They threaded past an elderly black couple in outdated fur-collared coats who hold each other's hands and stare at the malfunctioning board, uncomprehending in a circle of their scuffed old luggage piled around them battlement high. The pair of CIA spooks sat between them and a urine-stained street addict who'd made the bench his manger: syringe, spoon, and cotton on the floor a cruel mockery of holy gifts.

Angleton retrieved his pipe. Thumbed the bowl with his preferred Oriental blend. Struck his lighter. "Lockhart believed energy interdependence could stave off a second European world war. Believed the opposite could neutralize Japan."

Angleton lit his pipe.

Silas offered, "July, 1941. We cut off Japan's access to oil."

"And December seventh they delivered Pearl Harbor. And in Europe, total control of oil interdependence became not a brake, but a controlling purpose of the fight. It devastated Lockhart." Puff-puff. All smoke. "He did see some success post-World War Two stabilizing Middle East oil flows under secret treaties. Truman complimented him, but Lockhart lost his faith. That war he'd been handpicked to prevent had brought nuclear horror and made the casualties of the First World War look like a hangnail compared to the gaping wound of human destruction that had happened under his KALEIDOSCOPE. A prophet, not a savior, he saw the advent of Strategic Entropy—"

"Your CIA Kinetic Pax Americana."

Angleton—puff-puff—nodded.

"Train 96, Twilight Shoreliner to Boston, final call, Track 26..."

Whir. Clackety-clack. Buzz. Letters jumbled. Christmas surged.

"The original oil companies apotheosized into conglomerates, multinational, militarized, politicized. Lockhart Puff-the-magic-dragon'd KALEIDOSCOPE into OTRAC. Hid it there like a mustard seed he protected but wouldn't plant."

Shouting rose from the concourse. A wealthy man smacked his Red Cap porter with his hat because the fellow stopped and wasted time giving a pair of old clutching spinsters directions that in deafness, they listened but could not hear.

"President Truman signed the National Security Act in 1947, creating the CIA. Our fight against the Soviet Union full-bore, our Agency proved our utility, effectiveness—and although that war drags on—our CIA's utter importance to freedom from communist totalitarianism."

Silas watched two street kids steal popcorn from a vendor.

"Korea, on the other hand, radicalized US foreign policy. Our activities there, and in South America, in Southeast Asia—assassinations, coup d'etats, paramilitary armies, arms-for-drugs mafia money laundering—Truman worried CIA'd become 'operational' rather than focused on intelligence collection. We build the fires we justify our being in putting out."

A young married couple passed, bickering.

"In 1952, Truman remembered Lockhart. Set up a fund—presidential-discretionary/secret—an insurance policy they named Covenant 17. Gave it an innocuous OTRAC historical treaty advisement/oversight within CIA. A file tag. Did nothing. Bothered no one. And set Lockhart to finding his replacement."

"You."

"A counterintelligence spook made sense. We don't run covert actions. We wait and we watch. We guard against betrayal and treason from within. We believe in our institutions; hunt those who corrupt them from the inside. Preserve them by understanding their vulnerabilities. It's not defeating your enemy today in one violent cataclysm." He relit his pipe. "It's controlling how they think without their knowing you're in their mind. For decades. And they trusted—once—me. To know the real from the counterfeit. The loyalty. The rot." His eyes lifted to the ceiling, water-ringed and fluffed with mold like wet ash. Followed a dirty drip to the floor. Another. Another.

Drip (echo). Drip (echo). Drip.

"I've seen my every secret betrayed. Every victory, pyrrhic. Every alliance contaminated. My friend Philby, from across the puddle, a God damn Soviet spy *I* spilled secrets to. Who the hell am I? I missed altogether. They call me delusional—not behind my back, but to my face.

The trouble with counterintelligence, Silas, is that at the last, you suspect yourself most ardently and painfully. Were it not for KALEIDOSCOPE..." He railed off.

Sucked smoke. Blossomed it.

Assaulted his seasons past. "I took the view through a different optic. One where 'delusional' shifts to 'deluded'. To 'disillusioned'. The clarity to see that I gave my whole life to an institution that no longer believes America has a soul. Doesn't particularly want it to."

A crash and a cry rose above the hubbub. Both men witnessed a young woman in an ill-fitting teenager's blue windbreaker too small, too thin to be of any use against the winter outside. Two suitcases of the three she'd tried to carry, knocked to the floor. One spilled open. Its contents, cheap. Gaudy. Poor. She clutched a round vinyl box—converted from an old hair-dryer case—to her fat belly.

"KALEIDOSCOPE remembers America does have a soul." Puff-puff. "That's why KALEIDOSCOPE must keep turning."

Silas couldn't take his eyes off the raggedy young woman. No one bothered to help. They hardly looked. One who did, cussed her. Humanity hustled on to outpace Christmas. Even from this distance, Silas could see the glisten of welling tears. Silas felt her hopelessness.

"Sounds like the job you want me for, you'd be better offering to Elisabeth Kübler-Ross."

Angleton's eyes swished between Silas and the capture of his attention. His mouth cracked sideways. Smiled to himself. He'd made the right decision with Silas. "Only if you ascribe atheism to Kübler-Ross' concept of care for the dying. Of course, in *Death and*

Dying, that's not her point at all. She speaks of a good God."

The poor young woman let her other bag drop. She wasn't fat. She was pregnant. Christmas Eve. Pregnant and alone. She just stared at her crap at her feet, a sweat-soiled bra upturned like an empty beggar's cup, and only her throat moved—swallow, swallow—swallowing her fear, her pain, her pride lost. Her humility.

"Kübler-Ross teaches dignity that leads to peace, which clears the pathways to spiritual love. And isn't that Paul? His first letter to the Corinthians, chapter thirteen? Tuned in—or do we now say, 'turned on'—? To 'Feel love, feel God...'"

Silas wasn't feeling it. "Why did you bring me here?"

"'Love, do God's work...'"

Silas glanced at him, annoyed. Angleton's owl eyes blinked. "Didn't know you're a Christian, sir."

"My mother is Catholic. My father, agnostic." Puff-puff. "As for me—best you'll get is the accusation I am a rabid Zionist." Discerning—in that, telling. "Had you a Buddhist temple at your Foxtail Farm—Silas—instead of the chapel, I would quote you *Siddhartha* to make you see."

He checked his wristwatch. Silas noticed a hippie. Big. Muscular. Beard as rough as the cotton of his Mexican jerga. Rushing into the station. His battle-distressed but ever-trusted GI jungle boots slapped the marble he crossed.

Angleton led Silas from the benches. A train horn blasted from the depths of the tracks and as Silas followed him, he heard the defeated spy mumble the best Jimmy Stewart this side of the actor:

"There she blows." Glasses removed, Angleton swiveled his head on that worn collar that rubbed his neck. Jutted chin. Lips, the actor's insouciant pucker. Slapped one gloved hand into the other and, in that easy famous drawl, "You know what the three most exciting sounds in the world are? Anchor chains, train whistles, and Harvard nap bombs hitting the canopy."

Silas gaped. Angleton trudged for the night. Focused on the man, on the decision he knew he would make, Silas missed the hippie reach the girl in the blue windbreaker. Missed him lift her into his arms.

Her tangled hair brushed his mouth.

The hippie kissed it.

They clung together.

In each other's eyes, and inside of her, the truest star shone brightest and for the briefest moment, people paused and bore witness, but Silas and Angleton were already gone.

3.

THE LIVE NORWAY SPRUCE, though scraggly, soared and, when decorated, made a splendid National Christmas Tree. Carried America out of the turbulent 1960s into the birth of the "Me Decade."

Withered in March.

Senescent in June.

Dead and sawn to the ground in September.

1972's Natural Christmas Tree was a cut blue spruce from Pennsylvania. Tall and full, it tilted; the cut, just not quite right. But, boy: the red, white, and blue of its lights—big bulbs, nothing chintzy—heavy tinsel, silver and flashing, a golden star, incandescent, and sharp, and crowning. Nixon was bringing home 70,000 servicemen from Vietnam. Hadn't he said so at the illumination?

The heavy snow that had blown Silas and Angleton from Georgetown to Union Station danced here in flurries on playful gusts. Gave a magic appearance to the festivities unfurling and uplifting that filled this open park south of the White House and known to Americans as the Ellipse.

Because tonight was Christmas Eve, the hundreds of people who assembled for the school performances, church choir carolers, the military bands flashing tight with *esprit de corps*, the humorous speeches and homey homilies of friendly politicians and folksy preachers, packed tenfold around the stage, around the Tree and the National Creche beside.

The cheer was forced. The joy, anxious. Peace talks in Paris were failing. Watergate exploding. Trust in the government at an all-time low; although the war protesters weren't throwing rocks this year, more guards and helmeted federal police were on hand to make sure they didn't. So, the hope in smiles, though not artificial, was strained. Tired. Mistrust and watchfulness were on fathers' faces keening over the heads of hot chocolate children.

Silas noticed. Felt it in his gut. And the sparkle Silas met in the eyes of revelers around him: not all that different from the glassiness of terror he'd seen in a face in a Moscow alley less than six months before.

Already today, Angleton had revealed an empty past preserved in ruin, a rushing present consumed by impatience, self-importance, or surrendered blind to despair, and here, the future: bright and orchestrated. But hollow. Desperate to be filled. Cautious of what might fill it. In his strange offer, Angleton revealed to Silas the ghosts of his failures, the locked secrets of his aspirations.

But to take, now, Angleton's aspirations as my own?

To control peace—not by war—but by shaping beliefs; creating dependency on peace with no one ever knowing where the tipping pressure comes from. No one wanting it when it came.

To assume this as my own? Why the hell? How *the hell?!*

Wasn't his successful dangle/doubling to the Soviets, tripling back to Counterintelligence enough? Unspoken this whole day, this holy night—what about the most obvious and missing piece?

"Call me Kalaydoskop."

A parallel/opposite operation by my professional and personal enemy?

Angleton wasn't asking Silas to serve two masters—CIA, KALEIDOSCOPE—but serve one, be the master of the other, and go into battle against the single enemy poised against it all.

The infection in my wife's blood.

The infection in my son.

My dark mirror, Kolya Yurenev. Kalaydoskop.

Beside the tree, too white/too bright halogen spotlights showed the holy family made of wood. Too paint-faded. Made too menacing by the towering shadows the glare threw from them to loom over the crowd. As Silas waited for Angleton to return with hot coffee, he watched protesters wave signs: *No Church in State!/No Christ in Christmas!*; watched supporters wave signs: *Know Christ, Know Christmas!*; watched an anti-war couple push in front for news cameras, flashing peace signs and their own placards: *I'm a bum for peace* and *Peace Means Surrender* and felt his blood hot and knew with the certainty of passion:

If KALEIDOSCOPE is a mirror already broken, then from the shards, with bloody hands, let me forge a weapon not for justice but to shatter Kolya Yurenev—and call that peace.

A boy's chorale dressed as Victorian chimney sweeps finished a rousing *God Rest Ye Merry Gentlemen*. Traded places on the stage with a gospel choir who in scintillating robes of royal blue sequins filed up from the Pathway of Peace—fifty smaller trees, one for each state in the union—singing and swinging and snapping their fingers to *Hark! The Herald Angels Sing.* A yearly favorite, the crowd knew to clap and sing along. The people coalesced. Leaned into it. The view of the edges cleared, and Silas craned his neck. Scanned coffee carts, treats kiosks, and temporary tented gift boutiques for Angleton.

From behind him: "Silas! You're all right!"

He turned. Doris gliding toward him, boosted by a slip of ice, grasping into his arms.

"Doris? Why wouldn't I be?" Puzzlement. Laughter. All affection. He steadied her. Peered into her lovely face.

"Jim asked I leave everything, rush out and meet him here. I asked if you were with him and he just suggested, in that compulsive not-a-suggestion way, that I hurry. Are you with him?" Her head swung out around her husband, eyes searching.

"Hark! The herald angels sing, 'Glory to the newborn king!'"

Silas saw him first as Angleton came up with three steaming paper cups, up the path Doris had just come, as if, perhaps, he'd been tailing her.

"I'm right here, dear. And I'm very glad you've joined us. There is something Silas will rely on you for when he takes over, but while I am still in charge, we will benefit from you starting promptly. Have you ever had the chance to enjoy Switzerland—Geneva, specifically—in the winter?"

He passed out the hot drinks—mulled wine, in fact—and led them away from the throng, further south to the temporary Ellipse Skating Rink, where the electric light was softer and the skaters—tentative families, fluid couples, teenagers playing gleeful/raucous courtship games—orbited the rink counterclockwise on the glimmering ice; a lone figure skater all in black practiced his spins. Angleton sketched for Doris enough about KALEIDOSCOPE to arrive with her at Covenant 17. They reached a chilly bench, and Angleton removed from his shoulders the surtout cape. Swept the snow with a flourish. Spread it, red felt-side up for her to sit.

"No! I told you 'no.' At Barnard. And again at Yale. And *again*, when you sent Silas to Moscow. I will not be recruited!"

Angleton took the seat. He crossed his long legs. Held his cup between his black-gloved palms. "You dreamed of being an economist. You studied International Banking. Yale took you as the first female student into their International and Foreign Economic Administration program."

"I'm a mother, now, for Godsakes! And furthermore—" her angry eyes flashed between the two of them, including Silas as party to the offense— "I swore to both of you: I'll have nothing to do with your secret warfare, hot or cold, American or Soviet," her head nodded at both men, left-right/up-down, broad arcs with burning eyes: *Know me. Know who I am...and the man who sent me.*

Silas retreated a step from her ferocity. Angleton placed his hot-cup by his left shoe. Spread his hands. "More than all that. More than the two of us—" he fish-hooked the air, a crooked finger between himself and Silas— "you, Doris, yearn for justice. You know in your heart that only through justice—right for right's sake—will we ever near a state of grace where humanity may say with a hundred languages common-voiced, 'Let there be peace. Peace on Earth.'"

She flicked her wrist, tossing her hot wine just past his ear. "Don't you mock the holy spirit of this night."

She threw her empty cup on the ground and shuddered into herself. Silas wrapped a comforting arm around his wife's shoulder. Doris didn't lean into him but felt her husband's strength and, more important, his allegiance.

"You're breaking my heart, James Jesus Angleton." Because she had chosen this man to father her. To walk her down the wedding aisle at Foxtail Farm, trailing a queen's worth of his hand-grown orchid garlands in her train.

"I'm not mocking Christmas. I'm not mocking you or the treasured affection and trust you have placed in me. I yearn for peace—it is *all* that I want—and the singular thing I cannot bring to pass. I fight you on this point only because I know, because of who you are and who you love: you are the only one who can attempt to achieve it." His eyes offered a perfect glimpse of the beauty and power of what fire might look like if man could freeze it in time and place and clutch it cool in his hands.

For a long time, none of them moved, held to each other by their triangulated facet of the vision. Distant and carried snowflake to snowflake from the Ellipse, the rolling piano triplets of *O Holy Night*.

Angleton. "I want you to manage a fund of your own design. A lockbox on a fortune already established and growing which you will use to make vast. That you will protect from war and war-profit and profit's compromise."

Within the circle of his arm, Silas felt Doris's breath slow, become heavier as Angleton painted his dream.

"This isn't covert finance—one of Director Helms's untraceable accounts wired through Banque Lambert. It isn't gleaming troy ounces, bars in an alligator-shoed nuncio's alligator case, tucked into the folds of his holy skirt. It is a trust fund, Doris, you'll keep hidden from bribery and revolution, war and the wicked false promise of 'defending democracy' to line the pockets of the military-industrial complex." He reached forward. With two fingers, he removed a dead leaf from the sole of his shoe. "You remember my greenhouse?"

Her warming cerulean eyes told him, of course she did. Silas knew she wanted to speak, but knew that if she did, Angleton would have her. It's what spies do. What Angleton did best.

"You remember. Where you selected your wedding bouquet—I must have over two hundred varieties. If I may digress, I'd like to introduce you to one. The *Paphiopedilum sanderianum*. Common name, the Lady's Slipper." He described it, his hands weaving the air. "Her petals spiral like loose ribbon. Four feet long, they'll grow. Biding time. Borrowing time. Stealing time. It doesn't feed to pollinate. It seduces. No nectar. No sweetness. Just illusion. With its flower, it mimics the shape of a female insect. And one day, some poor bastard fly, thinking he's found what he most desires, lands on her. In trying to possess her, he gets coated in pollen. Leaves unfulfilled. But he carries her seed. It can take decades for the girl to reach full bloom."

She caught her breath and Angleton spread his thin, tight lips. "That is what I'm asking you to grow. This fund. This trust. A living instrument, not for profit, not for regime change. A gift. Not to be used—but to be *waited for*. Only when the global peace of the KALEIDOSCOPE promise meets its sticking point, will we release its treasure to the flies."

Doris. "When the time comes, how will it be released? What kind of expenditure?"

"Not as an expenditure, but as a magnificent gift. A gift like tonight's, a lifeline to peace but in the only language of faith left that people understand." Back to the Chesterfields. He lit up. Blew. "Free money," he said.

WHEN, AT FOXTAIL FARM, on Christmas morning, after the stockings, after the presents, after the morning meal while Silas sifted ashes in the common room fireplace and pushed the Yule log deeper into the embers, Doris finished putting Michael down for his morning nap and she came up behind her husband. Folded her arms up his chest from behind. In his ear: "Most banks of this sort, you know, launder dirty money—because that's what these funds will be, don't tell me otherwise—they launder dirty outward. Burning it into action, aggression, war. Pell and Glatisant will remain hidden because we'll do the opposite: launder our money inward."

He turned in her arms. Face to face. She said, "It will gather, compound, and I will hide it better than anyone has ever hidden a single dime. Not for chaos, but for creation."

Silas nodded; confident she would do just that. "An unusual name you've chosen for your bank."

"King Pellinore chased his Questing Beast, Glatisant, for so long that when he caught it, he couldn't slay it. He was in love with everything the dragon offered. He set it free and it followed him."

Silas, about to respond. Doris stopped him, her finger on his lips.

"You don't cage the thing you love. Silas, you guard its path."

SILAS ENTERED OTRAC. Not much changed from his first visit forty years earlier.

Nothing that happens here happens fast...

Well within the six o'clock hour, that brief still point neither dawn nor day, the tortoises (how Silas mentally referred to the men and women—young, old, in-between—those patient souls who soundless, steadfast and unswerving, kept KALDEIDOSCOPE advancing through the inhospitable and shifting shingles of Angleton's wilderness of mirrors; year after year; decade after decade) occupied every swivel seat under the false dome shells of the old Commerce hall. A faint light, gray and uncertain as a mouse, spread across the oval skylight. Tuned the dark cuts of glass from black to the adagio of color they would play/spray/kaleidoscope across the coming day.

"Coffee? Mmm-yes?" Meryl Hofmyer offered Silas a heavy mug.

"It's cold."

"Not two hours ago—hmm?—when I made it for you." She clicked her tongue to accent his fault in missing out.

"Slept in." He put the mug back into her hand. "Nuke it."

She signaled the tortoise in the closest chair who took to the task. "And please see it beats us to the chief's desk. You will with a 'Yes, ma'am?'"

"Yes, Ms. Hofmyer." He trundled off with the mug.

Meryl to Silas, "Harker's December first deadline, presuming you care—yes?/no?—fast approaches. You've yet to clue/hint/include me in, hm, his missive."

They walked now, Silas aimed for the farthest corner, furthest door.

"Not that I don't—" more Meryl— "and I do, entirely, have my hands full with your full plate of today's Baku." She shifted files pressed against her bosom.

Silas reached the door. Instead of its knob—"I'll take those—" he took the files in trade for his letter from Harker.

She skimmed the letter as he prioritized.

Caspian Crossroads – TCP Pipeline Stabilization vs. Bloc Capture

Siloviki/Yurenev Bloc Penetration: State/Corporate Fusion in Ashgabat

Cinder Crown – Wànhuātǒng Encroachment via Kurdish Transit

"I don't like the idea of the Chinese anywhere near Houton's group."

"And I don't like the idea of Drexler fishing with your son at Camp Abu Omar."

"Drexler never knocks things over when he's hunting a light switch. Hal's loyalty I'll never question. Has Houton been informed of the CCP sniffing around?"

"Mm-hm—" reading from the Harker of it all. "He has, indeed, yes... Hmm, this letter is quite—"

"Childish?"

"Harker plays at the child's level of playing with matches and gasoline." Silas nodded, gave her that. "Childish, Silas, until Chicago burns down around us."

"That was a cow, Meryl. And stop worrying about Drexler."

"Morton Drexler sharpens knives for you. He is not-never nor will ever be family."

Silas opened his office door in time to see through modern glass windows that fronted an inner suite, the tortoise sent with the coffee, doity-doitying away.

Silas's two office doors linked him past to the inevitable future: an action-area where KALEIDOSCOPE jackrabbit'd along the superhighway. Necessary. Silas didn't like it/trust it/ride it; whenever he studied it through the glass, his old-school displeasure displayed for anyone unlucky enough to look his way.

"*Wànhuātǒng* worries me." He dropped the blinds. "They had a house-cleaning in October." Silas shaped a hand like a gun. Fired off a half dozen imaginary rounds. "We any closer to discovering last-man-standing on that account?"

Meryl shook her head.

"Whomever it is, we'll need to know before Baku."

The coffee mug steamed from a hole shifted between reams of files and white papers on his desk. A miniature vision of the *HMS Terror* unable to find the Northwest Passage. He added his new files to the ice floes. Lifted the mug. Sipped. Felt better.

Meryl wagged Harker's letter. "We going to, yet, let *yet* another day pass without addressing this order? The government, at-large, larger sir than us, is real."

"Did you have a nice Thanksgiving?"

"Silas!"

He bobbed his head—*I'm getting there*—eased into his chair. "I had a thought. A disturbing thought. Great Britain—they'll be at the Oil Conference?"

"They always are, but little, eh, relevance to us."

"That old tortoise, Jilly Bregado, too busy to take on a special project for me?" Silas.

"Never."

"She's older than I—"

"Will die in her traces, I'm quite sure."

"Pleasant, Meryl. She was here 1970-ish?"

"Started in 1969. We celebrated her fortieth, mmmm—"

"Don't care. About that. Right now, I care about the Brits. 1968 through 1972. They weren't pinging us, and soon after, went all-in Gulf/North Sea oil interests. But right there, that short window: Jilly is going to dig out—where she knows needs digging—if they reached out to, or were reached out by, Kalaydoskop. Have her pay particular attention to any unusual contact with Yurenev/Moscow Station. Would you do that?"

"Directly, sir." She offered Harker's letter.

"Keep it. Frame it. I'm making it his obituary."

Silas leaned back. Folded hands behind his bullet head. Detailed his plan for bleeding out Harker by paper cuts. When he finished—Meryl Hofmyer half-out his door—he inquired, "Are you hearing any whispers out of Foreign Resources—? That Malkinson group, or Gravin's Seventh Floor suite on, um…?"

"Lynn."

"That's the one."

"I warned you about that calendar, Silas."

"Nothing, then, from the Azerbaijan Embassy?" Blithe.

"No. Would you like me to, you-know-mmm, add that to my list?"

A short noise between a snort and a laugh—not something you would do in front of the person you were doing it over—but Lynn wasn't there. Nor anywhere anyone knew. Silas brushed the air to brush Meryl out. "Do nothing. Better or worse, that girl always makes her presence known to me."

Friday, November Twenty-third

1.

MORTON DREXLER WAS NOT a Kingston. Not by blood. Not by license. Nowhere along his muddy Texas bloodline did a single Drexler merge beds or jump a bank into the Kingston river of blood. No link. No kinship sunk and secret. His mother's Grainey branch—withered to just him and his bachelorette sister Molly down in Texas—had never run especially wet. It had sprung, peculiar as lines sometimes do in Texas, from a dirty-red-headed brown-eyed girl born on the Kickapoo Reservation whose personal ancestry drew on a centuries-old kidnapping, who claimed "white/Irish" on her 1958 paperwork for employment as a laundress at the Spindletop salt-brine extraction development in Beaumont (a coincidence, that, with the name of the Kingston dog)— and married her way into the American mainstream. Nowhere along that runnel had Grainey and Kingston blood flowed together, mixed.

As for the other—Morton Drexler would never entertain the idea of marrying into the Kingston blight. And yet...

Name the man, or woman, more devoted to the Kingston name, than Morton Drexler.

But to the Foxtail Farm table, where he'd dined with Silas and his wife, had lifted his wine—the children their milk—to Doris and the Agency and "family," to all he believed that entailed, Morton Drexler had been denied a permanent seat. Morton Drexler, of orders followed without question. Of confidences sworn. Advice not only taken but modelled. Dirty secrets kept. Of KALEIDOSCOPE blind-eyed and, unasked but, when necessary, massaged/cultivated/unleashed inside Langley's walls.

Of knives twisted—

Sidelined. Left behind.

—and left dripping in backs.

Morton Drexler never to ascend and claim his rightful position earned at the head of the Counterintelligence Center. Abandoned in the position of Associate Director Counterintelligence with a Silas bone thrown his way. (After having left him floored.) A special designation. Specially created. *ADCI for Integrity and Liaison Review*. Stuck in his throat these last five years. And too late, Morton Drexler understood: the knight who guarded Silas Kingston's gate would always stand outside that gate.

Sidelined. Left behind. Shut out.

That early morning, the day after Thanksgiving, Drexler arrived at the CIC an hour before the night watch rotated out at five. At home, and earlier (though he didn't yet know, well-nigh the moment Lynn Kingston held Roman Sayadov's ruined head between bloody palms and another piece of her soul dashed against her Kingston legacy), he'd planned to enjoy the companionship of his long-time friend Deleta Manthorne and had rushed his holiday meal—a few thick slices of Boar's Head Hickory Smoked Black Forest deli turkey breast, and half a Sara Lee pumpkin pie; and half a Marie Callendar's pecan pie (each, best of their brands); Reddi Wip on both because it was only once a year (and Christmas Eve and Day and New Year's—each of them once a year, too—) but soured on the Deleta idea halfway through the can of jellied cranberry he'd forgotten he had also bought. Put aside his spoon. Cancelled with Ms. Manthorne as she was driving over. Promised her money anyway and though she cursed his fat ass to high heaven for wasting her best holiday after-midnight hour for his discount, he was good for the cash and a "recovery" tip and a reschedule.

Drexler meandered the CIC with faint hope of word from Camp Abu Omar. Faint worry Hal's CINDER CROWN legend backstopped sufficiently for Colonel Finn Houton, or if not, he needed to jump on damage control to protect his officer.

My officer. A Kingston. Son hunting the father, sent by me—a son who never was.

Sidelined. Shut out. Stomped down.

Did he honestly believe Silas Kingston a Soviet mole? James Jesus Angleton's hand-picked wonder boy all those years ago. Improbable. Highly unlikely. But his Silas-bestowed designation, *Integrity Review*, spoke to "internal compromise"; a sexy sounding dead end Silas kicked him into, he now used in hopes of shoving Silas's head into its wall.

Seven hours ahead, nothing from Iraq. CINDER CROWN safe. For now. Proceed as planned. For an instant, he sparked a wild notion to print out President

Lincoln's *Thanksgiving Address*. Inspire the Mission Center. Rouse the troops.

Might as well holler down a well.

No one took inspiration from Morton Drexler. Might be healthier to give a few orders—had he orders to give. Wandered the CIC bullpen. Didn't feel like dishing put-downs to anyone just to feed them his blues. Footprint'd the carpet. Displaced quiet dead air with a mien of pretend thankfulness, mean of gratitude, humility, and reconciliation. God or man. No matter how large he constructed himself, he diminished daily in impotent aggrievedness. His feet felt light with his passage. Found his way to his office. Dropped his briefcase. Dropped anchor at his desk.

And so it happened. Around the same time as Silas to Meryl Hofmyer, *"Are you hearing any whispers out of Foreign Resources?"* Morton Drexler caught a low-level communication. Per Vienna Convention protocols. Routed State Department Office of Foreign Missions/State Protocol Office's after-hours queue. Routed Diplomatic Security Service Watch-Desk. Mirrored across his Liaison Review/Counterintelligence console. Azerbaijan Embassy to US State Department.

PRELIMINARY WATCH-FLOW TRAFFIC

Usual/standard date and time. The origin. Distribution list. Source-tag, routing/traffic code, etcetera. Standard bell/standard whistle—

[CLASSIFIED//EYES ONLY]

—followed by the text:

IT IS OUR DEEPEST REGRET, THE EMBASSY OF THE REPUBLIC OF AZERBAIJAN MUST INFORM THE U.S. DEPARTMENT OF STATE OF A CRIMINAL INCIDENT INVOLVING AN INVITED AMER-

ICAN GUEST THAT TRANSPIRED AT 11:48 PM DURING OUR NATIONAL REVIVAL DAY CELEBRATION. THE MATTER IS UNDER REVIEW BY INTERNAL EMBASSY SECURITY. NO UNITED STATES HELP REQUESTED OR REQUIRED.

The nagging blues to crab-boil red alert. Five-bell fire alarm. Aerial bomb whistle.

Language: fire-alarm wrong. Not the *American guest* of it—only reason the traffic goes out. All diplomatic language is code, even what reads plain. "*Deepest*" regret. "*Criminal*" incident. No help "*requested*". That's severity flaunted, agency denied, cooperation defied. Drexler red-lights. The "*Transpired at 11:48 pm.*" Minute-specific. Indicates the necessity for a forensic timeline while the sent/received stamp of 5:45 AM—six hours after the fact—

Hey, America. How're you fit for an after-turkey afterthought?

—indicates *fuck off.*

But it's the last word. The tacked-on verb "*Required.*" Red flags. Fire alarms. Drexler red-light, red alert, boils red.

That's a God damn international threat. A diplomatic immunity/sovereign ground America butt out: your "citizen" belongs to us.

Phone in his fist. State Department. Bureau of Intelligence and Research. "Need Jolee Ganbe—" his liaison officer. "Now."

Her administrative assistant re: Ganbe: re: holiday weekend. Re: out. And she ain't scheduled to "in".

"Then you whip her up. I want Ms. Ganbe on this line faster than a sneeze through a screen door. Now patch me over to whomever isn't burping turkey in bed like your lazy-assed boss, and is acting Deputy Liaison Officer for Host-Nation Events and Clearance. Cut back into the line when you got Ganbe."

Call transferred. Connected. Low-totem-pole/short straw-puller only a couple rungs up the frog-raven-thunderbird stack, crab-appling he didn't get his stuffing, but with more authority than the *"Happy Day After!"* administrative assistant. Traffic read? Check. Red flags same? Check. Satisfied Drexler's urgency but only to a darker negative.

"Don't understand though, Mr. Drexler. Makes zero sense."

"Explain as if I'm stupid as you."

"So I was missing my holiday meal—2:30 pm—right here at this desk, sir—when the official cancellation of that particular event comes in from their embassy. Official cancellation."

"Whatdya mean? Obviously, it wasn't cancelled."

Some other-end key-clattering. *Ding*: Drexler's computer. Official cancellation. Rec'd: 2:30 in the PM, Thanksgiving Day.

"I'd say, someone got sandpapered." Drexler.

"Wasn't one of ours. We don't typically send anyone, this sort of event. Azerbaijan's shop or anyone else's."

"Typically?"

"Odd again. We did have two invites for this event. Confirmed. I made the RSVP a week ago. Confirmed the cancellations yesterday."

"Who?"

"An Energy Officer from our Bureau of Energy Resources was going with a Deputy Director of Energy Affairs. Happy not to, I'll say."

Every red drop of blood inside Morton Drexler froze glacier blue.

KALEIDOSCOPE.

"You're telling me—confirming hundred percent—they did not attend?"

"They did not. And I checked the rest of the guest list soon as the message came through—"

"You have the guest list? What else you check?"

"That's correct, sir. I do. No other American officials on it. But that doesn't mean someone foreign's plus-one couldn't have been an American civilian. They're listed, too—all the plus-ones—for everyone. But something like this, friendly nation, no need for a civvy to clear with us. They'd just need their passport to get inside. Requirement embossed on the invitation. Honestly, way-names-go, we have no idea; plus-ones could be anyone from anywhere."

Dazed. To the core.

"Send me that list. Right now."

Interruption— "I have Ms. Ganbe, Associate Director—"

Drexler slowly removed the phone from his ear. Slowly fit the receiver into its base. Crossed arms. Rocked slowly back in his chair. Breathed slowly, almost not breathing at all. Faint through nostrils. Out through the whistle formed by his lips. Except for his heavy breath, the slow and steady rise and fall of his chest, Morton Drexler was motionless.

Ding. Guest list.

Even if this is KALEIDOSCOPE—

(KALEIDOSCOPE: that small dormant acorn forever aching at the center of his mind/being/meaning suddenly a mighty oak in root and trunk and branches of imagination; a tree his every muscle quivered to meet with the ax of vendetta.)

—I am an Associate Director of the Central Intelligence Agency. No foreign hand will so much as touch an American, especially if this is an intelligence officer. So long as I draw breath.

KALEIDOSCOPE used outside contractors for most denied area access/alias insertion. Light-cover jobs: NGO or USAID operatives. Heavier work: the ex's. Ex-CIA, ex-FBI, ex-DIA, ex-military. Drexler didn't pretend that many times they weren't ex-anything at all, but current CIA seconded to KALEIDOSCOPE by byzantine TDY assignment eight miles down Department of Commerce corridors to a dim and faded sign: *Office of Treaty Regulation and Administrative Compliance*. No matter how deep their official or non-official cover was buried, their aliases, the nuts and bolts of their cover identities, were somewhere in-system. Registered. Protected.

Drexler ran each unverified name on those lists. Guests—Azeri, foreign allied/neutral/enemy verified; every unknown/unverified plus-one against transit activity logs. Queried agency watchlists. Queried SIGINT databases. Queried NOC legends. Queried credit pings on phony cards that went through black accounting administration. Paid particular attention to alias/cover kits assigned to the National Resource Division/Foreign Resource. And every leaf on every twig at the end of every branch of that mighty oak sprung from that acorn of resentment inside him, created a psithurism on the faint breeze of his ponderous breath.

Kingston/KALEIDOSCOPE... Kingston/KALEIDOSCOPE... Kingston/KALEIDOSCOPE...

Eyes popped. Last one. List bottom. *Layla Kingsbury.* Signature-easy/memorization-easy/slip-up recovery easy. Easy-pour/quick-cover-lite.

Lynn.

Had to be. Ran it.

Nothing. Drexler's gut quivered.

Good Lord. I'd eat anything right now that didn't eat me first.

The fat man ached, ravenous. Truth about that—about Morton Drexler's appetite—well, he gorged himself to black-out flashes of deep-ache psychic insignificance. Souls don't rot on their own; there's always a secret sharer. Even if they don't know it. Like any addiction, his true nature/inclination stared him right back in the face. Every waking moment of his adulthood. Like all addicts, he willfully stared back black-out blind.

She ain't so stupid to walk into a trap. Ha! Lynn? No way. That and a wooden nickel will buy you a ride on an empty field the day after the fair. A gut this big—take a niggle too far.

He sent a request to the floor. Deep dive "Layla Kingsbury." Retired aliases. Restricted aliases. KALEIDOSCOPE-blocked personnel files. Followed by a second: "Layla Kingsbury" public records.

Somebody else. Somebody real. Light cover too lite. A phonetic coincidence. (How they make it; no-think/light-cover.) Get a grip, fat man.

Set himself on traffic surveillance. Wide net. Metropolitan PD. Federal Protective Service. Requested a footage-pull from CIA's Technical Surveillance

Unit. Flagged them all PCT. Potential Counterterrorism Threat.

Get 'em dancing like a lizard on skillet.

Sweet Lord, that hunk of turkey breast sounds right good about this side of now. Second half a'pecan pie.

Pictured the crimped shiny sparkle of tinfoil. Hand's reach inside his briefcase. Thought—

Lynn Kingston. Gut-trust.

She worked Foreign Resource—did now, no way around that—but Lynn Kingston was KALEIDOSCOPE barred. He'd shut that barn door right in her face after Michael Kingston vanished during CLAVICLE; Drexler's unsuccessful attempt to draw her in his direction. Pit her against her own name. Pit her against Silas.

Throat wrapped and voiceless. She sits a wooden bench, front of the Centennial Street US Post Office, La Plata. I set myself beside her. Wooden slats bend beneath me.

"Whatever you, Michael, and your GI Joe brother are mixed up in, aims back at your father. You can either ride above it in the airplane or be on the ground when the bomb hits. I'm blowing up, Silas Kingston."

Lynn shows me her tablet: Not so nice a way to treat your second daddy.

I stand. Give her the pig eye. "Get that voice healed. If it comes down to it, it'll make interrogation/confession that much easier."

Silas pushed her hard from his side, too. Drexler couldn't believe he rode the same teeter-totter with that man, but together—

We might've catapulted her right into this.

Into Foreign Resources. Into crap job, crap work, hoping to force Lynn into a lengthier medical sabbatical until the Michael blowback blew over. Both of them responsible.

Foreign Resources: where losers throw pitches at foreign embassy kitchen staff.

Morton Drexler waited for surveillance. Chair back. Arms crossed. Chest heaving, O'ing that heavy subterranean breath. Thinking that tinfoil bundle. Fighting that craving.

Thirty-eight minutes—no footage returned—Drexler snapped his briefcase. Tore tinfoil. Wolfed. Swallowed. Stilled himself. Centered into his mass. Grabbed phone and cracked the whip.

In order: MPD, Metropolitan Police Department. Got hold of the Sergeant in Charge, Special Operations Division. Bit hard enough to get a line up to the Deputy Director of the Joint Operations Command Center. Dipped a Texas smile in Texas tone. Kind that denied all forms of happiness. "When this bumps to Tier One, do you really want your Chief Intelligence Liaison—what's his name?" Checked a list. "Carter Upkins—asking you why this video request sat on your desk forty-five minutes 'stead a'gettin' routed to me in the ten minutes that you, me, and the fly on the shit know you can get that li'l drag-'n'-drop job done? 'Cause when the fly bounces and the shit starts rollin'— ... Bless your heart, pal, that'll do the trick I'm lookin' for." Went direct with his next. Sally Dean-Killian. Assistant Director, Regional Operations/National Capital Region, FPS, Federal Protective Service. "Sally, I know you're buried in backlog. I get it. I do. I do. But this isn't just some embassy cocktail party with a wine stain on some cultural heritage, child-labor hand-stitched rug. The Director's already asking, 'Why's my fat man don't have eyes on this yet?' ... That's correct, ma'am, we're ruling in—not out—a terror component. Your footage may provide the ID our DCI needs his eyes on. Like, next time he blinks." Last call. In-house. Branch Chief, Covert Technical Operations. This was his "you never know" longshot. William Melendor (Drexler referred to in his head as the "Blow-tied Bow-job" based on his Classic Harvard Bowtie) was a suck-up, legendary for a streak of job paranoia; spent 24/7 looking over the city's shoulders. Drexler had him convinced whenever the opportunity arose, BTBJ's shoulder was getting the same treatment in his own chair.

"Lookit. I've got Gravin breathing down my neck. Last thing I want is to tell him's one of our own folk's dragging like a three-legged dog on a hot tar road."

"Do I even know what that means?"

"Billy: you know you don't want to make happen with DDO Gravin whatever it *does* mean. Hm?"

He didn't. Couldn't think of any ongoing ops in the neighborhood in question but jumped.

Drexler cradled his phone. Folded his hands (to keep them off the still-waiting pie). Stared at his computer screen, willing its doorbell *ding*.

O'd his lips. Got the bellows pumping inside him. Heavy, slow, soft. Knew he didn't hold Lynn Kingston in any affection.

Ridiculous. Obscene.

Two of them sparred over everything. Viciously, if opportunity granted. Words. Code-free.

Always only words.

And ideas/opinions; they instinctively disagreed on everything like cats disagree with dogs. Like a cat, he couldn't be bothered by her yapping. Like a cat—if cats were honest—and Morton Drexler considered himself honest, more than he needed to be at any rate, he secretly envied dogs their freedom. Their harmony with their emotions. Trust without that shame that masked aloofness to their simple needs and tender desires.

Embarrassment—more like it.

Nil from TSU; no drone, satellite, or CCTV assets positioned for other operations with LOS on the Azerbaijan Embassy or vicinity (came with a hint Drexler might mention BTBJ Melendor's swift response to DDO Gravin; Drexler of-course'd it; promptly remembered not to).

FPS capital city surveillance cameras ringed in next. Slider'd video capture.

A black Mercedes. (Lynn drives a Porsche.)

Typical East Asia rich-ass douche-mobile. It slows. Hits its blinker. Rolls into the middle and out of frame.

The Azerbaijan Embassy block. Driveway next, maybe two down.

Maybe a guest didn't get the "cancelled" message. Maybe an American guest inside the pimp-ride. Maybe caused a scene. Maybe that's the crime. Maybe nothing.

Slider'd back. Tried to isolate plates—*No, no, crap angles. No*—Caught it. Keyboarded it to the bullpen.

Drexler fed his face. Chewed hard. Didn't think (way he didn't look at his addiction) about Lynn.

He'd known her, precocious as a teenage girl. Limber legs up and down those dangerous beach stairs. Throwing a football with her brothers. With Silas. Drexler sympathized with the kid.

Then.

Her quiet despair over her father's viciousness. That despair that crushed her when she thought no one saw.

Kingston's get what Kingston's deserve. And I get meat and pie and I'm just glad I'm not one of them. Not by blood. Not by license.

Right thing to do, right now, alert National Resource Manager Malkinson. Bing-bang DDO Gravin, Seventh Floor the whole thing—woman's already his.

If it's gotta be her.

Didn't know. Never sloppy. Didn't do it. Pulled up Facebook. Magnifying glass. Search it. L-A-Y-L-A. K-I-N-G-S-B-U-R-Y. Hung a thick index finger over *Enter.*

Ding! MPD traffic cams. Facebook abandoned. Scrolled video panels. It didn't have to be Lynn. Isolated the pimp ride.

Computer *ding.* Separate window. Vehicle registration. 2009 Mercedes SLS, registered: *Kingsbury, Layla.*

Probably bimbo arm-candy for some shaved-head vanity-posted douche.

Didn't matter, one way or the other, who she was. Didn't matter crime or no crime. Didn't matter Lynn/not Lynn. Didn't matter. Glanced at the original Embassy watch-flow traffic—finished the chunk of turkey, moved to the pie—

A middle-fingered FU hostage note. Not in Morton Drexler's face. Nobody holds an American hostage.

Fast-forward video. Caught the black douche-mobile. Strike that—Layla Kingsbury's sugar-daddy-wheels.

Sure enough. Douchebag driving. Except that the driver had hair rather than a shave-top, beside him... Beside him...

Beside him: Lynn. That's panic—full panic—poor girl's face.

Hated face. Kingston's get what Kingston's deserve.

Morton Drexler ate to hide from his insignificance.

Call DDO Gravin. Push it off. Wipe hands. Gravin will save her. Gravin won't stop until Lynn's safe. Drexler swallowed. Felt supremely better. Any blind man could see: the illustrious Deputy Director of Operations Gary Gravin was hopelessly in love with Lynn Kingston.

I'll just finish this pie before I call.

While he lip-smacking did just that, Drexler jotted himself a note:

ATM. Deleta's cash.

Pushed from his mind the dirty thought—sometimes when she saddled him—times he pretended he wasn't hungry at all, he'd pretend he was young; fantasized himself still shy, still warm-hearted, still warm-feathered under Silas's wing out there at Foxtail Farm where the wind whistled the boughs of the high pines that loom over the strip of lawn where he'd been invited, once, to play badminton. (Before it became clear to the Kingstons, sports just weren't his thing.)

"Tell you this, Drexler. This strip of lawn—right here they're playing on—first Silvanus Kingston shot his own brother in a duel. Right here."

"Over a woman, sir?"

"You'd kill your own brother over something frivolous as that?"

Blushed. "I don't have a brother." Watches teenage Lynn bounce up for the shuttlecock. (His memory frames her lighter than air, simple, pure, colorful-clean as a balloon. Airborne forever.) "Sir."

"Slavery. American slavery."

Dinner around Mrs. Doris's table. Making that just-teenaged Lynn smile with something purposely stupid he might have said to get that smile, and Doris's sad, knowing look, that pure instant when he thought he had.

Damn fine roast that woman made. Succulent. Just the right amount of fat, cooked enough to dissolve on my tongue. That stupid thing I'd said— Lynn's smile is for Michael. Not me.

Doesn't notice me. Never has—not really. Never will.

And I avoid Silas's unblinking daggers and Doris touches my hand. "There's always a plate for you at this table, Morton. Always enough to eat, so don't be a stranger."

Her regard. Doris not Lynn. Never derision; consolation from the mother, what he wouldn't dream of receiving from the daughter. Doris Kingston was love. A good mother and kind. A wife who deserved better.

Silas never invited me back. Even if all I'd stolen was one kind look from those charitable eyes one night at her table, perfectly round.

Loyalty is a choice. Loyalty is a blind spot. Stubborn. And stupid. And why didn't Lynn grow into her?

Drexler ran the back of his hand across his lips. Crumbs and molasses-flavored corn syrup sticky.

"You stole my midnight money-hour! Fucking fat ass! You still gonna to pay me! Fuckin' want some sweet-ass

a'Deleta next-time-'round, you insensitive mutha-fuck-ah! Happy Thanks-givin'-yourself a handjob."

And, Deleta, sweet pea, you'll still smell like bourbon and "whoor-gardinia" like you call that shit perfume—

(Lynn. Dior Dune. Same as Doris.)

—and you'll still saddle up and squirm and squeal and moan, your touch dry without human warmth—

"There's always a place for you at this table, Morton," and Doris touches my hand

—and you'll never know I'm looking up at someone else, untouchable, I'll never see smiling at me when I'm smiling up hollow at you.

He'd hit *Enter* long ago; clicked through the legend photos—

Badminton to tennis. Porsche to Mercedes. Some old townhouse with a broken porch light. We used to say "pocket," now it's "social media" litter.

Copied the Layla Kingsbury's grinning profile picture.

Never smiled my way once.

Print-screen'd a Mercedes passenger seat Lynn/Layla panic jpeg. Email attached both. Dialed Deputy Director Gravin's office as he composed the man his report. Up to the Seventh. Drexler found Lynn, but Gravin would save her. Gravin was in love with Lynn Kingston. Any blind man could see that.

2.

SEVENTH FLOOR CORRIDOR. FAST between his Ops offices and the Director's Suite. Lynn Kingston: his officer. Suspect/prisoner inside the Azerbaijan Embassy. His fault. Every decision Deputy Director for Operations Gary Gravin had made regarding Lynn since Michael's disappearance in July: wrong. Too soft when he should have gone hard.

I massaged the Presidential Finding on CLAVICLE; almost lost her at Dulles.

Too hard when he should have gone soft.

"You went too far. Nothing I can do to help you now. You'll finish your medical leave, but you won't return to Ops. It's Foreign Resources for you. As far from KALEIDOSCOPE and your brothers as possible. You only have yourself to blame."

A confused rush to make it right when it all was falling apart.

Lynn—mischief-bright eyes— "Do you think my termination is going to go through or are you going to get Stephanie Malkinson off my back?"

"You're a piece of work, Lynn."

Come-on eyes. "And you haven't even touched on the sex of it all."

"I don't want to think of you that way. I think too much of you."

Devilish eyes. "In that way."

"I think too much of you, Lynn."

This whole code clerk op—too fast, too loose. Every step he'd encouraged. Approved.

The handle of the four-wheel combi-lock black leather document case was cheap plastic. Sharp-edged from its original *Made in China* mold. Gripped too tight, it hurt. Pain to cover emotion.

Inappropriate.

Unprofessional.

Sloppy. Two years flirtation; a dance of humming-birds. Swirling each other, rapier bills giving the appearance of aggression, of fight, but eyes fast on eyes, whole thing's a mating dance, whole time.

We never got involved. Never came close to acting on my feelings.

Not because I'm married. Because I am professional.

When he did flirt, Lynn called him out. Told him, *"No."*

But sometimes her "no's"—mine too—maybe all cover. Ghost money passed covertly as "maybe's" creeping up, daring each other to peek over the orchard wall and steal a "yes."

Now, Lynn faced criminal charges.

What the hell have I let happen?

One of Director Harker's body men from the Office of Security waited at the door. Nods traded. Security card/punch code. Door opened. "Deputy Director, sir."

Gary stepped past. An antechamber—security officer's desk, Director's door, secretarial assistant desk, door to the conference room, and Executive Administrative Assistant desk with Mrs. Polovetz, polite. Almost but never quite smiling. "It will be just one moment, Deputy Director. The Director is back from the President's Daily Brief and riding up now."

One moment later, another bodyguard opened the Director's office door. Stepped out. Stepped aside.

Mrs. Polovetz. "You may enter, Mr. Gravin."

CIA Director Jeremy Harker III flung himself into his chair in an obvious display of got-anger-to-burn displeasure. Shot his cuffs even though he'd just hung his suit jacket on its rack. Gary stood between the visitor chairs and the director's desk. Worked the lock on his document case.

Harker. "You are aware that the Syrian al-Omar oil fields have fallen to rebel forces?"

"To the al-Nusra Front extremists. Yes. The Deputy DDO for Middle East and North Africa Operations is holding the line for me with our Chief of Near East Operations and Special Activities Division. I'll debrief after this."

A red-foldered file. Briefing marked TOP SECRET//SCI//EYES ONLY. Vertical black and yellow caution stripe slashed the right margin. Codeword stamped black.

Harker took it. Opened it. Glanced. Gary could see Harker's pulse zigzag the vein prominent at his temple. Harker's smile: grimmer than Mrs. Polovetz. "Where I've just been—the president has decided to recognize al-Nusra as an al-Qaeda affiliate. Order has gone out this morning, Oval Office to State, to designate al-Nusra as a foreign terrorist organization."

Like this is something personal I've done to him?

Harker shut the file. "Gary, do you know what that does to President Obama's Red Line?" The DDO knew enough not to respond. "Blows it the fuck up is what that does."

Harker opened the file. The cable traffic. The Lynn/Mercedes surveillance photos. The Lynn/Layla Kingsbury legend kit. Some new material Gary added after Drexler.

"Director, sir, if I can say: right out the gate you advised the administration against that specific piece of rhetoric."

"Thank you, Gary, for remembering. Yes. I did. I advised him not to go there. Red Line theatrics. We go on record now, saying Assad is fighting our number one, worldwide enemy, Obama's emboldening Assad to hit al-Nusra as hard as he wants."

"We're already tracking increased activity around Assad's chemical weapons stockpiles."

"He is readying them. Gary, he's going to cross that red line. Remember *these* words. Once he does—if Obama's good to his word—we're right into committing troops."

"Not like we don't have Special Forces there already." Offhand. Gary eyeballed Director Harker to the briefing file.

Harker ignored. "I don't want another full-blown Mideast war. My job is to keep Syria's war from becoming *our* war. Let CIA do our job right, we keep regular troops out of it. Young men, women into the meat grinder. But I tell you, the looks I see between them—it's like they see some kind of profit in it. They've been bringing around that CENTCOM commander, ran things in Iraq." Harker stares through his glasses. Blinks a few times. Removes them. Spits on the lens. Cleans with his tie. "I shouldn't say any more. This is between us."

"Always, Jeremy."

Glasses held to the light. Squint-checked. Clear. Back on. Eyes back on his desktop but a final, almost whispered— "They want a general running this place. Now what is this? Kingston's daughter, huh? Officer with that extreme *laryngitis* at Dulles back on the Fourth."

Gary annoyed/heart-stabbed nodded vaguely; Harker wasn't looking at him.

Harker read in. Went on. "You moved her to Foreign Resources, if I remember correctly." Read on. Looked up, puzzled. "Silas wanted her there. FR. Specifically to keep her *away* from KALEIDOSCOPE."

"Lynn Kingston was running that recruitment by the book. Our book. But I will admit, she's unmoored and I should have seen it. For her, the embassy op wasn't about Sayadov—it was about what he could give her on KALEIDOSCOPE."

Harker closed the briefing book. "KALEIDOSCOPE is supposed to have CIA's back on energy conflict. Specifically oil. Our Syrian problem, our President's Red Line with Assad, one that's blowing up in my face? Al-Samir is the biggest oil field in Syria. I could have used some warning. Could have had some help. Instead, you're telling me Silas Kingston is piddling around up the street with the Azerbaijan Embassy?"

"I'm not telling you that. The embassy situation is all Lynn Kingston. Not Silas Kingston."

Harker let his frustration off the leash. "And Baku is about him running surveillance, wiretapping, bribery schemes, business deals—fucking industrial espionage we're not even chartered to engage—for some oil conference, and who-knows-what he's up to in Iraq? Training Iranian insurgents for God knows why. This administration is actively putting together a solution for Iran. With China. With Russia, France, the UK and Germany. This president is putting an end to Iran's nuclear ambitions and bringing them into the free-world light. Cash 'em out. My God, what is this?"

Gary pointed at the Lynn folder. Touched the codename. Harker bristled at it. Mocked. "What the hell is that anyway 'BORDEN SAINT?' What-what *is* that?"

"Well, I think it reflects she's either one or the other."

"A cow or a saint?"

"Drexler—I believe—meant *Lizzie* Borden. The murderess?"

"If she were the Borden part, she'd have already axed her father and half my problems—this *Agency's* problems—would be gone. And 'saint,' I'd say, speaks directly to your history of overestimating that woman's worth to this Agency."

He slumped. Out of steam. Waved Gary down. His cufflink swung at his wrist. "Sit. You bother me, hovering." Opened Lynn's file a third time. "Drexler took this in CIC?"

"Just before dawn."

"Got the surveillance? ID'd your officer?"

"He did."

"I like Drexler. My kind of company man. Always a thorough job."

"Yes. Sir. I followed up. Ran second contact back at the Azeris. Had DSS submit a non-escalatory/routine diplomatic request for more information."

Harker fished into one of the annex slots in the cover. Pulled two comms. Pulled an accompanying photograph. Pulled out his reading voice for the DSS outbound. "'We understand an American citizen was detained at your Thanksgiving function. Please confirm name, status, condition.' And..." Switched to the second cable. "This came back from the embassy." Read: "'The guest is not a civilian but a U.S. intelligence officer attempting espionage on Azerbaijani sovereign ground who has committed a deadly crime. We will not permit DSS investigation, but we are keeping you informed. We will share our murder investigation findings in due course.'"

The new photo returned from the embassy was Lynn Kingston. The Rock Creek Tennis Club Christmas calendar. "The club where she met her prospect. Pitched him."

Gary looked down. Small nod.

"What kind of cover were you running?"

Gary. Eye lift. "Moving fast. She'd only used the gym there years ago. Had no contact with any current employees in the past. Place her point of contact plays. Didn't like it. Made a judgment call. Best way in."

"'In.' I'll say. She's *in* their fucking calendar."

"Tennis club never produced a calendar before. We swept their social media and their computers. Lynn Kingston never had a picture taken there."

"Wrong." Waved the picture. "She did."

"I believe there might be more to that calendar..."

Troubled look between them.

"I agree." Haker subdued. "That's not our problem right this second... They say she's committed a murder, they know she's CIA. There's nothing offered on the supposed victim, nothing about this in the press?"

"Not theirs. Not ours."

"Russian? Chinese—always snooping."

"Nobody."

"Means they want to negotiate something."

"Except they're insistent we stay out of it."

"Telling us not to get involved."

"Not to get involved. That's right, sir."

"Why? What was she after?"

"Permanent access to an embassy cipher machine."

"Is everyone an idiot? If I am not mistaken—and I'm not—like almost every foreign embassy here in town, they use Crypto AG's cipher machines. Specifically the CX-52, which we've had a backdoor into for ten years through our RUBICON operation with the Germans. From where I'm sitting, that makes this entire shit-fest useless."

"I stand by my op."

"You will if something worse happens to your officer."

"This was a valid target worth the risk. This particular machine is the Azeri proprietary version of the Greta-coder 605 the Azerbaijan data encryptor dedicated to Russian traffic. We don't have a backdoor into that."

"Until you put a Kingston on it and she kills someone."

Gary waited. Harker cooled down.

Harker. "How?"

"How?"

"Is she supposed to have done that? Kill somebody."

"It's preposterous on the face. Gun to penknife: she wouldn't have had a weapon on her."

"They had the calendar. Cancelled the reception. All the earmarks of a trap."

"Secured by *them.* Minute it was sprung, she'd know to sit tight. How does she get the advantage? How does it escalate to violence?"

Harker. "She was under official cover. One thing about Kingstons: they don't scare. She wouldn't have done shit."

Now the bait.

"When we built it out, it was official cover."

Harker schoolmarm'd over his frames.

"Two days ago, that cover was KALEIDOSCOPE restricted."

I'm getting you back, Lynn.

"You said this *wasn't* KALEIDOSCOPE."

"Not her. Not me."

"Bullshit. Gary—she obviously was working for her fucking father. This—this—this will take him down."

Now the lie.

"The restriction is the same one we've seen on the Baku Caspian Oil Conference."

"Good. Silas is funneling everything to you on that, right? As I ordered him. That conference begins the day after Christmas."

Sprinkle of truth.

"Nothing definitive has come to my team."

"I swear to God—whether that man cooperates or not. He has been given orders. Firm dates for disclosure and a hearing. I am dismantling KALEIDOSCOPE."

The pitch that's going to mean everything. Don't blink. Don't breathe. Kill it.

"Let the daughter be his undoing. He put his stamp on her cover. Her cover is blown. I'd like your permission to oversee Silas Kingston handling this situation. If it is Baku related, I'll be there to find out exactly what he's up to as he negotiates her release."

"And if it blows up?"

"That would be the end of Silas Kingston and KALEIDOSCOPE all at once."

"It would. Wouldn't it?"

Haker's desk phone/intercom buzzed. Harker and Gary shared a look. Harker nodded him for the door, already silent-signaled, opened by the security man outside. As Gary passed through, he heard both sides of the exchange.

Mrs. Polovetz: "Silas Kingston will deliver a first set of the KALIEDOSCOPE documents you requested this afternoon."

Harker: "Really? When they arrive, have them brought directly to me."

The door shut behind Gary Gravin who stopped in the director's anteroom. As the corridor door opened, the body man outside shooting him the *move-it* look, Gary waited for Mrs. Polovetz's response.

"It's three trucks, Mr. Director."

"Three?"

"'Small moving trucks.' His words. In the essence of time, Mr. Kingston has engaged an outside transport company. They'll head down to the garage basement for mirrors, sniff-up, and search."

Gary Gravin smiled. Resigned. He'd heard the talk. About moving a general into the suite now sealed and guarded behind him. Thought back to his first field assignment twenty years earlier. Wondered if Silas Kingston would remember him, or even knew he'd seconded to KALEIDOSCOPE—

Who knows what or why

—off a DDO Harker China clusterfuck called SIDESHOW.

3.

GRAVIN. SECURE PHONE. HIS desk, Langley. Silas—connected on the *if you say so* secure number Harker had for him. Warehouse activity surround sound. Sounded unsecure but Silas vouched for it, Harker vouched by passing the digits, and Gravin, cautious always—purpose of this call—didn't care all that hard. He introduced himself. Silas didn't bother.

SILAS: "Been quite some time since the two of us spoke."

GRAVIN: "Over two decades."

SILAS: "You were instrumental in one of my successes. You've come a long way to what some call a lonely place. If I never thanked you, consider this that."

GRAVIN: "All I did was pass a file to one of our officers after the operation was already over. One of our officers and a civilian that Director Harker—when he held my position—rescued from a Chinese prison."

SILAS: "Is that how he tells it?"

GRAVIN: "That amuses you."

SILAS: "The real operation began only after you put that packet in Tom Bishop's hands and he opened it. Ran successfully—we might add to your small credit—for ten years. Until ATROPOS reared its ugly head in the

Malaysian jungle and I took Acting Director Harker's head in exchange. Unless he tells that story differently. Too?"

GRAVIN: "He is back as director."

SILAS: "Squids grow back tentacles."

GRAVIN: "I think it's octopus that regenerate."

SILAS: "I think I know of whom I am speaking. But let's cut through the BS. He's issued me compliance orders by one December, which my organization is complying with as we speak. I'm also directed to advise/include your directorate in our ongoing training operation at Camp Abu Omar, as well as our influence operation going into the Caspian Oil Conference, twenty-six December."

GRAVIN: "This call is not about that. Not directly. I don't believe—"

SILAS: "Meaning indirectly, you do believe."

GRAVIN: "Meaning maybe."

SILAS: "Meaning cut to the chase: Foreign Resources. Meaning Roman Sayadov. Meaning the Azerbaijan Embassy. Meaning my daughter got the short end cracking the turkey wishbone."

Blank air.

GRAVIN: "How do you know all that?"

SILAS: "What I know and how I know it is not for you. You called me about the girl. You have something you want to tell me? Tell me."

GRAVIN: "My officer, your daughter Lynn Kingston, has been accused of espionage and arrested/detained for murder. The Azerbaijan Embassy is claiming foreign sovereignty. Shutting us out."

SILAS: "How do we get from the first to the second?"

GRAVIN: "They have provided no details."

SILAS: "No law enforcement? No ambulance? No verification—an allowed inspection of evidence—nothing?"

GRAVIN: "Nothing."

SILAS: "I won't waste time discussing the obvious. Lynn didn't kill—by murder, accident, or sudden plague-contagion—anyone."

GRAVIN: "Zero chance. I agree."

SILAS: "Doesn't mean someone else who went in alive is not coming out in the same condition."

GRAVIN: "We have the entire compound under every form of surveillance. If Lynn or a body comes out, they will be intercepted."

SILAS: "Not going to happen. Can you confirm that she went inside with her target, Sayadov?"

GRAVIN: "One hundred percent."

SILAS: "Our girl was pushing him to treason, so, best guess—he won't be coming out either. I imagine his body and every piece of evidence would prove they did it. Not a game that hasn't played all over the globe—it's been played here. I'm certain of that. But never this way. Never with us. A very disturbing circumstance."

GRAVIN: "Director Harker thinks they want to negotiate something. My question is, *does* this bear weight on their Caspian Oil Conference? On KALEIDOSCOPE?"

SILAS (MIRTHLESS): "Does now."

GRAVIN: "Then it would be beneficial to all parties if you handle this with me."

SILAS: "You're not adverse to my taking the lead?"

GRAVIN: "I'd expect it. How would you like to open the approach?"

SILAS: "No approach. It's what they want. We start now *not* giving them anything of what they want."

GRAVIN: "I'm not looking for a pissing contest. I'd say getting Lynn back is our only priority and doing nothing does not help achieve that."

SILAS: "Then go knock on the door. Bring the DSS, bring the FBI, bring the army. Bring the fucking Canadian Mounties. And when they slam it again in your and your horse's face, you all can walk off the property with your dicks in your hands. If they were going to kill her, she'd have just disappeared. They don't want an international incident. Someone inside needs leverage. Might be personal; might be the need to cover that, but the only next step they have—by their very clear mistake of holding onto her—is to move from investigation to a hush-hush legal proceeding."

GRAVIN: "What do you mean 'hush-hush'?"

SILAS: "It's to their political advantage and your institutional advantage—nationally, both sides, and internationally—that this stays out of the press."

GRAVIN: "And what about Lynn? Her physical well-being?"

SILAS: "That's your fault. Rests entirely on whether she gets straight bread and water or they take pity and spike it with gin."

GRAVIN: "My officer is sober. I guarantee it. Since her accident, she hasn't touched a drop."

THIS TIME: MIRTH; laughing, Silas hung up the phone. Chuckled. Stared at it, shaking his head at the stupidity of others. Meryl Hofmyer approached from where three small U-Haul moving vans were filling with banker's boxes.

"Ms. Hofmyer. How far did you get?"

"Historical records 1945 to 1991. With, uh, your approval, Silas, that's these, the three trucks, mmm, ready to go—yes?"

"You bet. Good. Get your origami-ists folding more boxes. Tomorrow—Saturday—rent from a different company. We'll send over 1992 to 2011. Anything FOIA-cleared, and this next batch, because it's more recent, double the black-marker tortoises' efforts: everything is to be redacted to the point of absurd-slash-obscurity. For Sunday, I want to get him in from the golf course—"

"The Director—you will recall, and I will remind, eh, you—practices ballroom dancing."

"Meryl: it was a metaphor. Syria's blowing up. He's here on Sunday. Guaranteed. And he's shrewd enough to recognize a disclosure dump for what it is when the three trucks pull in tonight. Sunday, go in official-channels. Armed delivery. All the frills. I want Harker forced to stand there like it's an official ceremony with pine boxes. Send him every obsolete OTRAC treatise on pipeline diplomacy. Get our NGOs, our USAIDs, our think tanks—"

"People's Energy Collective, American Institute for Pragmatic Climate Solutions—"

"Yes—Horizon Initiative—all of them. All our useless cover work like it's the Holy Grail. We'll top off the one December tranche with a two-inch binder—I want it so full that the rings are bent and no matter what he does, pages will slip off those rings when Harker turns them."

"And, um, what do I fill it with?"

"Our glossary."

"We have a glossary? I know we don't, but did you—"

"Don't be purposely obtuse. I know you're delighting in all of this. I want a glossary created for every outdated piece of terminology, CIA, NSA, DIA, Department of Commerce, Interior, Pentagon. Focus on open source/obvious and archaic/obsolete. Skew, say, a fifth of them, so the definition is confusing."

"Oh, that's thoughtful. Lovely. Purpose?"

"My rabbit hole. They'll all point to a set of records—files, minutes, reports—from the NPC, specifically 1946-1948."

Although Meryl Hofmyer most resembled the Teletubby named LaLa, she did have a bit of a nose. Enough to tilt into the air and show it just a mite out of joint. "I'm not aware of our KALEIDOSCOPE, eh, historical involvement with the National Petroleum Council."

"Meryl, sometimes you bother the crap out of me."

"If you are to, shall we say, keep handing me shovels, they won't do you any good unless I have a map of the unmarked graves where I'm having our people excavate the bodies. Will they?"

"We're shoveling shit. Not bodies. Walk with me to my car." He moved. "After the horror of WWII, Truman preferred KALEIDOSCOPE. 'Hegemony Through Energy' Instead of relying on endless wars, the idea was to peacefully engineer dependency. Whoever controls energy controls development, and by extension, influences sovereignty. Truman preferred our methods to the CIA, but the CIA was inevitable. The National Petroleum Council was window-dressing, a cover to obfuscate and confuse oversight into KALEIDOSCOPE. Until—post-Angleton, post-Church Commission—Director Colby seized the NPC and siloed it inside Department of Energy. We have nothing to do with them, but the entire cover construct of KALEIDOSCOPE does. An empty house of cards; Harker'll see an ace, pull it, collapse it, spend a month playing fifty-one pick-up."

"Uh, fifty-two, sir."

"*Uh*, fifty-one: he thinks he holding an ace. DOE will treat Harker even worse than I."

He unlocked his Cadillac. Slid behind the wheel. Gave Meryl a curious look—profound exhaustion brought by deep sadness.

"Anything else, Silas?"

He didn't appreciate the tenderness she returned.

"Azeris have Lynn under lock and key—" he turned his key; his engine rumbled, bellowed with contained violence— "for murder no less. Funny, but that outcome never crossed my mind when I made her a calendar girl."

Had Meryl blinked she'd have missed it. Pain in her mentor's eyes. Silas squeezed his fist three times where his aged hand rested at his knee.

"Must be losing my touch."

A voice from a Moscow alley. From the steam devil swirl.

Disembodied.
Feminine.
"We're more than what we survive."

AT THREE IN THE MORNING, Saturday morning, Lynn Kingston's DTs began in earnest. Once the Russian SVR became involved in the interrogations—smuggled in unnoticed by the CIA stakeout on both embassies—small doses of forced alcohol kept Lynn in severe withdrawal well into the Yuletide season.

The Holiday Season

1.

"IT ISN'T REALLY MADE of cheese—the moon. That's just dumb, right, Mom?"

Three week to Christmas. Two days without snowfall. A melt started yesterday, snapped back deep freeze overnight. Foxtail Farm and all of St. Mary's County iced hard.

Rushing for the door, rushing sweaters, jackets, *where-are-your-mittens?/we-wear-gloves* rush-rush chaos, get out to the truck and off to buy wreaths—a Melody half-trick to get the twins someplace fun where she could buy the Christmas decorations and give the boys some holiday culture at the same time. "Gloves. Right. And, Li'l Silas: who says it is—the moon?"

"Not the moon. Jack."

"I didn't say the moon was cheese. And they're on the mud room chest where we got hot yesterday."

"They said it on your dumb cartoon, and you asked me."

"I didn't *hear*. I asked you what they said, and you said, 'The moon is made of green cheese,' Silas, maaaannn."

Little Silas wouldn't let go. "And, by the way, the moon and cheese aren't even green. They're yellow or white or orange."

Melody suppressed a laugh—the things these two found to argue—opened the door into the utility/mud room. Braced. Shivery cold. Ten degrees colder than the house; it would be at least another ten degrees worse outside.

"Come on. Zip jackets. Let's go." They zipped. Melody touched each boy's shoulder, guided them inside the mud room. "Mittens."

Both boys: "Gloves."

"Oh. Sorry." (They were mittens.)

The twins grabbed them. Grabbed their hats discarded yesterday on top of the old chest that contained old car blankets no one ever used. The old grassy lanolin smell, sweet and nostalgic, from blankets that once belonged to Silas's grandparents (when all cars stowed a blanket "just in case"), and Silas's parents, and Silas and Doris in turn, never got rid of them even after "just in case" became more "what's the point?" lingered ever-so-faintly in the frigid air. Seeking it, Melody noticed. Breathed. Drew into herself an essence of Foxtail Farm to untighten her chest. To take with. There was so much about it she loved. But there was also the other.

The Inward Light—

"Past, present, future: a black ball on a heavy black chain. It swings, and it wrecks its way through all three, knocking things down with indiscriminate and perfect accuracy." Starched shirt, dimpled necktie, DA Calvin Kirby.

—The Place of Blackness.

She thumbed the truck's *Start* button on her key fob. Frigid air knifed between the mismatched top and bottom of the Dutch door where a poor repair after some

"Halloween accident" (as Melody, told, didn't question) had left the two sections cracked to the unbound cold. Beyond, Billy Goat's Gruff, her big Dodge Ram, grumbled to life, pumped heat, ready to jounce them into town.

"Remember we once saw the moon red like it was on fire? When it was super big that time over the trees?" Little Silas.

"So cool. But I never saw a red cheese." Jack.

Melody wrapped her scarf. Grabbed her wool gloves from their hook on the rack.

"Wait! What about the Laughing Cow with the red plastic stuff and kind-of-a-stringy you pull it to open?" Little Silas; the boys back in tandem.

Melody said, "That's wax—the little red round pocket—and what I want to know is what kind of cow can even jump a little bit let alone over the moon?"

Both boys laughed, and Little Silas—"That show's dumb anyway—" and Jack overlapping, "When did Papa say we can start the Yule log in the fire?"

"According to him, we start it a day earlier, so we get a '*Thirteen* Days of Christmas' in this family. Extra special." Melody pulled on a cream-colored knit cap. She grabbed the heavy throw-bolt. "Hats, boys. Won't do you any good in your hands."

"I forget what day we start." Little Silas.

Jack. "No, you don't. Its first night is when Mom makes the cake."

"My Bûche De Noël. Christmas Eve, silly. C'mon, you guys ready or not?"

Hats on, she threw the bolt, the cold hit them as they slip-slid careful-fast to the big red rumbling truck.

Nat King Cole traded tracks with Dolly Parton. Traded with Frank Sinatra, the three of them spelling along those "J-I-N-G-L-E" bells; Julie Andrews counted favorite things, and Mariah Carey let them know for the one thousandth time this season that all she wanted for Christmas was everyone to listen to her one thousand times more.

They headed into town.

Melody liked Mariah; happy to be "you" in the song and "you" for everyone in her family but she turned down the volume and said out of nowhere (but right where she wanted them to be with Christmas/life), "I think it's fun to imagine the moon as cheese or anything else you want. *I* kind of think in the winter, when it's all silvery, that ol' moon's a giant snowball."

"Or a face hit by a giant snowball." Little Silas.

"Thrown by Mars—'cause he's a war god, right?"

"Just like your dad."

Twins twin'd, "Oorah!/Just like Dad."

She drove the back way into Old Town. Slowed at the rambling, historic and half-forgotten residential edge where the tall black gum trees, alligator bark sparkling with frost, stretched bare branches hanging icicle tinsel overhead in silvery handclasp with the thirty- forty- fifty-foot matching gums across the street. She glanced at her sons' faces filled with wonder. Signaled her turn into the Patuxent Historical Society driveway. Since Halloween, the poisonous yew tree had been culled of ghosts and skeletons, pruned conical, garlanded and lit with colorful lights and great big golden glass balls. The old Colonel Vickery House beyond. Named after its 18th century builder/owner, boon companion of Silvanus

Kingston III, who many Christmases would ride out to Foxtail Farm, a whisky jug and a sack of wooden toys for the slave children and coins for the male slaves. (Extra, if they won in the wrestling and boxing matches Kingston held annually for the plantation owners and the best of their stock men, Vickery running book.) Tucked back and waiting to be left alone, it glowed and sparkled and delighted Jack and Little Silas and Melody to see it transformed into a Colonial Christmas open house, crafts fair, festive time-machine that drew them in on warm-breathed inspiration.

"*This* is where we get the wreaths?"

"And a whole bunch of yummy stuff too, I'll bet. Maybe make your own decorations? I was told they'd be doing that—you know my friend Victoria—I mean, only if you *want* to."

"Will Santa be here?" Jack asked quietly for himself and for his brother because they were on the verge of losing that jolly old soul and were reluctant. Not this year. At least not till after Christmas morning and presents.

Melody smiled, warmer inside and out than the weather held any power to deny.

HAL KINGSTON HAULED the last bag of rice, truck to stacked pallet, pallet to the Class I storage locker. Empty crates, boxes of foodstuff waste, sacks of commissary rubbish went onto the empty pallets on his handcart. Out to the burn pit. Low and pale, the rising moon cast the rocky pitch behind Camp Abu Omar gray like a strewment of battlefield corpses. The burn pit, always smoldering, winked through smoke with the eyes of hell-summoned rats. A ghost provisioning for ghosts.

After his killing of the wannabe suicide bomber, Mojtaba Niavarani—deceived, lured, exploited into Hal's knife (murder when you put the fine point to it)—after Houton's receipt of Hal's manufactured "Corporal Henry Cooper" 201 file, after Houton dug back from that to Hal's General Discharge, and Houton pulled some strings he didn't know had already pulled him in: Houton's curiosity overplayed his caution. Coaxed him deeper into "Cooper's" discharge. Discovery of an excised "conduct unbecoming" report. Excessive aggression toward prisoners during a black ops forward deployment.

Admired and somewhat celebrated for wasting the Haji who would have wasted the rest of them, Corporal Cooper was deemed useful. Allowed more freedom of movement around the high-security training camp than a straight-paper commissary corps noncom ought to be given. Houton—Colonel Houton as at some time, somewhere, he'd done the Sanders bit and Colonel'd himself—allowed the extra movement. Wanted to watch where Cooper moved. Where he sniffed. What made his back bristle and what made him point. And so, Hal/Corporal Cooper moved. Between the grub cage and the barracks. Between mess tents and the rusted armory. A commissary ghost, slinging chow, pushing paper, hauling ammo crates, burning shit at the pit—and generally poking his nose in the places where things were said, places where Houton's training advisors would toss him occasional scraps, exchange testing/knowing looks, and Hal would listen and "Cooper" would smirk, and trust was earned in grunts and small confirming nods.

Their charges were Sunni militants; one hundred fifty-four Iranian Jundallah POWs. Shaved heads. Scarred wrists. Chain-bit, keloid-thick ankles. One hundred of these were racked out. Fifty ran night drill. Four to the Goat Shed. Not that Houten kept any goats at Abu Omar. The Goat Shed was for "recruits." For the recalcitrant—to make them less so—and Cooper carried the whispered reputation of a man who went too far with prisoners.

"Hey, Coops. We're taking care of a little problem t'night out at the Goat Shed. You might enjoy lendin' us a hand."

The Goat Shed. Hal used fists. The rubber hose. Boots. The battery. The waterboard. Mostly his fists. He didn't like it, but he knew where darkness lived inside him and he didn't hold back. These were three-way traitors. To Iran; to the Mahdi's Army they'd fought for in Iraq; to the mission they volunteered for to get out of US military incarceration in Baghdad. Four the first time. Another pair scared shitless—literally—end of November. Last night, a seventh who might have been just for advisor morale. Each of them revealed—not that anyone was asking; (when it got to the Goat Shed it was never about asking)—more about Operation CINDER CROWN than the last. More explicit than Houton's advisors hinted. The advisors watched/gauged Cooper's reaction.

These recruits weren't operators, weren't insurgents, weren't jihadis for one interpretation of the Quran over the other.

Cooper used fists. The rubber hose. His boots. Used the battery and the waterboard and Hal learned: these were throwaways. Trained to cross the Iranian border not for victory but for collapse. Self-destruction before compromise. Symbol before survival. Trained to burn bright and vanish and leave the smell of smoke in Tehran's air, in the name of some shimmering idea. Operation CINDER CROWN would light Iran's underbelly on fire. Not for Allah. Not for a free Iran. Not for America.

Simpler: Instability.

Was this KALEIDOSCOPE? Was this some involuntary suicide pact designed by his father, implemented by Houton?

He hit the burn pit. Dumped kitchen waste. Churned it with the hottest embers until flames leaped. Let it flare a minute. Gave it another two. Mixed char and ash and turned it under. Let the smoke build and billow into a thick column.

He'd met the two Dulles badass boys. Houton ran the camp; these two—names/maybe-just call signs, Bors and Vale—*were* the camp. Tactical khakis. No stripes. Handled all recruit files. Handled mission assignment. Oversaw live-fire. Ran all comms—physical, digital—and the little Hal heard them speak, half the time they spoke in code. Ghosts, too, but different from Hal; Bors and Vale were part of the op that almost killed his sister. That made Bors and Val cursed for eternity.

Smoke thick, smell unbearable, Hal accessed the PRC-343 waiting for him inside the false bottom of a scorched fuel drum. A tactical burst transmitter. He connected a thumb-sized token to the input pad, preloaded with a ROT13 shift-encoded short message update for Drexler. Thumbed *Send.*

The update included everything but this: whatever eventually happened for/with/to Hal at Abu Omar—whatever went down with CINDER CROWN in a rain of fire in Iran—before he closed out this operation, there was a personal debt to be paid. And Bors and Vale, already ghosts, wouldn't be left to haunt the Kingston ledger.

Burst transmitter stashed. Hal sat in the dent on the side of the drum concealment device. The flames danced. Smoke rose, dirty. Thick. Darker than night. He stirred waste embers, tending a fire that needed no tending. Warmed his boots, though his feet didn't need warming. December in Iraq didn't hold a candle to...

Christmas candles at Foxtail Farm. The holidays with my beautiful woman. My beautiful boys.

Little Silas, Jack—last December—with Papa, back of the tobacco drying shed ruins. The lee of the high, stone smithy wall where years back, Silas, Michael and I built the stable-style overhang. Roofed it with concrete-fiber tile. Three massive logs lie apart from the rest of the firewood. Each over six feet in length. A foot in diameter.

Silas: "This pignut hickory, I cut down two Octobers back. These two red maple trunks I pulled from the jungle—deadfall, from when-I-don't-know—but I pulled them out and they've been curing since. Which do you boys think?"

My twins look at Papa like he's king and the question bears the weight of the kingdom. The boys choose silently; a secret language of looks and nods and gestures they share. Little Silas speaks for them. "We like the pig one."

"Let's harness up your dad and he'll mule it to the house."

I bray and my beautiful boys and the log and the expectation of a fire that lasts for, not twelve, but thirteen days, is pure. And being a dad is beautiful. I let them ride the log behind me.

Today is four December. They'll be out there today, tomorrow, maybe Silas did it yesterday, picking this year's Yule log and getting it—somehow Dad'll figure a way, maybe old Mr. Claypoole or one of his sons, or nephews, or whoever they are—into the common room. Lean that old log against the big plastered-brick mantelpiece with its sooty cherubs and the running deer. Then Christmas Eve morning, Silas will lay the massive log one end into the firebox—

(Hide and seek, ready-or-not here I come.)

—the rest sticking out on the floor and into the room.

Somehow.

They'll get it done, and Melody will start her recipe for the log cake. Always something different she adds. Always something beautiful with the icing. The candles.

(I left Foxtail Farm before Melody went down to Arkansas. Wait, Alabama. I'm sure that didn't work out for the old father—if you could call the son-of-a-bitch that.)

And the old music. Mom's records. The old stereo turntable spinning round.

Ash swirled a mini-tornado around him. Never during a single deployment, where Melody was concerned, did Hal ever experience anxiety for her/for the kids—never felt it in the slightest. He stared at the column of smoke. Ash—failing to rise/falling back—coated his face. Clogged his nose.

CINDER CROWN. I'm fucking wearing one.

He cleared his nostrils, one after the other. The euphemistic farmers handkerchief.

The first tradition of Christmas Eve, Hal—if he was off-duty—would be to get the Yule log burning. And, later, the children—

Paige—adult now. Wow. Charlotte, Leigh. (Little Silas and Jack probably won't remember last year. Their first year doing it.) The long matches lit from the log and walked to Mom's portrait, Melody's cake on the landing. They'd light her candles. One for each of them.

("To Hal, my little one: for your uncommon fortitude." A different life a life ago.)

Gwen, every time: "Careful. It's fire."

Dad. Every. Time. "House is afraid of fire. Do it, children. Never be scared."

He pictured Silas. Each morning, each evening pushing the Yule log deeper into the embers, into the cinders, into the soot where it burned and shortened, burned and shortened, for thirteen days and thirteen nights until a mountain of ash was all that remained of Christmas.

Hal looked up at the black desert night and sent a two-word prayer— *"Thank you."*

As Corporal Cooper, he started back, inside the wire. Smoke clung to Hal the way it clung to the air inside Foxtail Farm the year his mother died.

Afraid of fire. The house hadn't burned when it should have.

Fire department—no explanation for why it hadn't. They offered it was impossible it didn't come down. Left it at that. All that remained of that deadly Halloween fire was the long char on the upstairs banister where Dad said Mom fell, burning, into the arms of death.

Everything should have turned to ash. But the collected breath of three hundred years bellowed, and gathered and, as though no more significant than a single birthday candle, blew out the Foxtail Farm fire.

SWEET AND SHARP the smell of orange and clove from pomander balls competed with the tang of fresh cut pine. The dominant aroma of the Colonel Vickery House, pine scent emanated from railing and doorframe, mantel to banister to festooned chandelier: bristly Scots, stiff pitch pine and shortleaf long-needle boughs braided with soft, feathery white pine intertwined with loblolly cones and walnuts. And yet, those spiced citrus balls hung with mistletoe, bowled on sideboards, in centerpieces, nested in the Christmas tree gave the holiday its spicy magic.

A plump-cheeked docent in a cream and mustard-gold polonaise gown, bunched around her Windsor chair like the children bunched around her slippered feet, read aloud:

"King John was not a good man,
He lived his live aloof;

Alone he thought a message out
While climbing up the roof..."

Sticky-fingered children paid slightly more attention to this poem than the usual reading of Clement Moore's *A Visit From St. Nicholas* which, as the saying goes, *If you've heard it once—you tend to stop listening,* their small fingers made stickier still as they pinched/pried/pulled at a sweetmeat pyramid in the parlor; made of sugared berries and crystalized grapefruit rinds that cupped candied apricots, pineapple rings, and glacé fig, preserved cherries and grapes; cone-shaped, it crumbled like the fall of a candy Mount Pelion.

Melody pointed out the Christmas miracle to Victoria as they shared a pewter ewer of wassail, backs to the glistering fire in the hearth behind them. None of the costumed museum staff scolded the mess. Only smiles at Christmas.

"The rug's Chinese. Walmart. Acrylic-synthetic, hundred percent plastic and petroleum please-spill-on-me reproduction. The Historical Society learned their lesson a long time ago... And it's only once a year." Victoria toasted Melody. Sipped. Passed their beverage back.

"This is nice. Having this; it's special. Hal's overseas. The twins are having a great time. Thank you for inviting us. I've been so busy since Thanksgiving." Melody sipped. Her eyes, over the urn's rim, tested.

Victoria opened her hand to the house. "We've all been underwater—or snow, right?" Flashed same-eyes back. *You sure?*

Melody. A tentative smile. "If you're selling faith, I'm buying..." Pointed: "Because I found it."

"You texted me that. Four-fourteen in the morning the day after Thanksgiving. You remember? You texted, 'I found it.' You never followed up. So..."

"I chickened out."

Victoria's bullshit meter twitched her nose.

"Awright. That's not really it." Melody gave Victoria the wine.

"No. What is 'it'?"

The fire popped. Melody flinched. They pretended she hadn't.

"Dark/bad family history come to life. Two directions—one, I've mentioned I can't tell you—"

"Is that a trust thing?"

"No-no-no. This is going to sound bigger than it is—probably—but that thing is safer you don't know."

Bone snapping. Mama howling from her broken, bloody face.

"If I told anyone, it'd be you, okay? It's just safer. It's the other thing that's the 'it.' Family history, buried under Foxtail Farm but come to life. I've chosen to accept it. To protect it. To keep it hidden, if I can."

"Your intelligence operation; you cracked the code."

"I think I was wrong with that."

"I don't think so. I haven't looked at any more of it, but definitely there's a coded secret embedded in the Kingston history of slavery."

"I don't need to know what that secret meant; I've been where the code ends. The Place of Blackness. It's a torture chamber. It's still stained. They *kept* it. Every generation. This gigantic—I can't even say 'sin' because that word is so small."

Victoria squeezed Melody's shoulder. A hand-hug. "I don't know, Melody. Why would they keep it? Evidence of such a horrible crime. Against humanity. Someone, somewhere along that Kingston line—"

"It's my line. It's my sons' line."

"Someone would have rid the place of all of that."

"The Kingston—" she searched for the word. *History* too forgiving. *Fortune* too cheap. *Legacy* too small—"*foundation* is literally built on it. I think there's a sense the whole Foxtail Farm would collapse to the last three nails without it. *I* got that sense."

Melody focused on her boys.

"Forget about the crackers, forget the candy..."

Tried to enjoy their enjoyment of the bad King's Christmas and the gifts he didn't receive. Smelled the pine. It smelled of turpentine.

My father's flask. Leaves me and Mom in the car. Carries Doris's portrait into Foxtail Farm. Into...

My home.

They were shoulder to shoulder, Melody and Victoria. Victoria tilted her head, bringing her lips close to Melody's ear. "Remember the slave, Cupid Williams?"

"Scrapefoot Williams. Who escaped."

"From the Jesuits at St. Ignatius Plantation, Cupid Scrapefoot Williams who Turkey John Swann captured and returned in 1716."

Lured, Melody faced her.

"I've been anxious to tell you. How he died—or didn't, depending on whether we believe the third Silvanus Kingston and Turkey John Swann, or if you believe the Jesuits. 1741. Cupid Scrapefoot Williams, sixty-six years old, escaped for the second and last time. Turkey John, ancient by then, tracked him down. Delivered him to your family's Place of Blackness. The priests had ordered and paid for his execution. Silvanus Kingston delivered his scalp to St. Ignatius while Turkey John buried what was left of the body in the mass grave of Turkey's Swan Song.

"But here's the thing, Mel. That bloody scalp was sheep's wool. Soaked in blood and tannins, animal brains and fish oil. A detailed process. In court, the Jesuits brought that up—to manufacture that counterfeit scalp, well, Silvanus or Turkey John, or both of them: they started a long time before Cupid Williams made his run."

"You're sure about that?"

"I've read the trial. Melody, the Jesuits opened it up to question every execution done at Foxtail Farm. Collected old scalps plantations saved. Swore they were sheep. Turned them over to the court for examination."

"Were they *all* sheep?"

Victoria shrugged her black eyebrows. "It never went that far. But I'm getting ahead of it. The court granted Jesuits an order to disinter Scrapefoot's remains. Silvanus fought that all the way to high court at Baltimore. The case went on for a year, then it was dismissed."

Melody watched the wisp of a smile play at the corners of her friend's mouth.

"Christmas Eve, 1742. St. Ignatius Plantation burned to the ground."

Melody lost the fire's heat. Her spine ran cold. "Silas told me about a Scrapefoot Williams massacre."

"I don't know about a massacre; our records don't cover St. Ignatius. It's a national historic center. They have an archive, but the government controls all the documents. I could get us in. But you can't blow me off. We'll get one look."

Tears stung the corners of Melody's eyes. "For what we're talking about it's probably the wrong emotion, but I want to give you a hug."

"For a massacre. Ha. You're somethin' else, Melody."

Melody blinked her tears and nodded and smiled, and Victoria chuckled as the plump-cheeked docent in the cream and mustard-gold polonaise gown gusto'd her finish:

"But, oh! Father Christmas, if you love me at all,
Bring me a big, red, India-rubber ball!"

On the woman's last word, from the perimeter of the children, costumed docents and volunteers shook/tossed/batted red ballons from pillowcases.

Old-fashioned red balloons.

Large and pear-shaped that those who remembered would recall similar to balloons they'd clutched on cotton strings—their own hands once-sticky—wandering the Enchanted Forest amusement park.

Children squealed and scrambled.

Red balloons bounced.

Red balloons floated.

Red balloons popped in the air releasing their stale breath. Melody swooped in to join Jack and Little Silas.

Little Silas noticed over the shoulder of his mother's hug, a hard, shabby man in flat cap and half-length sheepskin coat. Just inside the door, shoulders wet with snow, he made a pistol shape with a hand misshaped from seven years picking the state's cotton in Alabama swelter.

He cocked his thumb at Little Silas.

Mrs. Shelly, the blue heron Historical Society director, offered to take the strange man's coat—though her hands recoiled halfway; once elegant, the rat-colored leather, rubbed thin in places it would only wear by rubbing against the cold hard ground, the wool, patchy from moths and carpet beetles, silverfish infestation, cockroaches. Kind of coat fished from the Goodwill dumpster. Man didn't take his eyes from Little Silas but jerked his shoulder hard—assistance not required. Mrs. Shelly cleared her throat. The leathery man winked a faded eye, deep-set in his leathery face, a greeting, for the boy—

You're special, kid.

—and lumbered out, gulped into the weather's maw. A snowy gust through the closing door blew snow inside. A swirl of ash from the hearth. Children and parents squealed, startled, but it wasn't burning; the rug was temporary, made for stains. Accepting of ashes and made in China.

2.

TIMELESS. A CRYSTAL VESSEL. A liquid reliquary, all curves and convergence. No start, no stop to its form. A vessel of refraction. Of memory.

"Find the cognac. The bottle is the Holy Grail of this whole bloody mess."

Timeless. A vessel shaped like Paige's teardrop. Fallen from her lashes; mid-air frozen and a-shimmer in the dim-bulb wine cellar light.

"It's horrible. Never look in there!"

Open panel. Size of a playhouse door. Ossuary chamber for not-looking.

Timeless. Its blown crystal body encases the cognac like amber-in-motion inside a glass-hollowed breath. Catching light. Compromising light.

Place of Blackness in iPhone glow. The Spanish Spider: obscene tongs of sharpened arms—opened|closed; an arachnid's legs or a blooming flower—for cupping, gripping, biting, tearing flesh from slave women's chests.

Timeless. A kaleidoscope lens turned to the eye; every angle splits and bends the blonde|copper liquid inside.

Hennessy Timeless|morning time.

Clive blinked awake. The bedside clock. 6:40. Silas Kingston's bottles of Timeless.

Time to get up. Get up. Get up and get going...

Clive crashed his head back into his pillow. Drew a long breath and measured it out toward the moon-scape'd cottage cheese ceiling. Timeless: near as dammit to the situation he found himself in since Thanksgiving; a bloody time warp.

Alone, he rolled out of his Super 8 motel room bed. Bent the drapery. Window rimmed with wicked icicle teeth. Falling snow. Box haulers, some freight trucks, mostly civilian vehicles churn white snowfall into slush along Route 235.

Whole life, Cliver Lancer never minded sleeping alone. Life changed when he wasn't looking.

Or maybe I've never looked and only started once I started looking at Foxtail Farm. Looking at Paige.

Paige on her side, beneath the comforter she'd've shorted me anyway.

The curve of her thigh.

The string of her thong. Snap it—right about now—

"Wakey-wakey."

So what? One night alone. She was irritable and cross, anyhow.

She wasn't pulling away. She hadn't. Not exactly. Not with her body. But her gaze, her clarity—all last week—just off. Spacing out. Not while they made love but before and after. Almost like she was listening for something.

"Is Beaumont outside? Barking?"

"I don't hear him. I'm sure he's in his bed under the painting."

A countdown.

The tick of the grandfather clock.

The imagined summons of Christmas bells from out of the past or not yet rung.

The breath of the house or some new and invisible stranger breathing within it.

A countdown to what?

Timeless. Bottles. Photographs. The Silas risk.

Ol' Jolly Jack Ruddy Cheeks/B-309C's promise. *"Find the cognac. The bottle is the Holy Grail of this whole bloody mess."*

Found. Photo-snapped. Sent. Six Thomas Bastide Baccarat crystal decanters, the platinum band around the stoppers—in Clive Lancer accounting—a small, happy fortune themselves.

Labels etched into the glass, faint like the breath of a ghost—

Inward Light.

"Why do we have it?" Paige.

Silas. "It's always been here."

Melody: "Your ancestors tortured and murdered slaves in there."

Place of Blackness.

—Timeless with a lowercase "t." Serial numbers engraved on the base.

HT1289 Photo-flash and snap!

HT1290 Photo-flash and snap!

HT1291 Flash! Snap!

HT1292 Flash! Snap!

HT1293 Snap!

HT1294 Snap!

Transmitted to Legoland. Two weeks back. Too much time. He'd have figured out the gifts' provenance by now. He'd done his own research: only 2,000 bottle produced/sold. Each numbered. Each accounted for; tracked by the auction houses since the last bottle went out. $4,000 dollars US at point of sale. Christie's and Southeby's turned them around for as much as $9,000. Silas's six—five still sealed—would, with their presentation case, be rarest of rare. $50k easily. How long would it take the E-Branch econ-and-energy whizbangs to bang those numbers back from France?

A day?

If that.

Shared access with UK financial crimes and customs enforcement. EU protocols. GCHQ liaison request to the *Direction de la Surveillance du Territoire*. If the bottles were some kind of secret Russian gift, there'd be a shell company or five or who cares how many? Even a muppet could figure that one out.

But here we are. Fifteen days and not a whistle or a peep. No follow-up. No orders. Nothing.

Vertigo swept him as he climbed out of bed. Not so much a physical dizziness, but the feeling that something inside him—fundamental, like the ageless plate rock that is the thing, beneath the dirt and sand, people imprint their passage with fleeting feet—had shifted.

It's one thing to be trusted with the lie, a pro at running it down and living it. Be something, though, for once to stand still long enough to feel the truth rise up into me—heavy, like something Grand-mère Amie passed down between cowrie shells and trump cards, something she never once needed to name.

Even Fergus—Clive could tell—grew uneasy about their operation. He puttered around. Listened to the radio that broadcast old inactive channels, he claimed Cold War Soviet—

Yeah. Whatever. Fucking numpty.

Fergus made him spend the last week—whatever hours that half-drunk/whole-mad Scots could catch him—yapping into a digital recorder.

"Don't miss a fuckin' detail from any fucking room, hall, closet, crapper. Every doorknob and window latch and the bloody which-way they open."

The Clive Lancer narration of his Foxtail Farm map. Every inch. Every stick of furniture. Every rug—where it stretched and where it didn't. Every fireplace. Every shelf, cupboard, curtain, every cord. Every picture on every wall.

"Light switches and outlets. The circuit box. Double-check if you're unsure."

Everything. He didn't know whether his guided-tour came as a request from Legoland or was Fergus make-work torment, but Fergus's ask for Clive to conceal-camera it all had been denied back in the fall when he and Paige first went deep—too risky under the snoot of a legendary spook; this was the next best thing...

If someone's planning a hit inside the house.

Field officers don't do wet work—but someone does.

They scoot us out—Garde-Joyeuse, Maryland, America—and they slip in...

Too cold for a workout. Too cold for a shower. He threw on clothes, half of them fresh.

Lot of people in that house.

Kids.

Silas doesn't even sleep there.
Lot of—oops—mirrors, too.
(Playing with fire, that...)
Maybe I don't want to burn.

Dinners now—when he and Paige ate with Silas and Melody—the Timeless inevitably came out. Silas ritualized it. Warmed their snifters with a lit twig from the fireplace. He'd heat each of their glasses, the cognac inside. Fire bonded the four of them around the table, unwatched in ritual by the other empty chairs. Blow out the burning stick, and sometimes ash falling from the skeins of smoke, dusted the surface of Clive's drink.

"In this house it's good for what ails you. It's not poison. Drink it." A Silas en garde *with steeled gaze.*

Clive grabbed his keys and out the door'd it. He'd kiss Paige awake; take her mood's temperature with his lips.

Timeless: memory.

Paige: now.

His future: poisoned bait in a snap-shutting trap.

AFTER THEY MADE LOVE in her bed—not the horny/crazy sex of fall—but...

God-he-loves-me lovemaking

—and Clive drew Paige around the waist, into his lean, muscled side half-pillowing her back, and he interlaced her fingers into his below her belly button, she flinched. Shuddered. He'd felt her tense. Her spine lock. Felt her hips slightly—*it was so God damn slight*—buck away and that's what started their words. He didn't have to bring up Deeb, that was a low blow, but he'd seen her buck in a way like that before.

He regretted it immediately.

"Paige, I don't know why I said that. Why I'd ever be so stupid to bring him up. Equate myself to you with that knob. Quick, bite my head off or, quicker, move past it, because I'm—"

"Shhh. Sweet-sweetheart. Don't. Shh. I don't know why I did that. Okay? I'm just—Christmas and my family-all-in-ruins and you-an'-all-that." Bit-lip sulk. "Y'know— What might happen with Papa? I'm just a mess." A tender look that went beyond eyes meeting to her probing deep into the interior of his eyeballs. Earnest and selling him her honesty because all those things she said were true as well.

Upright with her. Stroked her hair. His eyes told her right back there's no easier counterfeit than selling love. "Mayb's you're one of those blue Christmas type girls they sing about."

Burned with her frown. "Never called that before."

"We both have a lot on our minds. That's for sure." Sighed. Northwind vast. Fetched his clothes. Stopped once his shorts were up to kiss her lips. Paige puckered but gave her cheek. He gently turned her chin and she hunched. Pouted. Rolled her eyes at herself.

"I don't know what's wrong with me." Gave him a real kiss to prove the "right" Paige was there too. Somewhere.

Clive lightened up. "I love you. Even blue, so fancy that."

"Fine, I'm blue." She laughed and hit him with her pillow.

"I'm going to sleep at my place tonight."

Clutched the pillow in her lap. "You're really going?"

"Don't be weird. Or blue. It's not like we're married."

"I would." Blurted—and I would*—and he knew that was true, and, on top of everything else, how would that even work? Mom, the least of my problems.*

Clive, Clive, Clive what've we gotten into? What are we going to do?

Paige sat down in the bathroom.

Now would be the best time...

But she had one day more until she missed again, and two negatives in the no-flow November.

Negatives are negatives and that's good, and there's lots of reasons to miss.

Stress. For one. AND I am blue and double bitchy and it's coming and you don't hope too hard for a thing you need to happen—right—? NEED to happen or you jinx it yourself.

(What if?)

Too late to think about it. If.

Beaumont wasn't on his bed, the stair landing beneath Doris's portrait. Paige's first thought was her sisters were back and walking him like they'd done every morning. Found Melody. Busy in the kitchen whipping up the twins' breakfast. "Where's Beaumont?"

"Clive's out with him. It's snowing."

A curious look, Melody's invitation to reveal. Melody high-tuned to the emotional breath of the house. Paige to the porch, through the door, the creaky screen.

Beaumont loved snow. Cavorted. Tried to be in all of it. Everywhere. At once. Shook his coat and swished his head back and forth to watch the snow fly.

Clive was a whole lot of laughing smiles. "Morning, luv! Watch this!"

He presented a snowball. Beaumont froze. Laser focus. His tail spun like a rubber-band-powered propeller. Clive hurled the snowball. Beaumont sailed. The snowball vanished in an explosion of white, but the dog couldn't care less. Scooped up a mouthful of snow and ran back with it, shaking his head and spitting it out, until mouth empty, tongue lolling, steam jetting, he waited for Clive to do it again.

They did it again. And again.

"He thinks he's fooling me."

"I think he is." And she threw her arms around Clive, squeezed and buried her face in his chest. Peered up.

"I'm not blue anymore."

"Your jacket is."

"And I selected it just for you to say that."

"Does it work?"

"What do you mean."

He meant—as he stuffed a snowball down her collar—"That."

"You dick!"

They tossed snow at each other until Beaumont got in on the act. Wide stance, front paws, shoveling snow and the dirt right below through his hind legs all over them.

Clive tackled the dog. Paige piled on. They all came up looking at each other.

"Why I was the way I was last night, and I-know-you-didn't-say-anything, but the last two days."

"Yeah. It's called blue."

"No. It might be called something else."

FROST IN FEATHERED PATTERNS. Large plumes across the glass, spread like open wings of a great horned owl across the front windows of the North Vista Outhouse. Fanned and filigreed from cold-captured drips, spread comb-like and serrated, fringed and velvety, ice that softened Silas's view and allowed him to observe without being observed. Paige. Clive. Beaumont—the dog spinning himself to pieces in the powder. An unqualified happiness radiated from the young couple; Silas remembered another Beaumont. Remembered Doris—almost a twin to Paige's sister—snowfalls long ago. The happy morning scene played opposite to what Silas might have expected after Clive's glum-glowered and smack-the-screen door slam-into-the-car Foxtail Farm exit the previous night. Something had changed overnight. It looked earned. Not borrowed. Unforced. Intuitively, he gave that to Clive.

"The bravest people are the ones who don't mind looking like cowards."

When the trigger moment comes. He'd told Paige to pass the White quote to Clive; he'd meant its coded message for Paige as well because when you pass intelligence you can't help but reflect a version of it back upon yourself. What did that make of his passing the message to her? Ownership mirrored; a third facet of the prism those words would work through.

Silas had slept in. Past six at any rate, which for him was late. A long night at OTRAC. With Meryl, the tortoises, the box-folders. Delivered a comprehensive index with summaries of everything he'd already sent Harker, forwarded to the Director of National Intelligence.

"Slap a preface on this shipment. Cite 1941's H.R. 1776 as an 'operative charter precursor.'"

Meryl tsk-tsk's. "The Lend Lease Act? Silas are you, how-shall-I-say 'serious?'"

"Say it just like that. Dead serious. There's nothing more terrifying to James Clapper than a document older than he is. And that man's just the kind of tool we need to screw Harker in place. Harker knows he can't unilaterally dismantle KALEIDOSCOPE. He needs sign-off or, at least, acquiescent silence from the DNI. Sign-post the whole thing so that Clapper and his DNI legal eagles understand that KALEIDOSCOPE operates under an interagency agreement predating the CIA's formation. That's important. That's his trapdoor: that we fall under 'treaty compliance monitoring,' technically housed in the Department of Commerce—outside any intel silo—throws a jurisdictional bone into the middle of this whole exercise. Top that off with a memo. Something like, 'In light of the December twenty-one deadline imposed by DCI Harker as a cut-off for material submission-slash-review, we respectfully request time for interdepartmental clearance—especially regarding classified activity adjacent to Presidential Emergency Action Documents, parenthetical 'PEADs', under the Atomic Energy Act of 1946. Then throw a C-C to the Honorable Judge E. Fortner Hopkins, retired, care of US District Court for the District of Columbia, independent

auditor for OTRAC/D-O-C. Parens ongoing.' Do you have it?"

"Yes, Amadeus. Confutadis. A-minor. Are we even under audit?"

*"Confu-*tat-*is. And again 'yes,' standard rule for when I walk into the fog and you remain: make it a rule to remain under federal audit. Always. Preferably with a retired treaty compliance inspector who needs the regular income badly enough to never finish. 'Audit' is a bilious word that agency heads believe breeds infection. Played right, this card will bring DNI blessing, not bulldozing."*

Meryl Hofmyer transcribes it all on the steno pad inside her perfectly round head with its odd spirals inside it, her bouncy, slightly wobbly walk, trailing Silas through the OTRAC main gallery. He stops in the center. Beneath the kaleidoscopically stained-glass skylight. His eyes sweep the compass points seeking a particular individual burrowed into one of the old-fashioned workstations, her hair bun pinned and bobbing above the sectional wall like a gray buoy.

"Clapper served as the Director of the National Geospatial-Intelligence Agency back in 2001. Those were his satellites Harker used to get a SEAL Team killed. A lost nuclear warhead found. Almost given to al Qaeda in Malaysia."

"OPERATION ATROPOS."

"Nathan Muir's Three Fates." His gaze lands. "That's her." He jerks his chin, follows it to Jilly Bregado. Her long line of a mouth bears the same upturned ends reminiscent of the "Come play with me!" expression a flippering bottlenose dolphin wears as it crashes into a shark, right behind its gills to kill it.

Jilly Bregado had found an innocuous conference badge in a Department of Commerce archive box. Energy Attaché Credentials / Cancelled Events / 1971. *A badge among the ephemera far from intercepts of diplomatic cables, ops analysis, white paper snow jobs. A box one step up from a trash bin retained only due to the excessiveness of bureaucratic recordkeeping and the need to justify large rooms constructed in large institutions for real estate value. A badge made out for* Evander Lott, Special Attaché, UK Delegation – Trans-Basin Energy Futures.

"But it's on the list, Silas. With everyone else long-gone who'd planned to be there. Did you know him?"

Her eyes tell me she does. And well.

A block of cheese pressed in a Soviet's hands. Safe, tactile, banal. Look: it's not a camera at all.

The white instead of the red.

The white instead of the pink.

The cheese instead of the camera instead of the meat instead of the texture of the splattered gray matter on the asphalt caulked cobbles, gun smoke wafting.

I stand alone, aged and smelling my own rot.

"Know him? Not really. I know of him. Might have met. Once."

My eyes tell Jilly: in this room, leave it at that.

"Not Lott. This *name on the list. Because you know him well." Jilly's lanolin soft, skeletal finger. Jilly taps its perfectly manicured, pink nail at a name buried in the Soviet delegation.* Grigor K. Alenichev. *"The Ghost did—" referring to Angleton who recruited both her and Silas long ago. "Grigor is on the attendee list. I found*

Grigor appearing here as well, which is where our James Jesus got a photo snapped."

She hands Silas a thin, yellowed report. Group photograph paperclipped. Attendees at post-Czechoslovakia USSR oil summit, 1969. The image of Grigor K. Alenichev is an image of Kolya Yurenez. Young, daring, simultaneously striking and alluring.

(Spitting image: Michael.)

"Coincidentally, but not, your Mr. Lott was in Prague that very same week. And another, I believe, not-coincidence: after Evander Lott's murder in Moscow—that would be June of 1971, Kalaydoskop retired the alias and Grigor K. Alenichev was added to the KALEIDOSCOPE Defunct Alias Registry—which, the portion thereof where I discovered it, has not been digitized due to over ninety percent of those defunct aliases users, that far back, long aged out, or died out of the business."

"Not him. Never Kolya. Thank you." Silas.

He left the North Vista Outhouse. Gave Paige and Clive a can't-be-bothered (so's not to bother them) "Good morning," and trotted through the snow, up the steps and through the porch door. Beaumont bayed once, realizing the old man wasn't stopping to play. Silas poked his head back out the door. Barked, "Beaumont!"

The dog froze. Snapped eyes.

Silas: "Boo." Paige laughed, Clive ambushed her with a snowball. Silas vanished inside.

Lott's head briefly/minutely turns. Kolya's eyes flicker a silent exchange.

In KALEIDOSCOPE there are no coincidences.

Explode blood. Explode brain and face.

Nothing is random.

I see Lott's head briefly/minutely turn. Straight look into Kolya's eyes.

Fatalistic. Familiar. Cruelty.

Right after that. Great Britain pivots from Eurasian oil. Goes all-in Gulf. All-in North Sea. But now they're creeping back. Back to Baku. And how does Kolya lock it?

Angleton whispers in my dream: "Bait."

Baits me with Michael: the cheese in the trap. Knowing Fergus Lott is listening. Knowing I'll reach for Kalaydoskop. Knowing Fergus and Clive will hear me and come for me to grind my bones. UK price of admission: the head of KALEIDOSCOPE—

"'I think we are in rats' alley. Where the dead men lost their bones.'"

Price of admission/cost of disclosure: the head of Silas Kingston snapped at the neck as I went for rat trap cheese.

1971. That Moscow rats' alley—Silas Kingston didn't know a thing about KALEIDOSCOPE. The malice in his heart he beat into a finger-pulse trigger-pull was more blooded and it ran purer than oil.

Pigfuckers-wanna-whack me—? 'Specially you, ya bloody Yank-fuck!

Especially me. Kolya was pleased when I selected you as my "irrevocable trust." It makes sense now—Kolya in context—but only Evander and I know why I blew out his brains.

"Melody?" Silas made his way into the kitchen. Turned at the sound of feet padding down the stairs. A moment, perfect stillness in the kitchen—

A bullet to balance accounts for an irremediable sin that will never be expunged in this life for its victims.

To Silas's way of thinking, Deuteronomy and Paul got it wrong: it's forgiveness for God to mete out on the sinful cursed.

Melody entered with the twins.

"Well, good morning my fine dragoons!"

"Morning, Papa!/We get to see the cousins tonight!"

And they scrambled for their eggs and cinnamon toast and Silas shaped his expression into a question mark.

"Gwen called. She feels awful about—"

"Everything?"

"Yes, Silas you can finish my sentence finishing hers. Sometimes I think it would help you to remember that Michael loved her and even though she divorced him, and he's gone right now, love that happened, that made your three beautiful granddaughters, should be remembered and recognized with grace."

Silas took a chair and helped himself; she'd made enough to feed him as well. "My heart is much smaller than you give it credit for."

"How come your heart's small, Papa? Are you sick?" Little Silas.

"I don't believe in getting sick. You like these eggs?" The boys *mm-hmm'd.* "Tell your mom; because her heart is so huge, we even out."

Melody scoffed. A single laugh/single shake of her head. Silas said: "Where is this family reunion to transpire?"

"The Old Town tree lighting. The girls are singing with the St. Pancras choir."

Jack. "You think Santa'll be there? He wasn't at the other thing."

"Ah. The Historical Society. They always send me an invitation for that." To the twins: "The guy who built that place was quite a character. You dig around by where the old barns were, you'll unearth some of his jugs."

"Why did he bury jugs?"

"They were empty. Fell out of his hands. Time buried them."

Melody jumped in. "Boys, Paige and Clive are playing with Beaumont out front. Finish up and bundle up and get in on the action."

Their forks became snow shovels; they cleared a path to escaping the kitchen. Melody cleared dishes. "Would you do me a favor?"

"Before you say it—I *didn't* say 'whisky' jugs, or 'dru nk.'"

Melody smiled at him. "Thank you for that, but you *can't* finish my sentence because that was already out of my mind."

"What would you like? Shoot."

"I'm going with my friend, Victoria, from the Historical Society, over to the St. Ignatius archives today. I need a few hours of you Papa-ing. If you're not going in to DC."

"No. The fate of the world will do without me. Today. I'm just glad whatever went on last night between Paige and her young squire got back on track. I need to recruit him to drag the Yule log inside. You hear anything from Hal?"

"No. He's doing what he's supposed to."

Silas loved how much she loved and trusted and how that peace it gave her she gave easily to others by expressing it. Since he certainly wasn't going to say that, he said, "You're going to find out about the Massacre. After what you saw Thanksgiving, I thought maybe you'd backed off."

"No you didn't."

Silas crunched cinnamon toast. "No, I didn't."

Melody pulled a chair. A deliberate turn to face him knee to knee as they'd done before. "The Place of Blackness and the Massacre. How do they connect?"

"Do they?"

"Cupid Scrapefoot Williams delivered men, women, even children to that door. Through that horrible door. In the end—and he was old, in his sixties which was extremely aged for a slave—he chose not to go through that door. He chose instead to return to the plantation he'd first arrived at."

"You blame him? Who'd want to go through that door?"

She held his hand. Squeezed it once. "I think many slaves wanted to go through that door. I think many of them chose to and did."

Just over the edge of not squeezing back, Silas's hand tremored in hers. "He went with others. With tomahawks and pikes. Murder in their hearts. Doris would have loved you. Me...I'm sorry for what you're going to find. Truly." Ahold of her hand, Silas stood Melody from her seat. "Come here."

THEY STOOD BENEATH DORIS'S PORTRAIT. Melody studied it before answering the question Silas had just asked of her.

"Who do you see when you look into that canvas?"

"You won't like my answer, Papa, but I see Doris and I see my father. And his lust for her."

Silas nodded. "I see both of those, but more and this is the magic of art—great art, which this painting unquestionably is—I didn't know it until after Boone Kelso left Foxtail Farm for the last time. Since I watched him drive away with you and your mother. But this is also a portrait of you. I'm sure you see that."

Silas watched the color drain from Melody's cheeks, the sunlight drifted-over by a cloud. She didn't move. Didn't take her eyes from Doris. Not, Silas sensed, because she was looking at the painting, but because she couldn't trust herself to look at him.

"I gotta get ready to meet Victoria."

He watched her up the stairs. When she was parallel with the level Doris's body burned on the silk kimono cord beneath the chandelier, Melody stopped.

"You can't save everyone, Silas. God gave us someone else to do that heavy lifting. But with you, I'm more than what I survived. I am. Thank you."

3.

PAINT PILES ON A palette, a kaleidoscope pattern of color brushed and knifed onto canvas, struggling to lock a singular vision, nothing into something and sealed in place. This is what the artist does. What Boone Kelso achieves in painting this portrait.

It is what Silas Kingston sees standing with Doris, handholding and expectant and awed as Boone Kelso drops the painter's cloth covering. Unveils.

No one makes a sound, then POP! Silas thumbs a champagne cork free of its bottleneck. Pours Doris, pours Boone—

"Hold that for a sec', sir." He adds his turpentine/absinthe mixture from his flask.

—pours for himself.

Silas raises the toast. "To the breathtaking and sublime."

Captured but uncaged by the gilt frame. Doris on canvas aspires before the three of them. Mid-turn in her crimson beaded gown. Red river lilies cradled in one hand throw brilliant sparks. One breath away from bursting off the canvas, igniting the stairwell. Her bare back. Her shoulder turned. Her figure absorbed into the depths of a mirror. Duplicated, not diminished, mortal yet immortal. The looking glass behind Doris suspends an infinity point as a haze or, better, a veil of gray ash. Light comes off her—not coming onto—coming from and coming out. Sunlight made manifest. Emergent from an hour unpainted/unknowable that Silas feels must be set at night. And Silas feels that if he blinks, love might step forward and laugh. Or walk past him, inviting him to follow by the tug of her cerulean glance.

They drink. Silas watches Boone Kelso watching Doris. Doris watches sunlight from the window bring life to her canvas self, her red flowers. Her red dress. Red lips.

"Let's go upstairs." Silas.

Boone Kelso. "We've business to settle, you and me."

Silas's study, Silas Kingston behind his desk, Boone: insouciant, legs crossed in a facing chair. Doris remains close to the door. Leans against its frame. Sips her sparkling wine. Distracted, curious and depleted by a feeling that part of her lifeforce remains in the stairwell, and will remain. Always. Uncomfortable but not unpleasant.

Silas writes out a check. The contractual $10,000 dollar amount. Boone denies the money. Claims he has painted Doris's soul, and Silas agrees and adds that there is no price to be put on Doris's soul, but that "There must be something you want in exchange."

"I've looked more deeply into it than you. A man needs to learn her, to earn her." Boone Kelso offers a trade. "This portrait is a birthday gift, not for Doris—for Doris is flesh and blood and bone and real. This is an object you commissioned for yourself. Your very best way to love Doris —and rather sad—is to pay money.

That is what you want. Love defiled by transaction. Monetary enslavement is a covenant with death. With this all around us. You don't appreciate, so you cannot know, nor do you want Doris as essence. See me, Silas Kingston. Feel me telling you this: the essence—" he lifts his flask, not in toast but some kind of proof— "essence aspires to live eternal above and beyond your enslavement covenant."

You don't cage the thing you love, Silas. You guard its path.

Boone Kelso's strange/drugged eyes bore into Silas with passion. Silas doesn't look at Doris. Doris's cerulean eyes are glazed in the manner eyes do when vision turns internal; she doesn't listen to either man because her inner ear is focused on her own voice coming from the floor below; a secret she'll never reveal.

Boone is correct: that she has given something of her eternal essence to his canvas. To his paint. Not through anything Boone has achieved but in his artistry of an imagined/perceived moment captured; fire would it be frozen, held to examination would be the same: a timeless and permanent, pure integrity of her identity—that essence—independently alive, attained in/by/of oil without need for explanation.

For justice. For cover.

"I see, Mr. Kelso." Silas temples his fingers. "But entertain a moment, my point of view. Doris offered you a glimpse into her soul—'essence', as you diminish the Maker from it—for me. She posed for your art knowing and fully intending you to capture her living soul in a moment of rhapsodic splendor for little ol' me. Not you, my friend."

Boone Kelso laughs. Unaffable. "I believe you've made God's point for me. That is all her soul Doris wants you to possess. I didn't paint it all. That essence she offered me. It is for me."

"I see; I understand you. Almost exactly."

"I knew you would."

"I get the painting. You get my wife. And your wife and little girl I noticed in the car when you pulled up. They're still down there, I imagine?"

"They are. I'm leaving them with you."

The only way Silas prevents the laughter about to burst at the absurdity of the artist seated before him is to draw strength from Doris. She wears a blank expression but meets his gaze and grounds him. Boone Kelso hasn't once looked her way since taking his chair. Remains relaxed into it.

"And you and Doris, if you don't mind my asking, will take that car and leave?"

"Yes, sir."

"And I'm to keep three things: the portrait and your wife and your daughter."

"To place them somewhere. With their people. I'm certainly not capable of that. You absolutely are."

"You would give up your flesh and blood and vows."

"Roberta violates them constantly. Fucks every man she meets. She disgusts me."

"You'd be rid of them to have my wife?"

"She's not your wife. That is only a transaction. A convention."

"Have you discussed this with Doris?"

"With her soul as I painted it, yes." Snappish. "I told you I have." Silas getting under his skin, penetrating his bizarre chrysalis. "Everything I am doing is for love!"

"What about Doris's love for her own children?"

"You and I are two forward-thinking people. Obviously, we both want the best for her. An arrangement can easily be made. Doris is unfaithful to you. Has always been unfaithful."

"She told you this?"

"Her soul screams it. I painted it. It's what you're witnessing looking at it but are too stupid to recognize!"

"Yes. I believe you captured that aspect. Of her soul."

"It's none of my business, but this isn't a marriage."

"But by your logic you would go from one unfaithful woman to another. You don't hold yourself, your own value, in very high esteem."

And Silas shifts. Turn the kaleidoscope that is this man: Silas explains to Boone that Boone is gifted. His gift is that he is an observer of unseen things and of emotions, but his curse is—and Boone must know this, must recognize it—that to practice this gift to create exquisite something from nothing, he is not allowed to be a participant.

"But now you've gone and made that mistake. You've cursed yourself, Mr. Kelso. That magnificent gift God gave to you, that you put in paint for us, you've destroyed it by betraying it; devalued it inside yourself by this desire to take what isn't yours. This is your last portrait. You'll never work again."

"You'll stop me?"

"No. You've already done that to yourself. That is why you want to take Doris; you'll take life because you've lost the ability to interpret it."

Silas watches Boone Kelso with exceeding carefulness.

The man is insane.

He drinks from his malodorous flask. Doesn't look, but says, "Doris, tell your husband."

"That I love him? He knows. That you've made a fool of yourself, Boone: he knows, you know."

Her voice is gentle, like a blade so perfectly honed that the cutting stroke comes so smoothly, the pain it causes cannot experience that it is happening.

"And I pity you, Boone, and feel only deep sympathy and compassion for that thing burning inside of you that allows you to do what you do. In all forms. And in all your boyish mistakes."

Hauntingly tender, perfect love that must be tragic because life is fatal. Silas has never heard this voice as Doris never has used it. Later, after tragedy takes her, this is the only voice Silas hears/remembers when she speaks from inside Boone Kelso's masterpiece.

When she whispers within the breath of Foxtail Farm, whispers through its respiring chimney stacks.

"You," she says. "Boone, you must go. Now. And take your family. And reject the fog of Foxtail Farm, the ash in the mirror, and that potion/poison you drink in slow suicide. Return to life. I urge you."

Boone Kelso never once looks at her. When her voice returns its silence inside her, he hunches forward. His head almost into his lap. He makes a strange, strangled noise. A cry between laughter and horror.

"I think you need to leave." Silas.

"My check?"

Silas writes another. Tears it from its book. "I've written it for 10-K and added another 10-K for your family. You want rid of them. This will pay for you to begin a new life as I am buying them as well. For this second ten thousand dollars, the girl and her mother will remain here."

Boone Kelso throws himself to his feet. He levels a finger at Silas and "SLAVERY! That is what I painted!" Spins to Doris, the finger aiming straight into her relaxed and majestic face. "This is what I painted! That is my secret I saved for you to save you!"

He snatches the check. Tears it in two. His head quirks. Eyes stare at the two pieces' fall. Horrified. Made small by what he's done. Both Doris and Silas share a vision of the man thrusting to his knees. Grabbing the pieces, begging for tape.

Boone Kelso straightens. "Keep your money."

He slams out the door. He slams out the house.

"You didn't need to antagonize him so much." Doris.

"That was the sound of my fury getting the better of me. I'm not sorry."

Silas steps to the window. Doris to him, her slender hands up his chest and cupping his shoulders from behind. "His genius and madness need each other; they live hand in hand, I think."

"No. You were right. He's poisoned his genius."

Silas watches Boone Keslo hurl himself into the front seat of his car. Barks at his wife. Roberta flinches. She argues. He mocks her with empty hands. She breaks into sobs over the steering wheel. Their daughter, in the backseat, cannot watch their mutual humiliation; Melody looks out the car window. Looks at the manor. Looks at Silas, looking at her. Her sundress, a faded yellow muslin, the look and texture of cheesecloth, accentuates the sunlight that Silas sees radiating from her tobacco shoulders, the sadness in her eyes.

"I'll make it right for the girl and her mother."

Anonymously, Silas Kingston will invest in Roberta Kelso. He will fund a contract with a clothing company for Roberta Kelso's designs.

"It will give her the freedom to take her child and escape. Leave Boone Kelso in his poisoned puddle."

It takes three months for the business to be secretly arranged. No fingerprints, no fingers to ever point back at Silas Kingston. It only takes three days more for Roberta Kelso to be found; charred in the wreckage of her cottage home. Husband and daughter vanished. Murdered by...

The papers only say Boone Kelso is the prime suspect. But in the smallest corner of Silas's heart, he knows that it was his finger that pulled the trigger.

4.

SHE DIDN'T WEAR CORSETS at wintertime to be sexy. Yes, the corsets were, technically, exceedingly sexy, but what—? Was she supposed to shop at *Grandma Winkies Sleep & Shapewear* where the only style sold were last grasp/gasp hold-it-all-together you're too old to hold your breath foundation? Gwen's holiday corsets were strictly La Perla. Luxury lingere. And you didn't just have to have sex to wear them. For chrissakes, she didn't wear them on the outside like some slutty popstar.

What's the phrase? Rhyme over reason?

She saw it like this: everyone agreed: the holiday season was a time of the heart; Gwen chose to sculpt that as her gift to the world. Art over biology. Or something that meant something like that. Fact was, women's winter outdoor clothing presented unappealing on Gwen. Due to the shape/size/thrust of her healthy breasts, winter outdoor clothing (if not made to rhyme smartly with her body) made Gwen look—any/everytime she stepped out in public—like a Whirlpool refrigerator box. Ridiculous pompom hat stuck on top. Promoted an unhealthy Gwen-look to the world.

And tonight, face it: the whole of Christmas.

To combat this, in winter Gwen wore corsets. Wore them tight. Created a smallest possible waistline over which she'd pull a V-neck ski sweater. (For the record: just because she didn't ski, did not mean she could be excluded; before Lululemon made yoga pants fashion-first/athletic-second, she promoted healthful exercise in bicycle pants. All-the-time. Everywhere. No one ever asked what kind of bike she rode.) Gwen knew the form-fit thermal sweater perfectly complemented the undercover health-appeal corset; she could (and did) accessorize with any type of winter jacket she wanted...as long as said jacket came with a serious-as-Wonder Woman belt. When Gwen went out into winter weather, the only box she presented had two rounded curves that tapered the aim down to a point like a heart-shaped box of candy.

"You gotta move, Mom. This is backstage."

"Honestly, Charlotte, it's not the Rockettes. We're outside and I'm behind a tree. And no one is looking at me."

"You're behind the Christmas Tree. This is the Tree Lighting. Everyone is looking, *and* you're leaning against our side of the stage!"

Gwen yanked her trench coat belt—*suck air, babe*—to the last nock.

"C'mon, Mom. Please? We're going on in two numbers!"

Leigh rolled her eyes at her older sister. She'd passed the point of being embarrassed by Mom when she was eight.

Gwen knew. Willed her smirk to be a smile. "I haven't seen the family since Thanksgiving. It's Christmas now and I want to make the best impression once they're here and waiting for me." She widened the space between her trench coat lapels.

"Mrs. Kingston?"

"Mmm?" Turning.

St. Pancras choir director. "This is backstage. The girls will do just fine. Please, let them have a moment to center for their performance and you can find a spot right in front."

"Exactly what I was telling them. Nerves—don't we all remember the days? Never know what boys might be watching."

"Now, Mrs. Kingston?"

"Break a'leg, girls—" She craned her neck around the city tree. Dammit. No Silas, no Paige, no Kingston nobody. She blew the St. Pancras choir a kiss— "And a ho-diddy-ho-ho-ho, you all!"

(Okay, Leigh is now, officially, embarrassed.)

Front of the stage. *Excuse'd me* her way into a spot. Broadened it with elbow room. "My family is joining me. If you don't mind." Mother's weren't as accommodating as fathers but, keen-eyed, the men hoisted hot-cocoa children onto shoulders, letting their watchful eyes linger on the Valentine's chocolate box effect Gwen's corset made within her half-open coat.

Clear your mind, Gwen. You need to prepare for Silas. Christmas thoughts...

She went to her go-to question. Overlooked and feminine and obvious:

Christmas is the spiritual season of motherhood. Joseph dragging Mary to Bethlehem for tax business, not caring she's pregnant, not booking a room. Then it's all about Jesus—which is right, later on—but there's no Jesus without Mary's spiritual victimhood.

The Christmas story always made her angry. This year, more so. If it hadn't been for her obnoxious lawyers, she wouldn't even have called Melody about the girls' performance. But her meetings with the lawyers weren't going easy. They kept trying to dig dirt on Michael—

"The fact, Gwen, is that Michael can always show up and blow the whole case to hell."

"How?"

"By being alive? Right? No death benefit and then your case against Silas, Hal, and Lynn stops being about you."

"I don't have any dirt on Michael. He's not dirty. Michael is a good man and a good father—"

"He didn't think so highly of you. He transferred power of attorney to his father."

"He had his reasons."

"Which would be...?"

"My God! I'm certainly not here to dirty myself."

Senator Ossani stepped in/stepped up the strategy. "Gwen, I want to change my recommendation on contact between you and Silas. He's our ultimate target and your shot at the biggest payout. What we need—you need—is an admission from him that he controlled Hal's changing his official statement from Michael alive to Michael dead. After which, Silas concealed his knowledge that Michael is alive, provable by his involvement with Hal going into the field a second time—without Presidential Finding—to acquire your husband."

Senator Ossani didn't need Silas to make a confession. All she needed for now (she'd stressed *for now*) was acknowledgment of involvement and a timestamp. If Gwen could get Silas simply to acknowledge Hal changed his statement on his advice, then confirm Silas had knowledge of a post-"death report" rescue attempt, the Senator and her committee could prove Silas Kingston concealed a rogue operation with national security implications. And *that* opened the box to everything.

Whatever "everything" that meant. Gwen had her question. And the amount of times they made her rehearse it she wasn't about to forget.

A group of teeny-boppers in reindeer headbands and tap shoes—might as well have been smashing ants—jerked and strained to *Rockin' Around the Christmas Tree*. Front of the stage, perfect vantage point to see everyone. Gwen turned her back on the dancers. Scanned the crowd. Basked a tidge—it's something to be in front of an audience and turn and see all those faces smiling and humming and singing back right at you. The snow had stopped falling within the last couple hours and the temperature had changed; fog rose from the ground. Some Christmas. Too many layers. She tugged at the top of her jacket. Lufted it all the way open above the seal of her made tight/made tiny belt. It was only at the last moment she caught sight of Silas leading the rest of the family past the cocoa and coffee carts, the ornament crafters' stalls. He stopped at the peppermint fudge lady who, foolishly, gave away pounds of the stuff each year. Silas took some and shared it. Everyone knew the peppermint lady didn't have a cent, and they put money in her cup when she water-colored on the green in the summers.

And here's mean old Silas taking food from the poor pigeon's mouth.

Gwen shook off the anger. Gave a quick practice for later—

"When Hal changed what he wrote—you were there, right? You must've—" Wait. Not you must've— *"You were there to talk him through it, right?"*

"Hi, you guys! You made it! Oh, Melody: what a charming..." Blank face; Melody always so blah. "Boots—cute. And look at you boys—you look great in your elf hats."

Jack and Little Silas gaped at her open jacket.

"Well, if it isn't Madonna." Silas (and everyone who looked) could see the red lacey ribbon on the corset's overbust edge.

Don't take the bait. Don't-fight-don't-fight-don't-fight.

Gwen's sugarplummiest: "Silas, I was just now thinking about the Virgin Mary."

Nice pivot!

Melody's fingertips tapped Silas's elbow. When he showed his teeth it was always in a smile.

"Christmas really is her season." Gwen continued. "When you stop and think about it. Does Madonna even have a Christmas CD?"

Clive gave Paige a deliberate look. Gwen copied Silas's toothy smile for Paige. "Paige, you two look so happy. Our Christmas miracle lovebirds."

Melody jumped in. "The tree this year is almost mystical with this fog. I can't wait for them to light it. What do you boys think?"

The twins *mmm-hmm'd* to that and anything else through mouths of peppermint fudge.

The St. Pancras choir filed onto the stage. As the director announced them, Little Silas pointed. "There's Leigh!" Jack: "I see Charlotte!"

The St. Pancras students gathered into sections and rows. The choir director stood behind a keyboard, her fingers turning triplets. And they sang. *O Holy Night.*

For years, it had been Silas's favorite. Angleton. The Ellipse. The skating rink and Doris, young and beautiful and impassioned. The given—yet never quite perfectly received—gift of KALEIDOSCOPE. The heraldic promise of Covenant 17. What a foolish thing for Gwen to say about Mary; but better the fool than wasting a lifetime chasing glory through clandestine mechanism, deception, violence when deceit (as maybe it always must) failed.

Melody eyed him. "You look like you've seen a ghost."

"If only I could."

"If I see her, you see her."

"Doris? When is she unseen among us? Why do you think I did that with the mirrors?" They both know he's not talking about Doris in the mirrors. "I meant the other ghost."

"Isn't that what Christmas is about—to renew our sight?"

Silas smiled placidly. Watched the choir a moment... "She liked coming to this. We'd bring the three kids." He tickled the backs of the twins' necks. They cringed. They giggled. They blew on their hot chocolate then sipped to clear their fudgy palates. "She'd be sad, this year—all three of them away."

Gwen faced him. Too fast. Too eager. A question on her lips. "When Hal—"

"You've had a lot to deal with this year, Gwen. And I've been unusually hard on you."

She blinked a sort of double-take. Her mouth hung open. No more words came out.

"Did you know, Doris worried about you?"

Gwen's eyes did their usual. "How?" She blinked moisture.

"You're incredibly beautiful—" Silas ignored the pressure of Melody's boot on his toe. "She thought it might be difficult for your daughters to measure up. But they've grown lovely too, haven't they? Charlotte looks more and more like her every day."

Blink-blink-blink. She nodded. The choir began their next song. Not a Christmas carol; more prayer than hymn.

"I don't know what to say, Silas."

"I know your lawyers want to keep us apart. And I understand you're doing what you feel is right."

"They want me to say terrible things about Michael. I'm the one who asked for the divorce."

"We all have our crosses. What I wanted to ask, this performance is Charlotte and Leigh's last school activity until the new year. Wouldn't it be nice for them to enjoy Christmas at Foxtail Farm?"

Melody gave Gwen the napkin from her coffee cup. Gwen blew her nose. "They've asked. Every day."

"Of course, we'd welcome you to come for Christmas Eve."

Melody. "We'd love that, Gwen. It's what Christmas is about."

Gwen fumbled for words. Gave up. The girls/the choir closed out with...

"'Peace and good will' / Thine own word increase; / Lord God of love / let us have peace!"

And the tree blazed. Lights all white, and Melody was right; in the swirl of fog, the electric bulbs appeared as candles flickering with primal and ancient flame serene and universal. Everyone saw and there was a simultaneous catching of breath, a public united, breathing as one, exhaling, some laughter, remarks, and that long/longing aspiration: life and happiness shared.

None of the Kingstons noticed Clive and Paige—who quelled at the idea of that life-affirming oxygen affirming an unseen presence that Clive all but convinced them an impossibility: now more than possible, Paige's period having once more not begun—slipping away.

Gwen slip-slid to Charlotte and Leigh, who waved her *go away*—they weren't finished on stage yet—but who jumped and clapped and squealed when she blurted how she twisted Papa's arm to let them return to Foxtail Farm for Christmas break; then the music swelled with the opening chords of *Joy to the World* and Melody kissed Silas on the cheek and whispered in his ear. "You laid it on pretty thick, you know."

"Only an idiot walks into an ambush." A bitter shake of his head. "Such a crybaby. It's really not sport."

"Mom?" Jack tugged Melody's pocket. "Where's Clive? He promised he'd give me a piggyback."

They all swiveled heads, and Little Silas said to himself: *There's the leathery man looking at me again.*

The leathery man raised a small, golden, rectangular-shaped and black-capped can. His other hand held a cheesecloth. With it, he unscrewed the cap. Intentional. Purposeful. *Watch my hands, kid.* He put the cheese cloth over the mouth of the can and strained the fluid into his mouth. Swish-swish. Made his cheeks bulge. Swallowed as multicolored beams of light streaked through the fog sweeping, dancing, bouncing, rotating with laser intensity. The massed crowd broke from singing to *ooh* and *ahh* the kaleidoscopic colored light and Little Silas's eyes sparkled as his gaze found the lasers' source: the Christmas star ablaze and turning slowly atop the noble fir like a disco ball. The boy glanced back. Glimpsed the leathery man fade into the jostling, singing, celebrating Christmas crowd, the churn of fog inhaling him without any movement of his own.

THE NAME OUT FRONT still read *Samuels Drugs* and although Doc Samuels had retired and sold, his wife (and Victoria's mother), Ellen, still worked the counter three shifts a week. The old customers liked having Ellen around and the new ones already liked her just as well. Paige knew Ellen by sight. Knew her by name by a thousand times reading her name tag. She and Clive were the only customers. Wished it wasn't old Ellen she'd be making her purchase from. She stood with Clive in the "Family Planning" section. *Before* and *after* kept her hand from touching the First Response Early Result Pregnancy Test box. Kidding around, Clive pushed her elbow. Her fingertips brushed the box.

"Don't do that."

"Come on, be brave. It's going to be negative. I think doing it, just one more time, getting that third negative's going to get 'Flo' flowing tomorrow."

She jerked her hand back. "Don't be so loud."

"Hey." Soft. "I love you, Paige."

"This changes everything. No matter what I do or want or dream or choose—if it's positive—my whole existence changes forever."

"You'd do the other?"

Eyes: hers up to him, his to hers down.

"Is that what you'd want, Clive?"

He thought: *Every time the chips were down, my best answers—my bloody best results—came from lies.*

He chose not to answer and, anyway, she pushed past the question with her next thought. She knew him too well. "I want to tell you something that I don't want to scare you."

"Luv, nothing you can say could ever scare me."

She thought: *"The bravest people are the ones who don't mind looking like cowards."*

"What I just said was a lie."

"What? Which?"

"If I am. You know. If I am. There's really only one choice that I know I have to do." She took the box. Her brave, brave, bravest smile.

Clive gave an exaggerated shrug. A goofy grin. "It's gonna be negative. Let's go, before you show the white feather."

"What's that?"

"White feather: the mark of the coward."

"You're weird." She tucked the phrase away. Another name for the thing she feared most.

Clive was paying. The quiet honor of that cast an exceedingly warm expression on Ellen's face. The door chimed. The pair hunched. Lowered heads. Ellen's hands moved fast getting the test kit into the bag for them while looking up and saying, "Melody! Victoria said you two had quite an interesting day at the St. Ignatius center. You're so nice to involve yourself in her historical mysteries!"

Clive and Paige stared at the counter. At the bag, inches from Paige's open grasp.

"Here you guys are. We've been looking all over."

Clive swept the bag into his jacket. Paige looked at Ellen. Ellen said, "These are yours, too?"

Melody put an arm around each of them. Hugged. "Paige is! Clive...we'd never need to buy a lottery ticket again. We'd have won."

"How nice." Ellen began straightening a counter display that didn't need to be touched.

Paige stared at her aunt.

"Paige, you're going to need to not have a guilty look when we walk out of here." She led them from the counter. "Good night, Ellen. Merry Christmas!"

"Merry Christmas!"

Paige and Clive echoed it like ghosts. Melody stopped at the door. Peered through the window. Scanned the sidewalk. "Did you lie to me, Clive, when we spoke on the beach?"

"No, Melody. I didn't lie to you."

"Well, life happens. Or not. You'll see. I'm going to make it not my business now and we're going to go out right..." Another eye-sweep. "Now." Door opened.

"Before Silas sees where we've come from. And you two can bring your sisters with you?"

"They're coming home?!"

Melody hustled them down the sidewalk away from the drugstore. "Christmas wonders never cease."

5.

A LITERAL STUMBLING UPON. Charlotte/Boone Kelso. Beaumont's morning walk. Sky clear. Air clean-crisp/breath-fogged. The snow beneath Charlotte's black Sorel Snow Angel boots sunk, cracked, sunk more between alternating layers of cornstarch powder and refrozen melt. She only moved when her boots gripped, their ridged rubber soles biting into the packed base. But Beaumont frisked. Beaumont yanked the leash. Strained to pull her onward or, looping back, entangled the girl in his ear-flopping circles. And it was tough going, where Charlotte was headed—extra careful with the heavy sharp scissors brought for the holly she planned to cut. She knew a small grove. Grew on the edge of the river palisade. The trees dwarfed and bent inland from the river wind, a steady bending breath their entire growth. Made the branches hang low. Easy to cut. Her dad usually took her to gather a grocery bag of sprigs they'd bring back and add to Aunt Melody's wreathes and garlands. Add to the bases of the candles that burned on the mantel in the common room where the Yule log would soon be lit.

"Everyone else gets twelve days of Christmas, but Kingstons get thirteen," she said to Beaumont, breath heavy from her snow trudge, to give herself excuse to say it aloud and hear a voice in the wind that blew over the river wall.

Charlotte entered the woods. Snow-draped bushes and bracken. Drifts Beaumont plunged between. Through. Moving faster now. Feet slipping just a bit.

"Slow down! Beaumont!"

He stopped. Did a thing like pointing and Charlotte blinked at the vision before her. A small, almost circular clearing. Unsure if she'd ever been here before, the pure snow, wind-washed outward from the center against the surrounding woods, made the circle appear to be a foaming bowl into the center of which a tulip poplar sapling, no more than five feet high, rose straight on its young gray trunk. Ridged and furrowed. Branches: a dazzling otherworldly red.

Northern cardinals pecked, snapped, ate the dried seeds from the brown clusters of the elongated samara pods.

Beaumont barked. Lunged. Charlotte floundered behind him. The birds burst, chittering, into the air to vanish into a high snowy hedgerow.

"Beaumont!" Charlotte lost her balance entirely. Twisted. Fell backwards into the hedge. Eyes briefly skyward.

The flight of cardinals appeared a release of red balloons to the sky.

Then she rolled, twigs and branches breaking around her, tangling her hair, scratching her cheeks, and—Beaumont putting up a furious racket—sprawled into the wet-jeaned ankles, the grasping leathery hands of a large (not tall, not fat, just sturdy/hard) man in a strange hobo sheepskin, his grip saving her face from impalement on an old jagged stump.

"Whoa! Whoa! Upsy-daisy, girl!"

Charlotte struggled backwards a few steps from Boone Kelso who leered with turpentine-ruined teeth. She looked at her hands. Empty. Beaumont dragged his leash and stood between them.

"My scissors?"

Boone Kelso wiggled them in his fist. The sword-pointed blades caught the sunlight. "Between that stump and these almost goin' in your belly, you're a lucky child to run into me."

Charlotte swallowed. They didn't look like scissors.

Aunt Linny's throat. The hole. The plastic tube.

They looked like murder.

Boone Kelso opened them, raised the blades to his faded eyes. Peered keen down the edge. "These oughta do much better."

They were among the holly trees. Charlotte watched him pull a pocketknife from the trunk of the tree she'd planned to cut her berry boughs. He'd been carving something and forgetting Charlotte, went back at it with the scissors. She stared at his rat-leather back. Frightened. Unable to catch her breath. Curious. Unable to come up with a plan..His coat was the color of wet stones and a quote from Papa's book came unbidden to her mind.

"Too dark to be light, too light to be dark."

"You can't just cut our tree."

He didn't bother looking. "I'm a friend of your papa." He continued to work.

"How? What are you doing here?"

"Knew him from the Army."

"He wasn't in the Army."

"Sure-bet he was 'cause I fought the war with him." He winked over his shoulder. Licked dry lips with a lizard tongue he bit back, held with yellow teeth. "Bet there's lots of things he did you don't know."

Beaumont whimpered. Snowy head followed his eyes. Tracked between Charlotte and Boone Kelso. Seeing her dog nervous made the girl stronger.

"My *dad's* in the same work as my papa. My dad's coming out right now to help me cut holly. You can tell him."

"That'd be Michael. Heard many good things about Michael." He pointed the scissors at her. Sap glistened on the blades. Aimed down them with his eye. "That'd make you Charlotte."

He grinned. Winked at her.

Something familiar, his eyes...

"Yeah. Maybe. So?"

"Charlotte: the bright one."

"Eh. That's my sister—"

"Paige."

"Paige is the smart one."

"But you're bright *and* you're pretty. Like your grandma Doris; the great beauty of her age. I'd say—now I've seen you close, pretty as a picture, feisty, brave, and bright, like I said: just like Doris. That kind of 'it.'"

Charlotte's cheeks burned. Didn't know why. Did. A little; the part of her that was growing up. Didn't like it.

Be brave. Be like Doris in the painting.

"Mister, why are you out here? Why didn't you come to the house—if you know Papa?"

"Thing is, I got lost. You found me." The blades flashed. Bark and chips of holly wood flew. "A bunch of his best Army pals are planning to come as a surprise for a Christmas visit."

"Papa doesn't like surprises. Where are your friends?"

"Ohhhh, they're not in town yet. I didn't have no proper directions but wanted to do a re-conny-since." He nodded at what he'd done to the tree. "Pretty as new paint." Spun.

The scissors snicker-snacked.

He flipped them in his hand and presented her the handle-rings.

"Be seein' ya', Charlotte." He merged into the thicket.

She thought he was gone. Exhaled. His leathery face peered back out.

"Remember, it's a surprise. Smart, bright, pretty girls get to grow up, those who know to keep a secret. Like Santa—" The branches sealed around the place his face had been. "I'll be watching."

Unsettled, Charlotte squatted next to Beaumont. Clutched him. Stroked his head. Clutched him more tightly. In her confusion she'd forgotten why she'd come. Then remembered she was here for holly. She opened, closed the scissors, testing. Stepped to the tree, reaching for the lowest branch with the reddest berries. She saw it. Boone Kelso had carved into the trunk:

One woman's light, one man's dark / Bound beneath the holly bark.

This couplet was done with the pocketknife, the letters tight and shallow. But what he'd carved with the scissors—deeper, precise, strong letters formed, stilled the girl's heart. She forgot all about her holly cuttings.

Grabbed Beaumont's leash from the snow. In case, he still watched, she didn't run. She shouldered through the bushes and left the mad and fallen artist's work bleeding sap in the crisp air.

Berries red, Beaumont dead, / If a single word is said.

Monday, December Tenth

1.

Photographs on a bedspread.

A medieval village. Stein am Rhein. Michael spreads out views of narrow, winding cobbled lanes. Timber-framed *Fachwerk* houses. Frescoed facades. Tucked shops and guest accommodations. A gothic church—its steeple thrust heavenward—offering distinct escape from the spinous/algous/gargoyled architecture. Time suspended on the banks of the Rhine, where the border—like everything here—was drawn in secrets. A town timeless in its survival; twenty-first century in its restoration: LED signs, neon glow; Mercedes and BMWs parked before motorcycle garages; high-end fashion windows gleaming beside mobile device retailers. A visual map to—

A flurry of fresh glossies.

A Cistercian priory—timeless stone reconstructed as a to-the-minute, every-ivy-leaf elitist boarding school.

The Lyceum Marrow. Contemplative courtyards. State-of-the-art athletic facilities. Vibrant, comprehensive libraries and bleeding-edge scientific labs. Separate male and female dormitories arranged on military-style quadrangles. A physical plant to rival a luxury ocean liner. And a motto carved in stone above the gates:

Ad Ossa Fidelis. *Faithful to the Bone.*

It's the physical plant that holds Michael's attention longest. But it's getting late. He's in his tuxedo. Music rises from the ground floor, and voice and laughter and—

Lulu.

Lost in a three-panel standing mirror. She arranged her snow tresses into a crown braid, its trailed end down the back of her neck. Switch. Across her shoulder. Like a white fur tail.

"You're going to be late to your own party." Michael stood at the balcony doors admiring the floodlit snowfield that stretched from the steaming swimming pool behind Lulu's dacha to the banks of the icy Skhodnya, a tributary of the Moskva River.

"It's not my party." Couldn't decide which shoulder to drape her braid. Left-right, back and forth. "In winter, all mirrors lie to me." A glance at Michael's back. "We trust them to show us the truth, but you think about it, what they display is really the exact opposite of the truth. In every way. Down to living and dead." Michael shrugged. Maybe/maybe not. "You were downstairs all day watching them arrange the icons. The *Znamenie*. This night we honor the Feast of the Icon of the Mother of God. Our Lady of the Sign."

"It's rather odd, though." He stared at the rising moon. "Her hands up. She isn't holding the baby Jesus. He's just kind of floating on her. A Russian Christmas thing? I'm not getting it."

"It isn't Christmas yet. Where would the baby be?"

He cast a sidelong glance. Went back to the moon. Silver-blue, it painted a snow-blanketed and endless forest beyond the black slashing river. Against the forest horizon line: the moon, massive.

Lulu switched her braid, shoulder-to-shoulder. A fit of pique, she unfastened it. Finger-combed. Let it all drape down her back. "The baby is still inside her womb."

"In the icon I saw, the kid's dressed!"

"And His eyes are opened; signifying divinity awakened to mankind within the holiest of temples: a woman." Lulu appreciated her reflection; folded the two outer panels in to cover the glass. Did a runway model's turn to draw her lover's attention. "It is where babies come from my-Michael-Misha."

"Aha!"

"Aha," she playfully mocked back.

"You ask me, your Holy Mother looks like the State Security Service has given her the 'hands up'."

"Maybe you're not wrong. Mary lifts her hands—not to bless, not to command—but to show she holds nothing. And that is surrender. Nothing is hidden. Her gesture says: 'I have no weapon. No deceit. Look and see me as I am.' That's why men find it so dangerous. Because if you see a woman as she is, you must answer for how you treat her."

"The girl with all the right answers." He went to a champagne bucket. Filled two flutes. "We should go down."

She joined him. Tapped his glass with hers like it was a magic wand. Like it gave her permission—and him—to do as they pleased. For this moment, anyhow.

"There's another question you could answer." Took her hand. Took her to the glass doors. "That forest—does it have a name?"

"*Les Dikiy*. The Forest Wild. Not romantic wild. Not storybook wild. Wild like what lives too long without kindness and lives only by violence." Sipped. Twinkle-eyed. "You'll see."

"I have enough on my plate."

"Then you asked because you have second sight."

"Believe me. I don't."

"Everyone does. Everyone uses it to a degree. The blind call it luck. The nearsighted call it instinct. Have you ever seen a ghost?"

He drank. He looked at the moon. Felt it looking back. "Everyone thinks they've seen a ghost some time or another."

"Have you seen one and believed it?"

He faced her. Took her glass. Set it aside with his. Regarded her, amused. "Lulu: every time I try to figure out what trick you have up your fancy sleeve for me, you somehow get me to trick myself."

Moonglow cast delight dancing in her eyes. "Is it tricking or trusting?"

Whenever Lulu said something like that—simple and profound—it filled Michael Kingston with love. Not for how she made him see himself, but in revealing the depth of her regard for things he hid from, lonely inside himself.

She must have read this love in his face. His welling desire to express it. She tapped his lips. "Don't say it." He kissed her fingertip. She pointed at the moon. "Do you like? My great big Russian moon?"

"Optical illusion—when it appears extra-large like that. They say it's a psychological trick of the human mind."

"Because there are other kinds of psychological tricks?"

"You know what I mean, Lu."

"Yes. And it's unique since all human beings' minds trick the exact same way. Psychology?"

"Awright. You tell me?"

She shrugged. She leaned backward into him. He held her.

She said: "What do you see when you look at it?"

"A block of cheese. A cheese with a great big grin."

She *mmm'd* her agreement. Thought for a minute. Caught her train of thought and looked backward, up into his eyes for him to punch its ticket.

I love her games. She makes me feel like we're children and in that I can trust myself as a man.

She said: "They look at the moon: no one says they see an elephant. Or a sailing—nah! A battleship. No one sees that—their own thing. No one group swears to see a howling wolf or some untouched/remote island population a flowerpot; modern civilization steps ashore and shakes hands and says, 'How do you do?' and 'what do you see?' and the islanders introduce them to their smiley-faced god of the moon they already know. All the planets—including Earth—and the sun and the stars are featureless geologies, chemicals, gases, but when we look out we see a cheery man smiling down on us. A 'psychological trick of the mind'? I see the same kind/friendly man in the moon that you see and every human being since the beginning has ever seen in the dark night sky." She turned in his arms. She held his shoulders. He held her waist. "Can you imagine the frightened existence of early man? Living in caves. Trees. Hollow holes along rivers. The entire environment designed to kill you. Most other creatures—those you hunt and eat want to hunt and eat you."

"Not much has changed in my life."

"You're a big baby. But think back. Darkness would be the worst hours. But the night has a moon that reflects the light of the sun. That would already be a comfort. And yet, there's a face on that moon: a cheerful, tender face watching over you, forever unchanging—no matter what you do—in its freely offered comfort. If that is something random, we are the luckiest species on the planet."

She kissed his lips. She indicated the photographs. "Put those away. We don't really know who in this house was sent to watch us. Watch you."

Michael nodded. "I think I've come up with a plan. For Alina."

"Never doubted." He shut them in her bedside safe beside her pistol. She said: "The moon: imagine how much worse we'd be if that random face glared and showed sharp teeth."

He joined her at the bedroom door. "Tell me you're not dragging me into your *Les Dikiy* tonight. Promise me."

"You're hardly ready tonight. But it's waiting for you."

He opened the door. She offered her arm. He took it and walked her through.

They walked down the hallway. Along the balcony. Below, two dozen guests enjoyed the Feast of Our Lady of the Sign; steam rose from rich hot dishes, samovars gleamed, candles flickered, and the roar of the central parlor-sized fireplace gave life to the folk art icons, the *Znamenie* prominently displayed. Guests' faces turned and bright-teeth smiled upward. Lulu put her lips to Michael's ear. "Remember, you're my Boy-Toy and this is the night we embarrass the country mice and the city mice into believing we have nothing to hide and ought to be more decent about that."

THE MUSIC WASN'T CANNED; local musicians *Dr. Zhivago*'d it up with *balalaika*, *dorma* lutes, *bayan* accordion, and *zhaleika*, a hypnotic folk clarinet played on a goose reed blown through a cow horn bell. Everyone but Michael could hum along. He bounced between neighbors from the oligarch set—not the oligarch's themselves, but the set that included their accountants and lawyers, physicians and surgeons as befit the second-rate first-class real estate of Skhodnya town. Yegor Surnin, the mayor was there, a short/round fellow, but for four comb-over gray hairs, bald and bearing the jolly face of Lulu's man in the moon while his wife, erect enough in bearing to make herself taller than her husband, looked down on all things with sharp teeth. The butcher, the baker, and the "handmade illumination specialist" were local guests—baker having arrived in his bright orange Lotus. The butcher, Tikhon Balakin, however, was truly no more than his job descriptor and ran the chatty local shop and quiet outback abattoir with aplomb;

Michael puzzled the phrase that everyone attached to Balakin: "Tikhon will dress old Skvoznyak for Christmas this year, for sure;" *Skvoznyak*—meant "breeze" or "draft", odd—meant nothing to Michael. The village priest, Father Vadim Zheldakov, curly-headed and spectacled like a schoolboy introduced his visiting sister—shy and somewhat schoolboyish herself—and Father Vadim attempted to explain to Michael his *Znamenie* service tonight would be short, but even with as good a grasp of conversational Russian as Michael held, chanted in Church Slavonic, Michael would be hard-pressed to understand it. Vadim attempted the history—Russians commemorate the Feast of Our Lady of the Sign, something about the protection of the city of Novgorod, an invasion in the 12th century—the story broken by babushka interruption, the old grandmother who ran Skhodnya's Michelin two-starred restaurant (she'd catered tonight's event) who had gotten into the Medovukha, honey-spirits, and kept stammering, insisting: "The *Znamenie's* hand is always up, see? She's not praying. She's saying 'Stop.' To protect the child, which is the city, which is Jesus Christ," which no one argued but her with herself in their faces. All night, Michael had felt like a rubber ball, and now he bounced away from the grandmother to a jokey banker named Kravtsov, whose wife asked:

"What do you do when you're not in Russia?"

"I do what I do in Russia. Consulting."

"What do you consult?"

"I specialize in systems that erase themselves."

"Oh. Computers?"

"Yes, but also, I leave room for everything else non-technological. Broad portfolio."

He bounced away but not fast enough to miss—"He doesn't do a thing except turn out as Lulu's American stallion"—for his rubber ball was attached to Lulu's rubber-band and she the paddle which he came up against, regularly and all the night, which when they did they made frisky displays of open lust until, too heavy the petting and pawing, she would bat him away.

Hammered church bells announced the religious service. For an instant, Michael swore he saw Lulu's monk on the mallets, but if it was him, outside the narcotic flash of Disco Chapel Perilous, he was an aged man of ninety. Everyone joined in a short (linguistically baffling for Michael) mass after which Michael's arm was trapped in the great paw of Lulu's Chechen. Pulled into a circle of the youngest, strongest, local men gathered around the back of the fireplace in footprints of ash.

"Mikhail Nikolaevich joins us for the toast."

Nods all around. Vodka shoved into Michael's fist. He lifted it, expectant. The butcher, Balakin, nodded encouragement. Hoisted his glass high. "We honor tradition. We give fair warning. Tomorrow the horns will signal each dawn. Ten blasts, one less each day to the last."

"Fair warning." Yegor Surnin chimed in, his cheerful cheeks sweat-glossed: "In ten days, as every year in Skhodnya town—"

"The Les Dikiy. Eight years now, on the Winter Solstice, we hunt the Skvoznyak."

"The Skvoznyak!" All cried. All drank. All glasses thrown into the fire. Hard. Shattering.

Michael pitched his into the flames.

The Chechen. "It must break."

They all watched Michael expectantly. He raised his foot, about to shove it in the flames, but Father Vadim pulled him back at the last instant. The Chechen dropped a wrinkle, center of his brow, intrigued, concerned, judging. Michael hesitated. Some nervous/knowing looks—*the Amerikanski doesn't have the nerve.* "Beer." Michael kept his toe up, held out his hand. Bottle to his lips. Opened his throat. Swallowed it like water. Boisterous drunk-men shouts/cheers.

Not his foot. Flash of the wrist. He knife-hurled the beer bottle into the flames exploding both the bottle and the vodka glass.

The Russians laughed. Shoved another beer into Michael's hand. Swigged, he drew the back of his hand across his mouth. "Explain: how do you propose to hunt the 'breeze'?"

Quiet. Judging. Serious. "The ancient weapons. Pike and leaf-blade spear." The Chechen.

A loose arm around Michael's shoulder. "We shoulder AKs. Just in case it blows into us first." Mayor Surnin took the vodka bottle. Toasted something. Drunk reverence. "The Skvoznyak."

Michael shifted eyes around the circle. Had to be a gag. Waited.

"In English, yes, Skvoznyak, translates to 'Crosswin d.'" The banker Kravtsov took the vodka. Offered it to Michael. Michael took it. Didn't hesitate. "Skvoznyak, in these parts, a superstition. Caught by a crosswind is to be put in a deathly situation. In Les Dikiy, Skvoznyak is the name of the beast with no fixed direction. For that is how he moves. From elsewhere expected. Kills like the cold—instantly and always from behind. He's a pig."

Balakin. "A very old boar. Last two years he has taken three dogs, two fingers, and one marriage."

"During the year, fools from Moscow, yellow-eyed shooting glasses and Gucci-flage come with heavy firepower. Boom, boom, ratta-tat-tat. Since 2006, four of these fools have wasted their lead and given their lives."

Michael: "The marriage?"

Kravtsov smirked. "Chuprikov, show him."

The ring finger and pinkie absent from the fancy candlestick man's left hand. "Skvoznyak ran off with his fingers; the ambulance driver ran off with his wife."

Michael swept the fire-lit/alcohol-hot faces. "I'm sure it's a great honor for an outsider to be invited."

They all worked fresh beer. No one met his gaze. A few slurred *Skvoznyak* as the vodka bottle made a circuit.

"I am not a hunter. I must respectfully decline."

"We bring you then for bait." The Chechen. Calm. Not kidding. No one laughing.

Lulu appeared behind them. She took Michael's arm. Possessive as a queen. Gave her Chechen a nod. He nodded back. Stepped back. She addressed the circle:

"Michael will kill the Skvoznyak. I dreamt it."

"Did he know this?" the banker's wife had followed her up.

"Michael never knows what I dream until he's already made it true."

Michael swished his eyes. They were staring again. A sudden cheer—all of them, all at once. Toasts. A few mutters. Father Vadim crossed himself.

Lulu turned to Michael. Stroked his face with her words. “I’ve drunk a little too much tonight, Michael. Take me to bed?” Her hand took the vodka bottle. Toasted him. Drank. Louder. “You’ve been the American guest long enough. Time to prove yourself a man.”

Michael tossed the men a casual salute. “We shall see each other on the wind of the solstice.”

The fire popped.

And in his wet, mossy wallow, far away in the snow-thick dark of Les Dikiy, Skvoznyak snuffled, grunted twice, and rolled over.

PARTY LEFT BEHIND. Lulu said it would continue without them until dawn. Balakin’s workers would bring the morning sausage fresh-stuffed and boiling in pails while Levka Rodyaevand’s bakery would supply the sweet and savory, buttery and fresh fruit jelly-filled breads/rolls/pastries.

“We don’t have to see them again.” Michael opened Lulu’s bedroom door. “I’m smashed.”

She nipped his jaw—teeth, then moist lips—said: “You held your own. But no. We won’t have to see any of them again until the hunt.”

“An astonishingly terrible idea.”

She pulled him inside, door closed with toe-tip, pulled his hands onto her. “Undress me.”

Michael obliged. “You heard what I said?”

Her perfectly white skin mirrored the moonlight, the snow reflection. Cast silver. Cast blue. “A perfectly terrible idea until you understand why it's the best idea." She spun and left him holding her dress. She spiraled onto the bed. "Are you going to pony around or prove the American thoroughbred—"

"I believe the word tonight was 'stallion.'"

"All right. Giddy-it-up, sir."

Amused. Michael undressed. Kicked off his shoes. Ripcorded his belt. Stepped out of his trousers and sat beside where she lay. Started on cufflinks/button hole studs. "Did we accomplish our mission? Find out who's spying on us?"

"Did you?"

"I figured they all are. Safest that way."

Lulu helped him out of his shirt. "Father Vadim's sister. I would say is not his sister. I would say, she is Kalaydoskop."

"Because she's the only stranger? That's not how it always works."

"Because I had my Chechen pull you into the hunt. Once she saw that, she encouraged Father Vadim to join the group."

"Sounded to me, he's a regular part of it."

"He gives a prayer and sends the men and dogs off. But as I insisted you were going into the Les Dikiy, she told everyone her brother would be hunting as well. He's asked me to come for a blessing before I leave for my visit to Alina—again, something new—and I predict he will urge me to give you your cover and send you on your way. Will urge the same thing on you in the forest as well."

Both of them nude, Michael half-slumped on the edge of the bed, Lulu snaked around and face-up, head-in-his-lap. The pools of her eyes sharing, knowing, inviting and her lips, full and pale pink and parted. Michael said, "It doesn't end." He said, "It doesn't stop. Everyone has an angle on me."

"How about you come with us? Me. Alina. Across the sea. Peace. Heal your wounds."

A sardonic huff. "Who's wounded? Unless I go in that damn forest."

Lulu's laughter was like hammered bells. "The most lethal wound a man can receive doesn't have to bleed at all." A leveraged hip. A push with her shoulder. She snaked up his chest. Her arms taking him, pinning him, as she threw a leg over his hip. "Hope will be the ruin of me," he said. "You have a new angle you want to try?"

The adoring smile. The laughter, like struck bronze. They reached for the light simultaneously. Lulu not wanting him to see and Michael afraid to look at her eyes. Click. In darkness, tears scrolled her cheeks, and they made love.

THE MOON SET. Darkness complete. Not even the outline of a back, a shoulder, a face for a human map.

LULU: "Are you asleep?"

MICHAEL: "Well, that's as worldwide and timeless as the cheese-man in the moon."

LULU: "What?"

MICHAEL: "The waking someone up asking if they're asleep."

LULU: "I want to talk."

MICHAEL: "So, I gather."

Reaches for light.

LULU: "Leave it off. That way we can pretend this never happened. Now put your hand on my heart."

He reached. She guided. His open palm placed flat above her breasts. Left of her breastbone.

LULU: "Now you'll know."

MICHAEL: "What will I know?"

LULU: "Telling is knowing's crutch. Shh. Walk all the way with me. I'm going to ask you questions but answer them silently."

Michael said nothing. Imagined her grin. Lulu's lungs filled beneath his hand. Air released. Her heart beat. Steady. And she seemed to be listening because she waited for Michael to breathe, take some of her air inside himself before she spoke.

LULU: "Love is the most important thing. Full love. Not love in pieces—romantic, affectionate, family, selfless or its opposite; self-love, playful love, obsessive, patriotic, misplaced love, enduring—so many different kinds we hold various amounts in pieces. *Not* piecemeal but whole love fully received from the universe and allowed to fully pour out. In/out on auto all the time. Love: Beatles to God to a child's first breath. Freedom to love what/how we love. Create/give/receiver-of-happiness-and-safety—? Does Kolya want any of that for you? In whole or even tiny scraps?"

He wants me to know he's my father and through that thinks I'll give or he'll take something else from me.

LULU: "He's made no indication he held any love for Doris, but he's used your love for your mother as bait. Since Turkey, he's gamed your every move, creating himself as a mirror image to love that you think you don't or never had, or now can't trust."

Her heartbeat increased beneath his hand. She'd given him the opposite of the *Znamenie*: not a sign of warning, but an offering. Not 'stop'—but 'go,' with my love in front of you. She breathed. Allowed it to slow; allowed him to respire her respiration into himself again.

LULU: "Is anything in this the act of a loving father? You fled your CIA but take it hard it's abandoned you. Because that's Silas—who, since you found out he's not your real father—has done everything to prove it. Showing how little he cares, as you've said he's shown you and your brother and sister's most of your lives."

Michael shifted uncomfortably.

I hate him. I hate Silas. I hate what he did to Mom, what he's done to Lynn, what he's made me be.

Lulu covered his hand with hers. Pressed. Held it in place. Her heart began to pound.

LULU: "Silas may not be blood—that's not a secret anymore—right now in the dark—where no one, not even me, can see how hurt you are, how small you feel, how love completely escapes you and it's all you have left and you don't even understand what it is. Ask yourself: is reacting to Kolya's bait, his revelation, his forcing this on you: is that the truest form of a father's love? A man can love so deeply he lets you hate him. Is that what your Silas did? And Kolya? I think, for him, blood is thinner than water."

Her words were finished, but her heart pounded inside her breast. With each beat held inside her chest by the palm of Michael's hand Michael knew.

MICHAEL: “He would have killed my mother and me at my birth if my father hadn’t bent to his will. He’s turning that kaleidoscope again. He’s walking me to my own death if I deny him. But if I join him... If I do exactly as Kolya wants... The man I’ve called my father; the man Doris chose to raise me. His life will be over. He’ll be worse than dead.”

Lulu rolled from under his hand. Fierce, she grabbed him and wrapped herself—arms and legs—crushing herself onto him.

“I wanted you to choose me. To save Alina and choose me and come with us and leave all of this, which killed my husband and my father, and probably thousands or more because that’s what this business of yours does for power and might and I thought I could convince you. But love is the most awful force in the universe. It leaves a man chasing the pieces of himself, long after he’s already broken.”

Tuesday, December Eleventh

THE DTs SLAMMED. JOUSTING lance straight through Lynn's chest. Hard shakes. Anxiety harder. Huddled on the cot, backed into a corner of the room, she sat, knees up to her chest, arms wrapped round them until the tremors in her arms went out of control. Lynn made fists. Shook her arms herself. Hard as she could. She'd control her pathetic, nerve-wrack; she beat the air in front of her face like hammers and hated that she had to watch herself reduced to this. Hated she'd groan if she didn't clench her jaw, but clenching brought pathetic chattering—

I'm not even fucking cold! I'm sweating and I'm freezing and I'm not cold, and I want to/won't scream anguish.

Her face pulled at itself, trying to rip its mask off her jaw. Her juttering chin. Forehead: harrow-furrowed, pulling down her nose, flaring her nostrils. Squeezed eyes, outside corners pulling down. Cheeks: muscles clenched/burning, pulling down. Mouth: horror-stretched, painful, pulling down.

My heart pulling down. I can't breathe.

She drummed the air, spastic with her fists. Hated the sight of them. Curled around her legs, hated fists burrowed behind her knees. She rocked. Flung herself onto her back on her cot, quivering legs stretched. She choked on a breath-rattling, wail that banged around inside her skull like the bullet inside of Roman's brain until it burst shrill/high-pitched/piercing:

Leigh. Bloody. Held in rubber gloves, bloody, between my legs. Lifted to my sight. Bloody/beautiful/alive. My tears. Her wail. My joy. My anguished shame.

Arms—convulsive—in the air. Juddered hands/flung hands like a primate railing at the moon.

Stop it! Fight!

She clutched the cot rails. Hammered her heels. Swirled into pathetic self-loathing.

(You [I] sure could use—) CAN'T USE! DON'T WANT!

(A drink.)

It won't be my choice when they force it. (Bless yourself [myself]. Pray.) I know I've quit. I've-quit/stopped/don't want.

(I deserve it. This. All.)

God! Why can't I just sleep?!

She pulled herself—

It's all pulling. Everything: body/mind/spirit: pulling-pulling-pulling.

—"Huh-hhh, huh-hhh, huh-hhh-hhh—" back into the corner. Arms around knees. Her hair hurt. The tops of her ears burned. She shakes.

Hammer the air. Beat it back.

Up in the corner. The cot smelled. Blanket: sweat, alcohol/camphor/mildew. Vomit. One dim fluorescent lightbulb. Under a thick plastic shield. Shield metal-strapped. Room for three more bulbs. Three slots empty.

Name of the father—

Silas. Looks down upon Doris's coffin. "Love and simplicity, you made worth having."

Name of the daughter—

"Year-round school!" Leigh laughs. I brush my hand across her cheek; she twists her lips to catch my knuckles with a kiss.

Mother ghost: blows out, folds her last birthday candle into my child-hand. "Lynn: your faith in yourself must never know—" The fire reignites. Flame plumes between my fingers.

Doris ignites at the end of her kimono silk cord noose.

I scream/Doris screams: "Fire/Lord, redeem me!"

Three lightbulb slots inaccessible. Black camera dome in another corner. Red light always on. Empty metal racks on two walls. A chair—hastily/inelegantly bolted near the empty wall opposite the door. Door handle removed. Hole: sheet-metal sealed. They bring a table in for interrogations.

They'd bring in a gin to begin. A gin to end it. I hate myself; I drink it. (Because I drink it, because I hate it, because I want it, because I need it, because—)

"I'm sorry! I'm sorry! I'M SORRY!"

Who cares?! Fuck it! I'm not sorry.

"NOT SORRY! Ahhhh!"

The Azeris kept her in the secure supply room. Told her she was next door to the code room.

Where Roman should be...would be if I hadn't infected him with my poisoned promise. My cold dirty lust.

(Layla loved him.)

"I want to settle something. Who kisses me the way you kiss me?"

"You know I'm pretending. Now pull over!"

"Who? Layla or Lynn?"

(Lynn. Too.)

"Layla or Lynn— If you'd asked. I would have helped you."

The overhead light burning since they locked her inside. That first night, Thanksgiving night, they strip-searched her. Poked inside her—no other reason than humiliation. Locked her in an office. Sweatpants. A T-shirt. A sweatshirt. No underwear. An injection—she let them jab her; knew what was coming—knocked out for however long it took to set up this room. Insomnia. Irregular meals. Sandwiches and water. No track of days or nights. Ten days? Twenty? Lynn had no idea.

When I get my period, I'll have a guess...

And a pair of facing mirrors. Like the chair, installed when one of the two women who tended (erratic/intermittent) to her hygienic needs, took her—blindfolded—for toilet, for shower.

And a pair of facing mirrors. Acrylic (discovered when her fists and feet couldn't shatter them). One secured to the wall beside the door. The other to the opposite wall behind the chair. A pair of mirrors. A black infinity point that match the place of blackness inside her, but better than television when she saw the tragi-comedy of her own suffering, when she watched her interrogations, when her mind/her DTs projected hallucinations.

TIME BENT. Mind bent.

One mirror watches me suffer. The other replays what brought me here. And between them, I flicker: not Lynn, not Layla.

Something blacker.

Something thinner.

Something flickering.

A ghost of "that girl" Silas made.

The mirror behind—only visible from the mirror in front—Roman bent his head around the corner of the shelving rack. Laughed.

Not at Lynn.

Stop staring. You did it to yourself. I had us out of here. Had you safe. Had you mine.

Not Roman.

She hissed. "Stop laughing, Silas..."

"Your bed's outside, you nut."

"Can't expect Melody to move it all tomorrow."

You're not even here.

Early in her confinement. Before the real shakes hit. After the Azerbaijan security officer—the one who shot Roman—and the female guard (bathroom/shower escort) finished the farcical incident report. Before she needed a drink so bad her mouth tasted like ash and embers—

"Where's the DSS? Where's State? I get a lawyer—where's my lawyer?"

She sat on the edge of the cot. He stood inside the door. The mirrors hadn't been installed. The knob not yet removed.

Elmin: undone. "What you know about me. My...outside life."

"Why does that matter? That doesn't matter anymore. I'm telling you right now: I don't know what you're talking about."

Whispered. Mumbly. Almost teary. Hand half-covered his mouth. "I don't know what I'm going to say—Aydin's cousin? He loved him like a brother. He put you two together. You reckless—!" Shook his head, his anger from his head. "This life..."

Shoved her bangle flask across the table. "Finish it. You bitch."

Lynn drank. One hit. Two. Empty. "Thank you."

He nodded. A dreg of sympathy. "I vetted you. Cleared you. I approved you." He shrugged. A private decision between himself, his heart, his future. Gripped the doorknob. Said to the door: "'The human heart plans...but the Lord deceives.'"

She never saw him again.

Then the DTs.

Then the interrogators. *Xarici Kəşfiyyat Xidməti*, Foreign Intelligence Service. Hardcore. A thousand questions. Three tones: suspicion, contempt, opportunity. The Agency, about penetration, methods, Langley flow charts, about training, about targets. About Russia.

"An attorney. I'm owed an attorney."

"You've not been officially charged."

"I'm under official cover; there are diplomatic conventions. Recognized international protocols!"

"Your State Department and your CIA have denied you. You're not even a number to any of them."

Watched her twitch, spasm, drool. Mocked her. Amped up her borderline psychotic anxiety. "Here, lady. Drink."

Gin. Not enough/just enough.

Severe withdrawal. Quivering, jumping, flat-out-horrified insomnia. When it quit, when sleep crept up: Christmas carols piped in. Jimmy Durante/hideous *Frosty* and Dean Martin's *Marshmallow World* on a loop that grabbed her head and shook it.

The Russians came. SVR. Slammed her around with questions that didn't matter.

"Did you personally authorize the classified request for Azerbaijani energy data?"

"Who saw the CX-52 manual? Did Sayadov let you photograph it?"

"How many times did you meet with Sayadov before the night of the shooting?"

The rhythm changed. Cold to cruel.

"Did you feel yourself come first the day you learned to lie, or the day the polygraph couldn't tell?"

"Is your brother, Michael, the father of your illegitimate brat?"

She blinked. Eyelids dry razorblades across her eyes. The mirror twitched.

"2001. You were Ops Planning. Silas Kingston still running CI. Were you aware he still reported to our Directorate S?"

Her whole being froze—body seized in sweat. No answer. No scream. No memory allowed to rise.

"Who is running your brother, Michael, in Moscow?"

"Why is the CIA so interested in who controls the Baku shipping lanes?"

"You were involved in the Venezuelan coup—2002. Did you inform the Ministry of Emergency Situations about your meeting with the Venezuelan attaché? Or was that another Foreign Resources signal routed off-books?"

"How many barrels of stolen Syrian oil run through your Kaleidoscope before Turkey finishes laundering it?"

Turkey/Michael. Father Cevik's photos; Mom's kaleidoscope man.

She curled into herself. Counted barrels, counted pipelines, counted how they launder ambition into energy, into hegemony. They weren't done.

"Tell me... when did you first realize he wasn't going to choose you? Not your father—Russell Aiken. Is the little piglet his?"

That shattered something.

Had she answered every question? Had she answered any of them?

"What is your agency's objective at the Caspian Oil Conference?"

"When the CIA retired your father... did Moscow retire him too?"

Did they see him in the mirror? Bent out behind the shelves. Bent out, bent light—

Bent me and time and bent Silas howling like one of those wild Claypoole hounds that run the woods. "Aah-oouu! Aa-oouuh!"

Or he'd stand there when it was just the two of them and the dim humming of each trickle of sweat like insects scuttling across her skin. He'd stand there—Silas—younger, smoking his pipe. Not laughing. Not smiling. Not speaking. Judging. Always the mirror behind. Lynn spun in the bed—

"Look at me directly, you motherfucker!"

—but he would be gone and now the mirror behind would not reflect her room/cell at all.

The Enchanted Forest. The Lady in the Lake. Water drips from her diadem-crown. From her bathing suit chain-mail.

Michael says from the mirror behind her—adult Michael— "If Arthur pulled the sword from the stone as Wart, how does the Lady in the Lake have it to give to him?"

Lynn whirled.

Michael leaps to the mirror behind.

Leigh holds his hand. Pure innocence peering up into his face. "It's not the sword that's magic. I mean, it is, because it gave Arthur a way to see power like God sees power."

Doris speaks.

Lynn whipped around.

The mirror empty. Doris behind her. "The scabbard makes it so Arthur can't bleed, but he forgets to wear it."

Behind her: Layla. Forest green raw silk, boho cocktail dress.

Zip.

Knee-high boots.

Zip.

Tight suede jacket.

Zip.

Lynn inched around. Ten minutes that felt an hour, lasted a second. Lynn and Layla face to face.

"She's pretty," says Michael. Somewhere not there.

The Lady in the Lake raises her face, water streaming diamonds. It is Nina Alvarez: Aiken's true love, his guiding light. My place of blackness.

The jousting knights collide.

Aiken impaled, tumbles in blood. His voice fills the room. "You'd never forget the sheathe if you never drew Excalibur."

And Layla—hunter green silk, knee high forest boots, deer suede jacket sits beside Lynn on the cot. Lynn cannot see the light. Cannot see the room. Only Layla, who cradles her head; Layla who was Doris, who was Leigh, who was Paige and Gwen and Melody, each a thread of the woman Lynn never managed to weave whole.

She is the *Znamenie*. *"I show you my hands, empty—because this is how love arrives."*

Everything else is a place of blackness and the doom of flesh.

Friday, December Fourteenth

1.

SERIOUS. GRAVE. EXTRAORDINARY. TRAGIC, regrettable, and explosive. Words Silas Kingston would later use to describe the Azerbaijan Ambassador, Yousef Safavi Orujov. The Napoleonesque diplomat used each of these adjectives (and their attendant facial expressions) so many times in their forty minutes together that by the end of their meeting he'd left little room to form any other opinion—though the "Napoleonesque" add-on Silas allowed him had everything to do with his small stature and not any display of grandiosity (except his use of "explosive" four or five times, that did seem a bit much). "Napoleonic" might have worked as there was an ineffable sense the man was fabulously anachronistic in his comprehension of modern espionage tactics/gamesmanship/geopolitics. And his haircut. And a strange harping on "destiny of nations." That was period too.

No matter. Although Ambassador Orujov did the majority of the speaking/adjective-ing, he was not the man in charge. Chaired and chairing from the side of the ambassador's gold-leafed (branched/treed; gobs of gold) desk, sat the long-fingered Mr. Elxan Khalil oglu Mammadov of the (unspoken/obvious) *Xarici Kəşfiyyat Xid-*

məti. Gorgeous eyes, feminine lashes, offset by an unsettling dent in his right cheek where the bone, obviously, had once been shot away. One of those *You should have seen the other guy* scars.

Silas Kingston and CIA Deputy Director Operations Gary Gravin, in formal/high-back small-seated and uncomfortable chairs faced Ambassador Orujov but had been summoned to open a negotiation with Mammadov.

An evidence-bagged, Turkish-manufactured, Zigana semi-automatic murder weapon with Lynn Kingston's fingerprints. Positive results of a gunshot residue test administered to Lynn Kingston, after the shooting, five eyewitnesses—

"...and CCTV of the murder. The crime perpetrated here, by your daughter, Mr. Kingston, on the night of our National Revival Day celebration is not at all in question or debatable."

"Very serious. Explosive and regrettable, this." Ambassador Orujov shook his flat-hair head.

Silas stared at Mammadov over the knuckles of his hands, folded and elbow propped on the little red velvet armrests of his chair. Said nothing aloud, though his eyes on the security officer's cheek said *I wouldn't have missed your forehead.*

Gary Gravin stepped in with his voice. "We would certainly require an independent examination and verification of all evidence/reports/statements to make our own determination, of course. Also, we request in the spirit of moving toward resolution and with the full acknowledgment that this would be an act of unrequired grace by the nation of Azerbaijan, a face-to-face interview with Ms. Kingston overseen by you and limited entirely to discussion of her health and well-being as a..." He searched for the appropriate term.

"Hostage." Silas.

Gravin. "Detainee. Of your nation's embassy."

The ambassador wrung his hands like a sopped handkerchief. "So grave, so seriously tragic an event."

"Not twice tragic. Not necessarily," the Foreign Intelligence Service officer said.

"Go on," Silas enjoined.

"The future development of our Caspian Sea oil fields have put our nation in a new strategic position—one I assume your officer was attempting to...pervert to your advantage."

He paused, not really hoping but allowing for DDO Gravin or Silas to offer something. They did not.

"This room, this moment, these stakes—" a pretty blink at Silas's direction— "No time for diplomatic masks. My nation balances the east and the west. 'Between'—yes, but also with our sudden and invaluable petroleum wealth as a fulcrum. Your nation, as much as ours and all others in the greater region, face consequences, potentially serious and kinetic, from the civil war in Syria. Malicious neighbors such as Iran. Sword-balancers such as Turkey. Russia-such-as-Russia. And resurgent al Qaeda bad actors with whatever name they don't try very hard to hide themselves or their radical agendas behind. All will find stability or chaos in the results of our upcoming Caspian Sea Oil Conference." Another pause. Another eye-bat. Another American dead silence. "We three in this room."

Orujov mumbled. Not really words. Not really—since he counted as the room's number four.

"The outcomes from the Baku oil conference will shape the region for decades. In our business, violent loss of life is never desired, rarely intended, and oftentimes subverts the intelligence goal set out to be achieved." Just gorgeous eyes.

Silas. Impatient. "We've all pulled up our chairs."

"In our business, when it does happen, it is rarely dealt with through normal channels. It is a loss of advantage and as such, leveraged." With a glance, he turned it over to the ambassador.

Ambassador Orujov gripped a file folder two-handed. A big red stamp on the cover in the Azerbainjani Turkic language didn't need to be written in English for Silas and Gravin to read *Top Secret* in its ink.

Orujov offered it, two-handed, saying "This is the deal terms and partners—formal and informal—"

Silas: "Secret?"

The Ambassador nodded. "For the Trans-Caspian Pipeline which will be the deal negotiated by the American oil interests to these specifications."

"Give your government's signed guarantee and you will leave here with Ms. Kingston." Mammadov.

"May I see that?"

Silas reached out, but DDO Gravin interjected. "Wait. We are an intelligence agency. We do not and will not engage in an industrial or economic influence to the benefit or detriment to US corporate concerns. We have come here in good faith over a legal issue between your nation and ours. There needs to be an alternative that stays closer to specific situation that has brought us together. I insist."

Insistence tempered by a slight—oh, so slight—twitch of his eye toward Silas.

Ambassador Orujov glanced at Mammadov. A nod. Extended his file straight at Silas. "We understand you're a civilian."

Silas nodded once. The mere fact that Mammadov knew to offer him, told Silas he knew KALEIDOSCOPE. Held up his hand. Refused the file. "What alternative are we looking at for Deputy Director Gravin's officer?"

The ambassador hadn't been briefed. Explosive eyes at Mammadov. Mammadov faked placid in his tight humorless smile.

Gravin stiffened in his seat. Didn't look at Silas, but his features hardened. Eyes burned. Read *sideswiped.* "Mr. Kingston has asked a question."

"We try your officer for murder committed in an act of espionage."

Gravin. Hot. "Just try to fly her out for that."

Ambassador Orujov cleared his throat.

The state security officer did the speaking. "We would fly in the tribunal and run the trial here on Azerbaijan soil. When convicted, Ms. Kingston's sentence would be carried out on this ground. She will be executed."

"That wouldn't look good in the press. Speaking for the US Government: it would be disastrous for our two nation's continued diplomatic relations."

"Worse for you, Mr. Gravin. For your government. The evidence is overwhelming and explicit. It shows your officer as a coldblooded killer who your agency set up as a sexual decoy. A honeytrap, as you people say.

In the press—we would be happy to go there—it would look entirely worse for America and your institution, regardless the bitter outcome." Pretty eyes turn deadliest. "Mr. Kingston, this is your daughter. This isn't a game."

"It is my daughter, so weigh my response to your threat against any movement you think you'll have on your Caspian Sea question. Have your trial. Convict her. Execute her. She is a patriot and knew the risks when she followed her father into this business."

"Sir. Watch your words. This explosive gravity of this situation—"

Mammarov cut off the Ambassador. "If this goes to trial, she stands zero chance."

Furious at everyone in the room, including himself, but most of all Silas Kingston, whom he'd not looked at once since Silas refused the blatant play at KALEIDOSCOPE, Gravin leaned forward. "In this circumstance, international law will allow us to give Ms. Kingston legal counsel."

Mammarov finished. Dismissive. Mentally out the door. "She will be represented by an Azeri attorney. But, sure—" he stretched the word, *suuurrreee*, derisively— "You may provide her an American attorney for guidance. For advice. Moral support." Shrugged. "Not a problem for us. If there is nothing more...?"

Silas was the first to his feet. "I will see my daughter now. Want to make sure you haven't shot her already." His stance, his tone left no room for argument.

A SPICED-CINNAMON boucle bead Teri Jon cocktail dress—half-sleeves, a crew neckline rough-edged and fringed—Lynn Kingston entered the conference room where Silas and Gary Gravin waited under the watchful, golden eyes of Mr. Elxan Khalil oglu Mammadov of the *Xarici Kəşfiyyat Xidməti*. They were already standing. Her shrunken frame barely held Layla Kingsbury's once-tight Thanksgiving dress. Thin, twitching, skin yellowish and brown. Raccoon rings around her sunken eyes. Gary gripped the back of the chair he stood behind. Silas didn't flinch.

Lynn tried to smile. Dragged from her fog a piece of her that was pure and brave. Still glowed life. Fight. To Gary: "Sorry I failed, boss." To Silas: "You know it's not possible for me to kill."

"I know exactly the girl you are."

She made a noise in her throat. His compliments always complaints.

"There's going to be a trial," Gary said. "They're going to allow us to provide you with supporting counsel. I will have the best—"

"Don't bother. I have an attorney."

"You'll need someone from our field, Lynn."

"I am aware." She looked at Mammarov. "May I be allowed the use of a telephone?"

"Do you know the number?"

"If it's the same it's always been."

"Would you like to call now?"

"Why not?"

Her usual female guard had followed her into the room. Helped her into a chair. Lynn leaned back into its leather upholstery. Shut her eyes. Smiled for real. "That's nice." Then she picked up the receiver and dialed.

A U STREET CORRIDOR three-level railroad house. The Duke Ellington historical area. The telephone rang. Russell Aiken answered.

2.

Most Reverend Father Franz Retz, Superior General of the Society of Jesus in Rome

The Sacred Congregation for the Propagation of the Faith

Filed by the Hand of Reverend Matthais Laurents, Provincial Baltimore,

January the Second, Anno Domini 1743

Being an Account of the Christmastide Violence at Saint Ignatius Plantation, Saint Mary's County, Maryland Colony

To the Most Reverend Father Franz Retz, Superior General of the Society of Jesus, Rome:

With anguished heart and spirit atremble, it is with the heaviest burden ever laid upon this hand I write of a wickedness secretly seeded, diabolically cultivated, and treacherously grown to flourish on consecrated soil. On the Vigil Night of Our Lord's Nativity, December 24th in the Year of Grace 1742, a premediated rebellion and most grievous barbarism was committed against the tobacco barns and houses; the mission house, cloister, and chapel; and the Brethren of the Society of Jesus at the St. Ignatius Plantation by eight Negro slaves led by St. Ignatius bondsman, ***Cupid Williams****. Property of* *the brethren through the purchase of his father,* ***Pedro Kwame*** *(Trinidad, 1678) and baptized* ***Peter Williams*** *(Baltimore, Maryland Colony, 1679; deceased),* ***Son of Pedro Kwame*** *baptized* ***Cupid William*** *(St. Ignatius, 1685), since his fifth year under close instruction, religiously trained and educated as an agriculturalist, and commonly called* ***Scrapefoot****, trusted servant and bearer of a 10-mile pass from* ***Governor Colonel Nathaniel Blakiston****, organized and armed five of the insurrectionists and led them in attack at the second bell after Compline. What follows is a procession of abominations:*

1. *Ingress made through tampered locks and latches of the plantation apothecary; immediate violence was enacted with the strangulation and subsequent mutilation of* ***Brother Roberto Savarin*** *discovered with his tongue cut from his mouth and crucifix embedded in its place. His death was near-instantaneous. His body stripped and arranged grotesquely on the examination table, arms and legs outspread. His servant boy* ***Moses*** *(age 9, unbaptized and mute) either willingly or coerced was given an Indian hatchet. He joined the cabal which moved, en masse, to the refectory.*

2. ***Brother Devereux*** *and* ***Father Charles*** *retired to the refectory for cold victuals.* ***Brother Devereux*** *was assaulted from behind by the thrust of no fewer than three pikes.* ***Brother Devereux*** *bleed to death from the neck across his open Scriptures.* ***Father Charles*** *(aged 90 and former*

pedagogue to the ***Son of Kwame*** *from age of 6 to his 12th year) escaped through the door and into the cloister. A fire was set by* ***Bett*** *(approximate age 25), a domestic of the Claypoole Plantation, and the raiding party split into two groups.*

3. *The devil was with* ***Scrapefoot****. He led* ***Phibby*** *(approximate age 20), a cook leased from the Claypoole Plantation.* ***Scrapefoot*** *used his tobacco knife (recovered; a childhood gift from* ***Father Charles****) to castrate the elder priest. The mute boy,* ***Moses****, was left with* ***Father Charles****. Rather than administer Christian Comfort or Beg Forgiveness, the servant boy tormented the dying man with the branches of cut roses until he was joined by* ***Samuel*** *(age 12), property of St. Ignatius who stabbed him twenty-five times with a pruning hook.*

4. ***Ajax*** *(aged 25), a St. Ignatius owned tobacco curer, and* ***Dinah*** *(age approximately 40) a local freedwoman washerwoman, led* ***Bett*** *and* ***Cicero*** *(age 27) a stable groom, into the dormitory. While* ***Dinah*** *set fire to linens and threw them bundled into our novice's rooms,* ***Ajax*** *struck anyone who attempted escape with pike and hammer forcing them back inside. Their cells were hammered shut. Four novices burned to death. Two were mortally wounded by pike. Ten others remain gravely wounded from burning and the breathing of ash and from smoke damages to their lungs. These victims have requested*

and received Last Rites. ***Bett*** *and* ***Cicero*** *found the dormitory apartment of* ***Father Pierre Demarest*** *(age 46). His skull was cloven by an Indian tomahawk while he shielded his personal servant* ***Titus*** *(age 12), arms wrapped lovingly around him.* ***Father Demarest*** *was unable to protect the boy, and his paper knife was found embedded in the child's throat, murdered at the hands of* ***Bett****, of whom it has been determined and verified, was the boy's own mother.*

5. ***Scrapefoot*** *and* ***Phibby*** *proceeded to the chapel. On their way,* ***Father Pons*** *(aged 39), who kept the library, was bludgeoned and throat-slit by the tobacco knife.* ***Brother Jerome*** *(aged 53) was dragged from the scriptorium and disemboweled before the statue of Our Lady.*

6. *The alarm bell rung by a lay brother, the sight of fleeing property, and the rising curtain of flame alerted a militia from the Claypoole Plantation. Armed with muskets and sabers and upon horseback, they made haste to St. Ignatius.*

7. *The chapel was broken into by* ***Phibby****, alone, through the sacristy. The tabernacle was torn open. The ciborium overturned. Consecrated hosts trampled under her dancing feet. She used Latin sacramentals to ignite a bonfire of missals, altar cloths, and the fragment of the True Cross brought from the Holy Land by* ***Mission Superior, Reverand Father Alban Thule*** *(aged 69) and preserved in the St. Ignatius reliquary.*

***Scrapefoot** returned with **Reverend Father Thule**, the hands of the Mission Superior bound with his rosary. He was made to kneel before the fire. The slave **Phibby** attempted to cut his throat, but the old slave **Scrapefoot** stayed her hand. It was at this moment that gunfire broke out in the orchard. The slave **Phibby** turned in its direction. **Brother John Gervase** used the distraction to knock that murderous slave senseless and into the blaze where she perished. **Reverend Father Thule**, who had been spared, rose to his feet and took command of the Brethren and Novices, unharmed and now gathered. A fire detail was organized. Others assigned rescue and injury treatment. **Cupid Scrapefoot Williams** was gone.*

8. *The **Claypoole Militia** spent the consequent hour hunting down the rebel cabal. **Bett** and **Cicero** shot dead by musket ball in the orchard. **Moses**, bayoneted among the roses in the cloister garden. **Samuel**, caught stealing cold meat from **Father Charles's** plate in the refectory, shot and killed by musket. The washerwoman, **Dinah**, perished in the dormitory fire. The tobacco curer **Ajax**, discovered stealing a mule, surrendered and was cut down by militia saber.*

9. *The Negro bondsman, leader of the insurrection **Cupid Scrapefoot Williams** discovered inside the seed shed where he had received much of his agricultural training. On his knees and blas-*

pheming the Holy Ghost with false prayer. He surrendered his tomahawk and went peacefully before ***Mission Superior, Reverend Father Alban Thule*** *who condemned him to death. Of the many witnesses, there is disagreement over the content of his last words.*

10. *At three in the morning of Christmas Day, in the smoldering ruins of the chapel fire,* ***Colonel Thaddaus Claypoole*** *of the St. Mary's Militia, carried out the sentence.* ***Scrapefoot's*** *dying words are remarked either to have been,* ***"The Lord giveth. Father hold my soul,"*** *or* ***"The Lord giveth, fathers stole my soul."*** *The rope hauled,* ***Colonel Claypoole*** *and two unnamed militiamen hanged by the neck the bloodthirsty malefactor from the iron bell frame under Jesuit Authority, his body left as an example until the Twelfth Day of Christmas.*

11. *Evidence suggests prolonged planning and secret coordination between domestic and field slaves across multiple estates. Particular blame rests in the latitude afforded* ***Cupid Williams*** *under his 10-mile free passage liberty. No evidence of Protestant influence has been found, but further investigation is recommended.*

I beseech your Holiness to offer indulgence for the slain, to pray for the repose of the martyrs, and to dispatch word to Lisbon and Port of Spain that no more Caribbean-born bondsmen be permitted within ecclesiastical estates, as their natures are proven unruly and their passions inflamed by false teaching and heathen memory.

In Our Lord Jesus Christ, your humble servant,

Reverend Matthais Laurents, Provincial Baltimore, Society of Jesus

WHAT HAD MELODY HOPED to find? A massacre made in kindness? A barbaric desecration of the holy made in grace? She yearned to see and understand the larger picture in her understanding of her family's place in a bloody and evil history it had founded and participated in, but emptiness overwhelmed her when the long view she craved offered only fragments and each of them, examined in pieces, yielded large patterns of sin and evil with nothing whole called mercy at its end. Her day with Victoria at the St. Ignatius National Historical Center located inside the gates of the Patuxent Naval Air Station ended muted and depressed.

The parking lot overlooked the heavy black waters and icy rim of the mouth of the St. Mary's River. "Will we see each other again before Christmas?" A frigid wind swatted at Victoria's hair poking out from the furry flaps of her trapper hat.

"It gets worse and worse. I have zero hope I'm going to find any goodness in any of this that outweighs the horror." Needle ice stung Melody's cheeks.

"It's supposed to be the Season of Hope."

She couldn't hold Victoria's gaze. She engaged her truck's engine from her pocket.

"We came away with new names. These could lead to something overlooked in the Foxtail Farm records. Those slaves could have arrived at Turkey John's wharf. Like Cupid Williams they could have been slated to run through the Place of Blackness escape route."

"'Rendered'? 'Rendered Unto God'? after what we read today, I don't see much difference and I definitely can't see God—not as I want to conceive him. I'm not like you, or Silas, or my biological father. I'm not just like my mother or Cupid Williams and those African slaves. I'm caught in the middle. Because that doesn't just fit together in me, but is my whole, I think I've let some stupid 'fitting together' thing drive me. But there is no fit. I'm not seeing the hope this year."

Melody opened the Ram's door. Victoria softly touched it. Pressure. *Not yet* eyes on Melody. *Please.*

Victoria said, "I'm a 'Merry Christmas'/'Happy Easter' Christian—if-I-am-at-all—on my mom's side. My dad's a lifelong, dedicated, non-practicing Jew. I don't get or have room to conceive how you see you-and-God and grace and hope—and mercy—and what-all, and how that moves you. I'm more like my dad than my mom that way. I don't get Jesus and I don't go in for God."

Melody shook her head. Disappointed it had gone there. Tried again to open her driver's door. Victoria held it.

"I wasn't finished. I see it in you and I admire it. I love it about you. And am both a little jealous, and maybe—" a nervous laugh— "kinda frightened by it, but it's like a well of love that flows from you and it quenches a kind of psychic thirst inside me—so the jealous part—I want to help you to dig and feed and dose out that well-water."

Melody. A wistful look. "Thanks. I needed that."

Victoria pulled the door. "Here, it's too cold. Get in—and don't drive off. I'm going to hop in on the other side. There was one thing I was thinking about— Well, two things. I'm not trying to convince you into anything, but I have context you don't have."

Inside. Melody cranked the heat.

Victoria said, "It's the women. Bett, Dinah, Phibby, and Nika."

"Nika? Turkey John's Nika? She wasn't mentioned."

"She was there. I brought this." Victoria unzipped her backpack. A plastic sleeve protected a Patuxent Historical Society folder. Thin enough to appear empty.

"You're the worst."

Victoria: sly grin. Melody: fake tough smile. Stared at the ice like a sandblast against the windshield. Shook her head. "You going to let me see it?"

"In Colonial America and, later, the United States, there were something like two-hundred-fifty slave uprisings. From the Stono Rebellion to the New York Slave Revolt, to Nat Turner's massacre. Female slaves were involved. Yes. Absolutely. But not as perpetrators of violence or arson. They ran—your favorite, family word—the intelligence operations behind these events. Marched in some of the country road farm burning parades—marched but didn't murder. They did best those events as spies. Never violent actors. In this St. Ignatius event, of the six originally involved—"

"Not counting the two boys."

"Actually, there's three boys. But of the six, and one being Scrapefoot—so there's five slaves who chose certain death, they knew what they were getting into (and from your Christian perspective, I'd like to know why they chose Christmas Eve)—the majority of his recruits were women. Two from the Claypoole plantation and one who is referred to as a freedwoman. Free. It's very uncomfortable and I'm sure that's why this history is left buried. But why the hell did they join and go and do what they did?"

"The one, Bett, killed the boy Titus—knifed him in the neck. The report said it was her own son."

"C'mon, Melody. You're a mother. You think she went there to kill her own son?"

I hold the gun.

"Give me the gun, Mel." Boone.

Sight and sound tumble like slipping on ice too fast. His snatching hands. My scuttling back. Mama convulsing. Hands lumped on the back of her chair.

"I'll kill you!" I shout so loud at my father I never hear the gunshot when I pull the trigger. Mama slams backwards into the sink and drops.

I am ten years old and I've just killed my mother I loved more than the world.

"You're a mother, Melody. It was the priest's paper knife. How would she have gotten it while he held Titus."

Dark understanding flashed Melody's eyes. "He wasn't shielding the boy. He was using him as a shield."

"Makes more sense that way to me."

"May I see that?"

Victoria opened the protective sleeve. Opened the folder. "This was with Doris's research boxes."

"How many boxes do you have?"

"Two. A file box and a shoebox."

"What all's in them?"

"Honestly, I don't know—I mean, much. As curator and archivist I focus on the historical record. Every time—and I'm talking for decades—we get collections donated, some kindly old blue-hair writes very wispy/heartfelt, nostalgic or revisionist letters. Booklets. 'Lost Cause' essays."

"Doris wasn't yet fifty when she died. I never met her."

"She did a lot of the work we're doing. I think in some ways she was ahead of us. I think she left this for you."

"Well, for someone in the family."

"No. For you. Specifically."

A Doris yellow Post-it. Two words. *Melody Returns.* Sticky-stuck to a page from Nika's diary.

FEEBLEMINDED. The decision of the court. The basis for Father Alban Thule to bestow the Sacrament of Reconciliation upon me with no other act of participation on my part other than my kneeling in court and my quiet singing of 'O God, Our Help in Ages Past' to avoid blasphemy committed by answering to his charade.

I sing because it is all God and the Great Spirit gave me, not to confess my sins, but to profess my abundant thanks. To share my happiness with mankind—my family, my friends, my strangers met: all loved.

To sing is the best of me, and I know my song holds glory and notes glorification for all that has been, is, and will be.

I sing, therefore I am feebleminded. Therefore I am set free to the confinement for the length of my days breath-

ing to Foxtail Farm and the custody of Silvanus Kingston III, and my ancient father, Turkey John Swann—a last chief of the Piscataway.

Cupid Scrapefoot Williams, Son of Pedro Kwame. Good man, bad man, freed man, slave: his soul gone to judgment but his corpse to hang and rot for Twelve Days of Christmas to frighten, humiliate. To shame.

Singing I came. Singing I watched. Singing I waited through the screams until the fire raged.

With song, I cut him down as the smoke billowed and the Bethlehem Star faded with the dawn of Christmas. With song, I carried Cupid Scrapefoot Williams from St. Ignatius. In harmony, his soul sang with me. It gave me strength to drag him the last two miles to Foxtail Farm. Singing, I prepared his body; singing I planted him in the ground and listened as his music fled to heaven and was to be heard no more on Earth.

Singing: I am feebleminded. What part of me, I ask, is feeble? My free white Claypoole blood? My slave African blood? The unchained spirit of the Algonquin heart given me by my adoptive father—the part of me I know best and live most—whose blood runs back to the place of still and peaceful blackness before time, to the chiefs of his lineage who lived in this country when the Great Spirit was only man and animal, forest and stream, and rock and air, and God had not been kidnapped into St. Ignatius torture chambers of perversion of flesh?

"You will bring me home when my labor is through?"

"My father and Silvanus have stolen you your freedom. We can go and have our life and I can sing to you."

"If I could have, I would have loved you, Nikamon—my song, my melody—and asked you to be my wife."

"I know that, Son of Kwame."

"Physical freedom is meaningless when love is murdered inside you as a child. That freedom—to love and to be loved, to touch and hold—was murdered by those men."

"I will bring you to my father's empty field and I will bury you in the soft warm dirt of Turkey's Swan Song."

Convicted thus, I, Nikamon Swann, shall be paroled unto the custody of Silvanus Kingston III and confined to the borders of Foxtail Farm Plantation for the length of my born days. It is a condition for the good of this community, the good of this town, good of this county, this good Maryland Colony, Nikamon Swann—the I of me, Nika—is never to be heard in song again. Or shall face sentencing for my part in the St. Ignatius Massacre which shall, in full force of the Laws of this Colony and—said—the Laws of God, be death by fire at the stake.

I go now to meet the morning in defiance! To meet the ships on my father's wharf, to whisper where I can: "The Lord Giveth; the water show us forth!" I will meet each day henceforth with gladness, full-throated in song. I will sing. For all my days.

May my song be heard by as many people as my voice can reach and I defy any man feeble in their false cloak of holy or of law: dare you by the power of the Great Spirit of my people's land: come to Foxtail Farm. Come and try to kill me.

THAT NIGHT WAS THE NIGHT Melody hustled Silas and the twins to the Old Town green for Charlotte and Leigh's concert and the lighting of the town tree. Gwen and the girls: the joy of their return: mistrust of her sister-in-law's motives. She'd watched the performance, the illumination—the hideous and haunted massacre report, the haunting diary letter left her (possible/impossible) by Doris.

How is it two Melody's come randomly to this place; not one race or the other; adopted into the Kingston's of Foxtail Farm? God? The devil? The quantum nature of the universe?

The girls sang *O Holy Night* and Melody focused on the laser-gizmo'd cheesy star dark; focused on waiting.

"Long lay the world in sin and error pining, 'til He appeared and the soul felt its worth.A thrill of hope the weary world rejoices..."

Hope. The season of hope. And it came to her, then, a kind of message crept up behind, catching Melody off guard, a thought fully formed, disconnected from anything she'd been thinking and whispered into her mind as sudden knowledge as music sometimes can and will.

We get it wrong, she thought, *in our modern times. Don't fully appreciate the original meaning of hope to Christmas...*

We talk about the Season of Hope as a smiley-faced Christmas Eve heavenly gift; a soft and fuzzy baby bundle we cherish and awe to and warm our souls to until we celebrate that hope's fulfilment of forgiveness of sins and eternal life. Modern faith comes without fear because we know exactly what we're hoping for. But that holy night—that O Holy Night—Jesus is born and humankind is given hope but there was no/none/zero explanation of how/where that gift of hope was going to take us. God's original plan was for us not to know at all. To make it the most difficult Hope Test ever.

Modern Hope versus Original Hope.

Modern Hope is bright hope. Is safe hope. Is known-outcome hope: Easter.

Original Hope is awful hope.

Reverential wonder mixed with fear because the original gift of hope is to not know and to see it dashed in betrayal, watch hope defiled and tortured and murdered and dead.

Hope that must be met with that reverential wonder/fear because Original Christmas Hope was hope for something unknown/unknowable/unrevealed that must be tested and beaten into submission by evil. Only then can the gift of faith be born.

The song was over. Gwen babbled and the tree blazed, and Melody was right: in the swirl of fog, the electric bulbs appeared as candles flickering with the ancient flame of original hope as fragile as a birthday candle extinguishable by the faintest puff. For an instant on that snowy green: everyone saw and there was a simultaneous catching of breath, a public united, breathing as one, exhaling, some laughter and remarks and that aspiration: life and happiness shared.

The girls joined them—

Coming home. Coming home for Christmas.

—and they divided up and set off to find Paige and Clive.

"Did you lie to me, Clive, when we spoke on the beach?"

"No, Melody. I didn't lie to you."

Unto us... Hope.

"Christmas wonders never cease."

BACK AT THE PATUXENT HISTORICAL SOCIETY. Back in the reading room warm and still. Back, the white gloves. Comfort to her tobacco hands. While Victoria, staff, and docents, the heronesque Mrs. Shelly, ritualized the season, snow-washed Maryland history with daily open houses celebrating a Colonel Vickery who probably never knew in life a Christmas like the snow globe/orange-cloved one they rendered him in magi splendor. Set up with the Foxtail Farm archive. Set up with Doris's two personal boxes.

She made the decision she would wait until after Christmas to dig any further into the raw wound of history; the documentary evidence of the historical record in the larger box.

But the shoebox with its label drawing of ballroom slippers, red, Doris wore for her portrait. It's Post-It note: *Melody Returns.* That was comfort, too, and she lifted the lid.

Its contents were a record of a public donation Doris Kingston made to the town of Lexington Park. A minor stained-glass window for the renovation in 1998 of Saint Mary the Virgin Episcopal Church. The proposal: Mary and Jesus, a pietà but—and there's always a "but" with art—depicted in a modern/progressive fashion. Mary as a local/regional Native American of the Piscataway Tribe. A Jesus depicted as an African American slave unchained.

Concept: approved. Vestry recommendation: It would be more meaningful if we were able to identify the figures with historical individuals.

Nika Swann, daughter of a Piscataway descendant of tribal chiefs.

Cupid Williams, an educated slave who introduced the agricultural innovations that allowed the region to flourish.

Historical context: approved.

Arts Council, Commissioner's of St. Mary's County: approved.

Glass artist: approved/contracted.

Design: approved by church; approved by council commission.

Mixed-medium design: Murano glass from Italy; sea glass from the Patuxent shore.

Italian glass cut. Sea glass collected, polished. The mock-up presented.

The lawsuit. St. Alban's Catholic Church. Official records presented. A Catholic massacre. Doris's donation money returned. And yet, the stained-glass artisan's contract fulfilled. Marked in Doris's bold hand: *Delivered.*

Melody visited Saint Mary's. The Doris/Nika/Scrapefoot window never installed. Melody understood. Went home, picked up the twins, the girls—checked in on Paige—

"Hi?"

"Hi, Mel. I'm scared."

She held her niece. Then raced the others to the car. They blew-up their shopping list; filled Billy Goat's Gruff with more presents, more food, more "extra" decorations than they had room for.

Clive and Silas lugged the Yule log inside and the boys climbed on it all night. It was the night of the eighteenth. At 4:14 the morning of the nineteenth, Melody's eyes opened. She grabbed her down robe. She shoved her feet into her Uggs.

Down the upstairs hallway. Doris aglow in every mirror, filling each frame every step ahead of her. Down the stairs. Under the portrait—Beaumont, awakened, on his feet, padded after her. Out into the darkness. Out into a drifting snow that curled, rolled on the susurrus of night. Melody walked to the chapel. Around both sides. Around the back. High in the stone wall a half-circle stained-glass window shone black.

She went inside and Beaumont followed her as if he knew more than she and Melody knew he did. Inside the chapel. A box of matches. A candle. Around behind the altar. She struck a match. She lit the taper. She held it high.

It was not a pietà. It was Nika. A walk along the river shore. Crooked stairs to Foxtail Farm rise behind her. Shells and beach glass gleam in the sand—white, blue, green, and red. In her open palm is the small black hand of the son of Kwame. Pure love radiates from his face, a Trinidad child, he toddles beside her leading the way.

3.

*N*O EASY WAY OUT. *A whole new kind of game; a not-this-time kind of game.*

There's always *an easy way out.*

Nothing is difficult. No difficulty permanent. Never has to be.

To take a life. That's as permanent as it gets.

Every step I've taken—hop and a skip and a jump over/around any difficulty in my path. Hop-skip-jump and an absolute corker of a lie. Or two.

A whole blasted thousand lies. And not a scrap of truth between. But show me the bloke who ever said, Clive Lancer didn't always give it a punt. Never turned tail and ran. Not I. Not once. Not like my own father: found out Ma Sylvie carried me and swept his cards and dice, his chips and cash into his straw hat and jumped the next boat off the island.

I'm not him.

(Liars, the both of us.)

I face a door. Doors don't scare me. Stepped through every one.

(Always count on a window to climb out of.)

Chairs lined the walls. Center line, chair back to chair back—twenty, maybe thirty. An intake counter with a bug-eyed receptionist, a buzz of nurses in and out behind her. Half a dozen young women fidgeted or tried not to, or slouched paralyzed and numb, or clowned with the friend they brought—*So you can find out what it's like when it's your turn*—or friendless, grinned at an empty universe like they're going to walk away from this thing without a wound. A couple younger girls, dazed, frightened, depressed. One embarrassed her mom by weeping.

And Clive Lancer. Whatta guy. Tortola didn't have a Planned Parenthood. This room didn't have a window. Just a door. Beyond that, medical bays for women who, like Clive Lancer, hadn't planned.

TURN THE KALEIDOSCOPE. Refractions of London. Fractures of MI6. A colorless room. No windows either. No view. Recessed pinspots cast narrow cones around each chair. Each beam isolated its occupant: bright enough to read by, too dim to see who's lying. An octagonal table. Too many sides to feel the order of a square. Not smooth enough for unity in the round. No head. No hierarchy. But a deliberateness: always a between line, between seat spaces, between people; anywhere you look you don't have to look at anyone. Six chairs. Three occupants: three "anonymous" from extralegal affairs. Anton Hector, known to his colleagues as Mr. Brown; the purposely prim (she cultivated the manner, the don't-talk-to-me-about style), Ms. Wilson; and Davies, who'd insisted they drop the *Mr.* the first time this team convened nine cases ago. A hotshot-type. Mr. Brown and Ms. Wilson called him "Mr. Toff'y" behind his back. Each had three files: *Clive Lancer. Fergus Lott. Operation FELL KING.*

A pitcher. Crystal clear filtered water. Three water glasses—spotless—and a wall clock. Oversized, sweep-second, high-end institutional.

"ANONYMOUS" TOFF'Y: "Unusual, this."

"ANONYMOUS" WILSON: "We hold a most unusual job."

"ANONYMOUS" BROWN: "Most unusual assignment in an unusual job—unless any of you have confronted this circumstance in other working groups?"

He waited out their blank looks.

"ANONYMOUS" WILSON: "Please, Mr. Brown. Not something any of us could divulge. If we had—which I am not self-attributing."

"ANONYMOUS" TOFF'Y: "Helpful, Ms. Wilson. Rather put it this way. It would be impossible for me to divulge a secret I've never been asked before to keep. Get it? Good. So, yes: I share your discomfort with the ask. I eschew slang in all forms and this is the perfect example because 'bloody bonkers' doesn't get me halfway to where my appalledness meets my bafflement."

Mr. Brown and Ms. Wilson touched eyes. She couldn't help herself.

"ANONYMOUS" WILSON: "Davies, as 'appalledness' isn't a word, it may as well be considered slang."

Ms. Wilson's posture wasn't rigid. A dead, lifeless word—*rigid*—that a lifetime of rehearsal had imbued with a century's worth of applied rules allowed her a straight-to-silence disagreement the way a coachwhip upright in its stand forces equine cooperation most times without ever being handed and snapped. Toff'y called her "Austen" behind her back but, while Mr. Brown nodded in placation, Anton Hector silently disagreed. A bit unfair to Miss Jane and the Janeites.

"ANONYMOUS" BROWN: "I'm not here for a bicker. We're here to hang a man. Unanimity on Clive Lancer. That's the brief."

An octagon table. Chosen by committee. No one leads. No one follows. And everyone votes to disappear the man not in the room.

"ANONYMOUS" WILSON: "It is, perhaps, a truth insufficiently acknowledged that a man marked for death must first be found inconvenient."

CLIVE LANCER STARED without seeing. A waiting room poster. A single-line cartoon guy, arms wide, running full-tilt into a single-line cartoon girl, arms wider running full-tilt at him. Their speed animated such that—so much for embraces—without a doubt they are going to smash heads hard and go flying.

One more step, those smiles are going to be bounced off each other's face.

The caption read: *LOVE Carefully!*

"Clive?" Paige, interior door spring-shutting behind her. Hands full of paperwork. Face pale, like she'd just been hard-scrubbed.

Clive shot to his feet. Unlike the cartoon, their steps together, tentative. He clasped both her hands in both of his, the paperwork a bouquet of the done and irrevocable between them. His heart hammered. Her eyes glistened. They were going to crash. Hard.

"Yes?" Clive. A thousand thoughts flashed his brain. In a millisecond, synthesized into a thought.

My own one anonymous chance to do something—

"Saying goodbyes—final goodbyes—"

—courageous, ardent and worthy.

"—are for our child. Him or her. To say to us."

True.

"Many years—" Paige pecked his cheek— "fingers crossed—from now."

THE CLOCK KEPT PERFECT TIME. Swiss movement. No tick. No tock. No before, no after, no space for second thoughts to fall between. Sweep second movement. Like the release of a final breath that goes on but is already something dead.

"ANONYMOUS" BROWN: "Last we met, Mr. Lancer's engagement file before us, our determination ended two to one in favor of continued employment. Whichever of us previously voted for separation is immaterial and not to be divulged in this room. We have been provided with new intelligence from Mr. Lott claiming Mr. Lancer has broken cover with the Kingston granddaughter, may have even tipped off the target, and has for all intents and purposes, abandoned the operation to 'shack up,' as the Yanks put it, with the girl."

"ANONYMOUS" WILSON: "How gratifying that intelligence work now permits the language of the schoolyard.

Under the rules of this department, the decision already made that spared Mr. Lancer's life did not need unanimity at the time, nor would a vote today that draws that result, fail to change the determination already made. Mr. Lott, on the other hand, who already received from us a unanimous decision—due to his personal obsession with the target, his inability to be circumspect in speech to colleagues/strangers alike, his alcoholism, the delicacy of the target's nationality and terminal nature of that individual's fate now in the final planning stages—that—for the good of the nation, the government, and all the etcetera's—that give the Crown cover from our American cousins. I agree with Mr. Brown. Our purview has been nullified and our order for Mr. Lancer is obvious."

"ANONYMOUS" TOFF'Y: "On with it. They want a Roman thumbs-down—three hands, two heads. Don't want a fresh opinion; require merely our hand towel." He flipped his forearm and checked his wristwatch worn vanity-air-ace on the underside, timepiece over his pulse point. Said: "Aye."

"ANONYMOUS" BROWN: "I won't dignify this with a spoken vote. Since it doesn't mean shite, I'd already planned to write the affirmative without forcing either of you to say it. What I'd like to get to is the second addendum requested."

"ANONYMOUS" WILSON (TO DAVIES): "I presume it's what you referred to as the 'bonkers' of it all?"

Smirked. Shrugged. Hid again in his watch-face.

"ANONYMOUS" BROWN: "We are asked to make the recommendation Fergus Lott render our decision for Clive Lancer."

"ANONYMOUS" WILSON: "I've never been asked that before. I hate it."

Not revulsive hate but the exasperation of a woman who kept etiquette manuals beside her bed. Likewise, Ms. Wilson didn't say it was unjust. Meant she knew it was.

"ANONYMOUS" WILSON: "We may operate in shadow, but we are not without mirrors. If the Americans discover FELL KING and Silas Kingston perished at our hands, they'll investigate the murder of the granddaughter's beau—"

"ANONYMOUS" TOFF'Y: "Most certainly will bubble up."

Davies checked his watch.

"ANONYMOUS" WILSON: "Would you please stop peering at your wristwatch? There is a perfectly good clock on the wall. You're doing it to annoy me."

"ANONYMOUS" TOFF'Y: "Mine ticks. Helps me remember there's space between moments. The space between good and bad decisions where ordinary minds, in ordinary circumstances, still have free will. Once we leave this room, where that space is simply not this space, where unanimous becomes un-anonymous, I'll be able to count down the time *we* have left."

Ms. Wilson didn't like that. Davies didn't like her. Mr. Brown had a job to do, and Anton Hector wished he'd been a fisherman like his pa.

A second chance. All I'd wanted for that bright, misguided/MI6-misplaced island kid. But that's not good enough when you're tilting against the American dragon.

He tapped fingertips on *Clive Lancer* and *Fergus Lott* reduced to bloodless paper in file folders that weighed less than a dead dung beetle. Looked at his companions in their little pyramids of light. They waited on each other.

The irony? The three of them chosen through psych profiling to be incompatible. Put around a table where they weren't meant to fit. Yet somehow, today they did. From any/all angles—fit in the worst way possible. Like mismatched teeth that always manage to click shut. No friction. No error. Closure. Whatever they'd circled the first go-round with this pair/this operation—a check, a brake—was gone. Now at the center as winter raged they'd been ordered to tie themselves to a pole with pretty spring ribbons of festival color. A Maypole mandate. A dance for new life, rebirth from earth seeded with the corpses of past mistakes made right. Every ancient rite dressed in petals was first rooted in blood and license. Ritual made from something older, darker. Something primal pretended to order but fed with lust.

Anton Hector's eyes lifted to the infernal single-direction time machine on the wall. Reminded himself of the "Swiss Cuckoo Clock" of Made-in-China manufacture he and his wife hung—must be nineteen years now—in the boys' nursery. Big, ugly, plastic thing. A push-button to a silicon chip could schedule a summoning. Cheap motorized knights, clattering out on spring-loaded trays. Bouncing puppets mimicking/mocking life for a moment, then vanishing. His sons loved it. Way back once in childhood pretend times.

Innocent minds adore the illusion. The rest of us just yearn for the "Gone Fishing" sign to bar our door. Escape our lives.

No escape for you, kid.

He spread his thumb and forefinger along the bottom edge of his caterpillar moustache, smoothing stray, rough hairs.

Sorry I couldn't be more help.

"ANONYMOUS" BROWN: "When this bubbles up, it may well pop against us. But think how many bubbles we have in our tub? Pop one, they all begin popping. And once they've all exploded what you have is a basin of filthy water. I'd say we have an entire government and even some joint work with the Americans that makes it to everyone's benefit we keep the bubbles shimmering little rainbows in the bath."

The three gathered their folders. Rolled back their chairs. Cheap motorized knights, they filed to the burn cabinet. Sealed government incinerator behind a double-locked fireproof vault. No ceremony. No goodbyes. Just slide in the truth, the lies and the lives and twist the handle. Davies's hand secured the latch. Lingered.

"ANONYMOUS" TOFF'Y: "We've got plaques for Blunt. Docents for Burgess. Philby, who ended up with KGB general's boards on his shoulders is bloody admired, some kind of Byronic hero with sycophant books and ga-ga documentaries every year, and here we are, scheduling the quiet kill of one of our own for shagging the wrong girl."

Ms. Wilson pulled on fawn-skin gloves. Each finger wiggled snug to the tip.

"ANONYMOUS" WILSON: "The Cambridge Five betrayed their country but never their class. Mr. Lancer confused loyalty with love. That, my dears, is never forgiven."

Fire hissed.

Sent to discredit a ghost.

Anton watched paper burn.

A summer errand to satisfy a man we all know is mad. Lancer did it properly. Once more'd it into the breach. Found in the Timeless the only piece of proof we ever had. A Hennessy Holy Grail linked back to an old KGB account; a frigging Silas Kingston retirement gift for a job well done. But without the Evander Lott piece of the puzzle—Silas Kingston a traitor—? That's an American problem. God help me, but since when do we kill our own young men for that?

Justice/injustice, retribution-righteous or vengeance pitiful. He'd write the order later. The flames would say it now: everything returns to ash.

ANOTHER TURN of the kaleidoscope. Watch the black and white past drop in bits. The colored beads of present strung. The lives, the souls, the fires and the ash, the faces, red balloons and jousting knights and dead drops: tumbling scintillations in future met light; seek and find a mirror's reflection.

Silas Kingston.

Jilly Bregado.

CIA Moscow Station, 1971.

Jilly a kind of Lynn to Silas's Michael. Running a tail on Evander Lott; out of MI6 Moscow Station; better to teach Silas how not to get exposed by an ally—as cheesed-off as that might make the cousins—first week behind the Iron Curtain, than captured by the KGB.

Starbucks. Night before last.

Jilly. Peppermint Latte: "You were younger than me. You were better than me. I was jealous of you. You ever wish you hadn't been so good? Had lost him?"

Silas. Black hat, black gloves, black scarf, black coffee—

"Size?"

"Medium, please."

"We only have three sizes: Tall, Grande, or Venti."

"The one in the middle; medium size."

"Grande."

"Yes. Large but medium."

"Name, sir?"

"Zittlebee: the one 'e' version."

—black heart. Black silence. Kind of black in Silas that's the thing Jilly respects the most. Kind of the thing that's kept her four-decades in her banker's wooden swivel in the central OTRAC hall. He, pushing out of his sixties, she already past that: still the "big sis" watching "kid brother's" back.

1972. OTRAC.

Angleton: "I believe you two know each other from Moscow Station."

Silas shakes Jilly's lanolin soft hand. It's the never-let-go grip of her eyes that holds him in its vice. I'll only let go when you release me, kid. I'll always hold your hand.

Angleton says, "Silas will one day take over from me."

"From all of us: best choice we could have."

Silas. Tonight. Ten minutes before tomorrow. Walking the Old Town green. Stops at the Christmas tree. Adds an ornament.

A wooden snowman with a long black pipe poking out of his face.

Easy-to-pick-out telephoto lens/low-light optics. Easy for Fergus Lott to cover it all with photographs.

To wait.

Breakfast hour. (Fergus/Legoland never will get an identity with facial recognition), Jilly Bregado meanders across the green.

Photo-snap, photo-snap, photo-snap.

1972. OTRAC

"He's suited for a position where one doesn't ask permission and never has to tell." Jilly: Hard eyes. Fire's trust.

Night before last, Starbucks.

"You knew I wasn't under orders. You never called me out."

"I saw what you saw in Moscow. Some evil isn't geopolitical."

After breakfast. Old Town green. Jilly facing the tree.

Fergus: Photo-snap.

Extra close to the tree.

Photo-snap, Jilly gone, photo-snap, the Frosty ornament.

Photo-snap: Pipe broken from the snowman's mouth.

Moscow, 1971. Evander Lott doesn't see his tail—Americans at practice—as he ducks through a loading dock door.

"You did well, Silas." Jilly. "Probably an agent meet. We can't be anywhere near."

But Silas is moving. He's going near. Exasperated huff: Jilly tails Silas. Past the loading dock. Up some barrels. Up some crates. Peers through soot-streaked glass.

Harsh whisper from below: "You don't come now it's going to be worse than a write-up for you."

Silas turns. Face pale. Eyes the size of half-dollar. He wags his finger twice.

Starbucks. Night before last. Silas slides the coded confession he worked up from Doris's book. "You'll ask for this edition—"

Fergus surveils Jilly from the town center to *Twelve Leaves Antiquarian Books – Bought & Sold*—Jilly in/Jilly out. A brown wrapped book. Jilly to the Hilton, Lexington Park.

Moscow, 1971, Jilly: mad as hell: up to the window. Jilly: Silas's hand clamped over her mouth. It is an agent meet. Some sort of Soviet—doesn't really matter—he's there for his payout.

He doesn't accept money. Evander provides better. Signals a couple dirtbags from the office. They wrestle one; only need to prod the two more docile children. Two girls. One boy. None yet in puberty. Siberia or some kind of Asian cast to them. That's what Silas and Jilly can tell from their terrorized faces. The rest of their naked bodies are just kids' naked bodies.

Evander Lott's Russian agent is giddy with excitement. He takes all three of them back into the office. Lott pays off the two dirtbags.

Starbucks. Peppermint Latte. Sip. "Was that the only time?"

Black coffee. Swallow. "Three times. Siberian, then Moscow orphans. Evander Lott knew how to get them...because he *knew* how to get them." Traced his finger on the cup's handwritten *Zittlebee.* "Then an opportunity came my way to stop it."

She drops Silas's confession into her purse. Snaps it. Confirms. "This goes to the brother."

"He's not that kind of problem. A son of a bitch, but not the devil of his brother. That said, I do need to make his life hell."

"Happy to." She rose from her café chair. Turned to go. Turned back. Shook her head in disbelief. "It was always KALEIDOSCOPE?"

"No matter how this world turns, it all falls into pattern. Thanks, Jilly. I owe you one."

"No. You don't. Merry Christmas, kiddo."

Fergus watches until night. While he watches, he calls *Twelve Leaves.*

"Of course, I remember her. A T.H. White. The Once and Future King. *Collins, UK, 1958. The* official *first edition. Not to be confused with the US edition, dated one month earlier the same year. But, oh-well, Merlyn did live time backwards."* Nerd chuckle.

THE OLD WOMAN went out late that night. Drove a rental car from Delaware. No surprise: rented through a shell company that traced to a shell company that tracked to a shell company. Empty, empty, empty good ol' shell game.

Earlier, Fergus paid the bell captain. Verified the old bitch had come from the airport. SwissAir tags on luggage. And, yes, she did have an East European accent.

Back on the mobile with the bookseller. *"I told you before: of course, I remember. It was just this morning. What do you think, I'm Barnes and Noble here with the foot traffic? Of course, I heard her accent. Eastern European—no doubt about it."*

Now it's late night. Now he's driving. Now he's followed her to the snowy entrance to an abandoned amusement park. Decrepit sign: *The Enchanted Forest.* Place Clive tapped the Kingston slut. He couldn't follow her inside. She was alone; fresh snow—she'd see his tracks.

Forty minutes later, his car tucked beneath a snowbound tree, watched her drive out.

Followed her tire tracks in. Followed her footprints in.

Ramshackle place. No doubt it was haunted. The decayed medieval main street to the crumbling snow-covered castle. Footprints right inside. This woman—if she'd ever been a pro, she'd bloody lost her fucking touch.

Chicken wire, plaster, and Fergus; some ducking around fallen framing lumber. Oddly, his imagination flashed a funny mental image—

The castle new. Merry children, parents, gaudy acid-trip Day-Glo paint. And two little ones. A brother and sister holding hands. An inner door marked "NO ENTRY."

Same doorway. Door broken beneath his feet in the snow-drifted wreckage; Fergus stepped through its crooked frame.

A man's hand beckons the two children inside. The door seals behind them.

Weird shite that. Mind playing tricks. Fergus shook it off.

The old woman's footprints ended at a low brick shelf. Lower, a loose brick. Behind it, a letter in a sealed envelope. Fergus yanked off his gloves. Pulled an ivory blade from his parka zipper pocket. Checked the parcel for the obvious (and the less obvious) traps. None.

Freezing his ass off, took an hour with the ivory blade.

Envelope undamaged. Letter open. Photo-snap, photo-snap every damning page of the document. Random sets of numbers you get from a book cipher. But Fergus had the key.

Soon London would have it all.

He resealed the letter: perfect. When Silas retrieved his Moscow orders, he would never know. Fergus could already smell the cordite.

Thursday, December Twentieth

THE GIN "DRIP" OVER, Lynn's captors shot her now with a thiamine-rich vitamin cocktail, glucose, electrolytes. Crappy sandwiches replaced by three balanced meals she mostly kept down. Still, she wouldn't be cleared by the Embassy Medical Officer until her alcohol withdrawal recovery was complete. Her first meeting with Russell Aiken back on Monday, happened via secure internal video link. Makeup, lights, the limited frame: one hundred percent stage managed, and their conversation reflected this—Lynn, once again brought by her minder into the conference room and wearing her Layla Kingsbury outfit, dry-cleaned and tailored to a better fit, and Aiken in lawyerly three-piece houndstooth in a small security section meeting room—they let their eyes convey the personal expressions they would have shared in person. Lynn: profound gratefulness, trust, devotion; Aiken: compassion, steadfast commitment, faithfulness deeper than cause and duty but born of the intimacy of their shared and private humanity. Their smiles and greetings were formal, perfunctory, performative; both understood and acknowledged, again, solely by their gaze, the many levels of scrutiny—diplomatic, legal, Azeri security and Russian intelligence surveillance—their contact engendered.

"I've met twice with your attorney, Ms. Nermin Jalilova."

"One more meeting than they've given me. She didn't succumb to my charms."

"Probably not an appropriate figure of speech, Lynn."

"I don't get the feeling she likes me very much."

"Not important. She believes you're innocent of the murder charge. As they will not allow her access to the CCTV of the event, will not allow independent examination of the murder weapon, fingerprints, your GSR test, she believes your statement. The charges related to the violence and death of Roman Sayadov are fabricated. In your trial she can hammer the lack of due process. We were very lucky the former chief of security, Elmin Hasanov, before his resignation, claimed the CCTV feed clearly showed the murder from three different angles. The fact that the prosecution is not admitting the video into evidence—only relying on eyewitness testimony—is equivalent to a Brady violation, a failure to disclose potentially exculpatory evidence. At the very least, evidence tampering."

"Could she win on that?"

"It's a collegium system, a three-judge panel. She would have to convince two out of the three." His expression: unflinching in discouragement.

Lynn crossed her arms. Sat back. Shut her mouth. Wasn't worth it to say another word. Aiken had come to her, the hospital after Dulles. Her coma. She'd not seen him, but she'd heard his voice, she'd held his hand, she'd felt his lips upon her brow, his essence enveloping her in its protective spirit. The same Aiken who held her once and physically loved her with a transcendent psychic depth that fused them together in a child. "Rusty?"

His eyes gleamed. "It's Russell. Please."

"You've always been right. When no one—especially me—didn't believe in you: you always were. I know this is a no-win. A show trial where both sides—us/Agency/U-S and them—are happy to hide the show. She must have some plan—or you gave her one—and I'll do whatever you tell me I need to do."

"We've been in places where there was absolutely no way out, and yet—"

"We're in another one. Just like old times." She made him smile.

"Ms. Jalilova recommends—and I agree with her—you submit a guilty plea to the five espionage-related charges and no contest to the murder charges; she will attempt to get you a prison sentence. It would be life. But because the embassy and Azerbaijan government suffers no illusion they could successfully remove you from this property you would serve your sentence here."

"Where I already have so many good friends."

"It would be agreed to that your terms of confinement would not be without some comfort as they would not be allowed to build a jail. It would be a kind of house arrest. Throughout the Cold War, situations like this came up from time to time, and of course, there's the situation in Great Britain right now with Wikileaks founder, that Assange hacker—thorn in our agency's side and the FBI's paw, years now—self-imprisoned inside the Ecuadorian Embassy."

"Visitors?"

"Ms. Jalilova does not believe it would be allowed. Feels to ask would be contumelious—"

"Come on, Rusty! There's no way she used that word, if it even is one, and remember *me*? Not a crossword puzzle gal?"

"Trust me, it is the exact word for how they would receive the request." He didn't elaborate though he couldn't completely hide his impish grin.

Lynn spread her hands. "Okay."

"On 'contumelious'?"

"Okay to the plea." A hint of her old devil-may-care back in her tone.

Aiken nodded. Satisfied. Glad. "She doesn't care—your lawyer—but did allow that as you are a pawn in a larger, inconvenient geopolitical brinksmanship, your circumstances could change for any number of reasons, and you'd be freed."

That was Monday. By Wednesday, Lynn's vitals had stabilized, her appetite returned. The Medical Officer cleared her for limited supervised in-person contact Thursday. This time Lynn and Aiken met in person. Physically alone but without illusion they were alone at all. The conference room where Lynn had met with Silas and Gary Gravin.

They came together. Didn't speak. Embraced and held on long enough to allow their touch, their press of bodies to say: lovers once, colleagues of a well-fought private past the world will never know but they will never forget, and deeper: friends who, whatever awaits, will walk together into it. A final clutch. Lynn's fingers into the tops of his shoulders. His hands, crossed at the wrists. Crossing her back. Flat. Pressing against her shoulder blades one final squeeze that was better than lovers. It was love. Lynn slipped away. They didn't sit. She said: "I expected it to be a 'no.'"

"And it was. Your trial will be in four days."

"Christmas Eve."

"Just to be extra-asshole. Their holiday comes in January. December twenty-fourth is just another Monday to them."

"I'm to be sentenced to death. Executed on foreign ground three miles from the White House." Lynn sniggered. Extra contemptuous the rasp of her damaged vocal cords.

Aiken steeled her with a penetrating look. Intense. Insightful. *Get ready for this*: "Before it gets there—and listen, room, I'm not shitting you!—I will make this an international incident." Calmly took Lynn's hand. Modulated, but still for the room. "KALEIDSCOPE won't let that happen. And if I learned one thing from Nathan Muir, it's that KALEIDOSCOPE is bigger than the Agency, bigger than this embassy, and bigger—because these Azeris have their own home-grown Kalaydoskop breathing down their necks—bigger even than the SVR thugs hanging about this place, puppeteering this show-trial."

"I hate to disagree with salvation, but Mr. Kaleidoscope himself-my-father got this ball rolling by practically ordering them to kill me. And Nathan Muir— I know you see things."

"Hallucination free for a decade if you want to know."

"Honey-sweet-man: he's been dead a long, long time."

"Even dead, Muir beat Silas Kingston. Not once, but twice. And I've never told you this, but his last words were that you Lynn Kingston—not me, which, I'll be honest, nettled me—were all of our future. Protected at all cost, because you were the one chosen to dismantle and destroy the entire leviathan—Silas's, Kolya Yurenev, and I hate to tell you, the Chinese mirror that will soon dwarf the US and Russia as the biggest kaleidoscopic threat of all."

Lynn cocked her head. Scowled. Always loved him, but knew Aiken was nutty and while he got the details right everywhere and every time it counted, his big picture grasp—photographic in high-resolution in his three-time damaged mind—was fucking Picasso on LSD to anyone else, Lynn—

God, how I love this man's faith in the insane!

—dropped backwards, thunked her bottom into a leather swivel chair. Kicked the one beside it out from the table. Pointed him to sit.

"If I can oblige the world in that, I'll be happy to, but Rusty—and don't correct me—this is the end for me. I'm pretty sure about that. And I'm okay with it."

Lowering into the seat, indignity brimming, Aiken: "There is no way you are going to be executed—"

"Of course there is. But listen to me. This is where I'm meant to be. Not for this thing I *didn't* do, but for all I have done. It's Christmas time. I'm okay to face my three spirits."

"That's what I'm saying! Scrooge lives! Gets a second chance to change everything!"

"Not what I meant by spirits, Rusty. Jesus cries with me, God cries over me. But the Holy Spirit protects me beyond the physicality of living and dead. If there was a way out, you would be the one to find it, my Rusty knight. But afterward, find Silas, wouldja? There's something I can't tell you, but for all his flaws, all the trouble he ever caused me or you, his heart is in the right place for what he'll have to pass on to you. He will do the absolute right thing."

"I'm going to have to pass on that. I have no worse enemy than Silas Kingston."

"That's why it's perfect." It was her turn to take his hand. "You won't understand this, and I didn't then, but these are the last words my mother said to me. Before she died. I'm saying them now, so you'll remember what I remember. Not for me. Not for you. Silas will show you. Okay?"

It hit him. He knew.

"Go Lynn, say anything you want to me."

"Do you know how much I love you?"

"Is that it? What your mother said?"

Lynn smiled softly. "No. I just didn't want to forget to tell you."

"Yes. I know. It's easy to know. Because it's as much as I love Nina."

"I'm glad. Okay. Here it is. And you got to remember it. 'Jenny's sins against her husband are complete. She accepts her death sentence. But Arthur won't. Arthur must not free her, or his Round Table—justice for the sake of right, for the sake of justice—will be destroyed. As much as Arthur prays it, as it always happens throughout time, Lance must not rescue Guenever.'"

"I don't think that's how the story quite goes."

"It has to. For some reason, it must. Can you repeat it back?"

"Yes," he said, and promptly couldn't.

He got it after four more tries and a quibble about syntax.

Then Russell Aiken said goodbye to Lynn Kingston. She said goodbye to him. Went back to the room of her captivity. She lay upon her cot. Pictured Leigh. The one time, right after birth, where she'd held her naked newborn body to her own naked breast and feed her first nourishment. She drifted off, peacefully, and saw in her dreams Leigh grown lovely, a bride on the arm of her father, the man Lynn held over all others sacred in her soul.

Friday, December Twenty-first

1.

A PistenBully 100 churned along the snowy service road. Michael and the Chechen inside. Three of the Chechen's laikas, bristle-coated red, gray, and brown, wolfish in snout and jaw, rode steady in plastic kennels in back. Braced and steady with every lurch. Every jounce. Anxious unblinking eyes. Windows to their souls which was the hunt. Intent on a wide metal-barred crate in front of them. Inside, a pepper-and-salt Laika lay panting. Every so often, the pepper-and-salt laika glanced back. Almond-shaped dark eyes cut across the other dogs. Set them to whining. She was the pack leader. A bitch scarred from two of her four encounters with Skvoznyak. The shoulder as a pup; her first hunt and eager and stupid. Four years later, grown fast, smart, and lethal, took a hoof to her head that because the claw was cloven carved two deep furrows from forehead to nose but missed her eye. Back two Christmas's, she'd gotten her teeth deep into Skvoznyak's jowl. Since then, bringing the boar to bay was not the hound's primary goal; Grítsa needed to kill the pig and ever since cared less about cornering the beast than going in with her teeth where each time since found herself beaten and cast like rotten fruit or a bag of old bones.

Grítsa, Tigress. From her cage bars—while Michael loaded the snow cat in morning twilight—her teeth gleamed and snapped, wet and full, at him; her lips pulled, her snout wrinkled she growled/barked/lunged.

"It isn't you, Mikhail Nikolaevich. Until she's on the scent, she has no patience for anything she doesn't associate with the hunt."

"Do me a favor. Let her know, once we're there, I'm part of the association."

The PistenBully made tracks between the Skhodnya River—blacker than the still dark sky—and the forest. Michael's and the Chechen's fogged breath mingled in the cab. Michael observed the river through plexi-window. It rolled with heavy certainty; fast enough not to ice over, inexorable power that denied the ice but rarely hinted a ripple. They crossed an icy wooden bridge that rumbled like war drums.

Les Dikiy. The Forest Wild.

Endless dense. Impenetrable. A wall of fat trunks thick with bulging bark, streaked silver with wicked frost and shouldering huge, twisted branches, snow-piled in coniferous towers. Les Dikiy's wasn't power like the river, contained by banks. It was doom. No matter where sections showed pockmarked recesses where loggers hacked and ran or woodcutters stole firewood, and ran, fingerling saplings lanced the air in clusters four, five, and ten around each stump. A rusting axe head jutted from one, bleached pale as bone by frost and time, its broken handle raveled by brambles. Les Dikiy covered its losses fast. Anything that lingered became part of it.

Hung on the rifle rack behind them: two AK47s, and a short-barreled shotgun. Their hunting spears, six feet of iron each with a seventeen-inch leaf-shaped thrusting/cutting head (when Michael dressed at 3 a.m., he listened to the high-octave whine of the Chechen grinding their blades; imagined the shower of sparks in the dark confines of the vehicle shed), cross-barred below with thick heavy lugs because without, the Chechen told him, the boar will charge down the length of your spear killing itself to kill you. Long and sharp. Black-iron cruel as death. The spears lay between the dog crates.

The gears ground. The engine surged. Loud. Diesel. Treads spun opposite—one forward, one back—vomiting ice. Snow. Earth. The PistenBully faced Les Dikiy. Michael could not see how the Chechen could possibly enter it, then the snow cat plunged through a snow-filled ditch. Grating, scraping. Rocks hammered the cab. Snow muck covered the windshield faster than its arm-length wipers could clear their vision. Soprano hysteria of the dogs joined the cacophony until the nose of the cab pitched level, the screen cleared in two swipes, the Chechen grinned, and Michael awed. Like some hidden/sealed gate swung wide, they ran a seam between high tree walls. The snow cat's treads pulverized this cart road's edges side to side. High above, daylight crept behind clouds of white and gray, but Michael understood: light, even on the sunniest of summer days, was an unwanted guest.

"Lulu calls him Uncle Kolya. With fear rather than affection. You worked with the man?"

"No one works with Kolya Yurenev. Nothing collaborative about him. Only orders you follow; given without interest or care or desire for your input. You become a node of execution. You succeed by embracing a machine logic of obedience. Personal thought/emotion, moral imagination, love—these things are discarded in his system. Someone like me, it was my life twenty-four/seven. Someone like Lulu's father? Ranked—you understand?" Michael nodded. "You step in and out of his machine and it can work. It worked for Pinwheel. It would not have worked for me. Pinwheel saw this. With the rise of the oligarchs and their threat to Kalaydoskop, he freed me to this life I have now devoted to your woman."

My woman?

Does this goliath want that—my pledge? Or does that get me fed to his dogs or worse in these wilds? His rival for Lulu, who will never choose him. Dead.

"Hmm. You mention love. Why didn't he take Doris? Marry her."

"Kolya was already married."

"To the Soviet Union?"

The Chechen turned into the trees and though Michael now could not discern a path, the forest accepted them. They ground deeper into Les Dikiy, further from the artifice of calendared/patterned time. Into the endless circle of constancy that requires only day to follow night, spring to follow winter and never to stop, eternal recurrence the entirety of existence.

"He's married to the Rodina."

"The motherland."

"The motherland. No matter the State, the power—king, general, premier, politburo, the oligarchs: the Rodina is Kolya's bride and by this transcends the political."

"Did he ever love my mother?"

"He may have. She believed it. But I only know one story of Kolya ever feeling/expressing love. A daughter. Long before Doris entered the picture. He was very young, the mother died. He turned her over to the State when he entered the KGB. He was seventeen and he was chosen for his brilliance, and he was lied to—they say—and when he returned from the Higher Intelligence School in Moscow to Leningrad where he came from, she was gone."

"Adopted?"

"He claimed she'd gotten sick and had died. But Pinwheel told me, once, that was a lie Kolya spread because the true manner of death was unspeakable."

The Chechen worked the dual-action treads turning into a clearing. Already there were snowmobiles—spiffy and overpriced with fancy stereo systems you could blast only when you weren't operating the vehicle, standing around in freezing temperature. They blasted now and the men from Lulu's party were there, fire crackling. The butcher, Tikhon Balakin, provided pork chops the hunters ate from the bone. Their clusters of leashed dogs held by handlers barked and whined, disinterested in the meat; they'd caught the boar's scent and were anxious to run.

Grins. Waves. Fluffy snow suits. AKs, spears, vodka air-toasted/guzzled/passed. Shouts: *"Mikhail Nikolaevich!"* Toasts: *"The Skvoznyak!"*

The Chechen cranked the brake. His body turned. Faced Michael.

"I'm glad you asked. About love. You reminded me that story and the answer to it, the end that never comes: Kolya needs to believe the wound of losing that child—however horrifically he did—was worth it. For that, he keeps it open; judges everything by the vision of that wound gaping in his empty chest. So, there's a side of Kolya that wants to inflict that pain while at the same time prove to himself that the choices he made that caused his loss brought power; through power: might. Might: enough to enforce a Russian peace."

MICHAEL ALONE REFUSED THE BOTTLE. A small defiance in a party devoted to forgetting what hunted them. Bottle finished, the men geared up. Boar spears. AKs. Shotguns with slug rounds. Those that weren't manufactured short-barrel were sawed-off; everyone hung one from their belt. The Chechen gave him a Kalashnikov.

The banker Kravtsov. The AK. "Not something you know your way around, your consulting business?"

Michael made a production of examining the weapon. "Seen kids on the news—all over the world—working one of these."

"One of our best exports, I am sad to say."

"Don't be." Michael primed it, thumbed the selector to single fire—"Going live!" Shouldered the assault rifle and shot three pinecones from three trees at graduated distance in two seconds. Made the weapon safe. Slung it. "Practically works itself."

He joined the Chechen with the dogs, already frenzied, whipped up by the largest, a black borzoi, loud and muscled, snarling across the crates. Its handler fought to control it as the wolfhound snapped jaws at Grítsa.

"Might as well get this over. Mayor?" The Chechen reached for Grítsa's collar.

Mayor Yegor Surnin, who owned the borzoi, nodded reluctantly for his dog handler to release the borzoi.

Grítsa and the much larger black hound crashed together with snarling, slobbering ferocity. How it happened, happened in a blur of boxing paws and gnashing teeth, twisting/rolling/pinning. Thirty seconds later, Grítsa had the borzoi on his back. Her paw on his throat. Her jaws ready to close around it if it so much as twitched. The borzoi's growl became a whimper and Grítsa let him up. The master of the hounds blew his horn. Grítsa answered, baying first, the others followed, clips clicked off collars. The dogs bolted.

A loud and sustained "Ura!" went up from the hunters and the forest swallowed their voices, accepted their charge as they rushed through the snow after the diminishing sound of their dogs.

Without snowshoes, their heavy boots made running brutal on lungs and hearts. The hunters spread out in an elongated line while the dog handlers, beaters of sorts, ranged their flanks. Twenty minutes, Michael bent over. Gasped air. The Chechen had continued ahead and Michael found himself alone with the village priest, Father Vadim Zheldakov.

He offered Michael water. At least, clear and liquid. Michael choked on a long draught of vodka. The priest laughed.

"You don't have water."

He helped Michael sit on a deadfall log. Sat beside him. Passed him a plastic Russian Evian rip-off. Michael downed half. Offered it back.

"Keep it. But now that I have your attention and we are alone, I have a message from Kalaydoskop. It is time to leave your love nest. Lulu is a losing proposition for you. Your destiny is in Baku. Your presence is required the day after Christmas."

"You never know. Lulu might want me to stay. We seem to be enjoying each other."

"She is being spoken with today. When you return, she'll have changed her mind. She will hand you your documents, your cover, tonight after the hunt."

He stood. Offered Michael his hand. Michael pushed to his feet without help.

"What happened to the leave-anytime ticket?"

"There have been... developments involving your sister. It's made everything more difficult."

Michael grabbed him in gloved fists. Snowsuit tight, choking at his throat. "My sister—what the fuck? What about her?"

Father Vadim released his spear. Clutched Michael's wrists. "What would I know?! I'm a messenger. Cut out of any loop. Receive your message, sir!"

Michael flung open his hands. Wanted no part of the man. Nor the message, or what it meant he would have to do next. Stepped back. The priest bent for his weapon. Muttered, robotic: "If, after you meet Kolya, you want no part of his offer you will receive passage out of Baku."

"What if I want to come back here?"

"The banker, Kravtsov. The people he represents will not allow that. Your association has already put the two of you in more danger than is healthful."

The yapping of the dogs took a new and fervent, high-pitched, almost human scream. Reluctance and indecision, most, but Grítsa—Michael already knew her voice—trilled jubilant and implacable. A crashing of wood and bracken, of snow thumping from cracking branches, the chorus of hounds divided. Far ahead, Michael glimpsed them: a moil of fury, forking two directions. One pack led by Grítsa moved away from the sound of forest wreckage, breaking from the chase, the other—

"Mayor Surnin's wolfhound's taken the lead!"

—strung out, a chain of howling madness directly after the destruction.

The Chechen, suddenly at Michael's side, grabbed his arm. Pulled him after his dog, away from the chase. Michael glanced back at Father Vadim. Almost childish the way the priest clutched his spear—a rigid port arms of indecision. The priest ran blindly after the main group. The Chechen gave a last tug then released Michael. Grítsa wailed. Neither would be kept waiting.

She's the only one who's hit the wind, bit into it before and lived.

Doris. Indistinct. A terrier in her hands. Beyond the ribbed bars of a crib. "Wake up, Michael. Beaumont wants to say good morning."

Hazy/distant/indistinct. Real. But Michael didn't recognize/grasp this memory, far out of his categorized timeline. Jogged to keep the Chechen's long stride, gasping: "I've hunted enough squirrel and possum, enough deer back home to know the kill happens when the dogs tree the prey or run it to ground."

"The Skvoznyak is no animal. He's the crosswind of bad luck and lost opportunity. Grítsa has tasted his blood. Knows how he blows. Knows to go where he blows next."

There was mist, and there was smell that clung to the mist. Not the smell of the dogs that boiled around the Chechen and Michael, anxious to put their whimpering selves behind the men, but drawn by loyalty to Grítsa, slunk between the two men's legs and back around them trying to move to the front *and* stay behind, as those two men scrambled through a thick thorny bramble. Hard twisted vines. Python-fat. Snow-shook and bloody-spiked. Made passable only by the destruction of the beast whose smell, not even animal, polluted the mist: a fetid pungency linked to the birth of nature's true disorder. Not so much a clearing as a rooted/pawed-through snow sludge. They staggered into a mossy wallow at the base of a flat-topped knoll that stretched twenty feet to two toppled stones. Natural Stonehenge monoliths in an inverted V. The opening yawned shadows. The mouth of the boar's den. Skvoznyak stood in front of his grot.

Five feet tall at shoulder. The space between its front hooves and tail covered at least seven feet of ground. Four hundred/five hundred pounds, at least. Its fur was long, thick, snagged with thorns and brush; Michael would swear he saw broken arrow shafts sticking from more than one place. Steam boiled from its snout. Its red eyes were more than mean; immortal evil like the eyes of the devil, and its tusks were mighty. Razor sharp. Drenched and dripping Grítsa's blood, the dog alive and disemboweled at the monster's feet.

Skvoznyak wanted to see them. To know them. To curse them and sear into Michael and the Chechen's mind the truth about Les Dikiy and immortality. Neither man moved. Not even to raise their leaf-blade spears. Skvoznyak snorted. Globs of pink foam, distended from black rubbery lips, hit the ground. Melted into the snow. Skvoznyak clopped around. Swished its tail. Pushed through the curtain of mist that veiled the opening to its den. Vanished.

"We dare go up and get Grítsa?" Michael.

The Chechen. "When its over. This is the beginning."

He instructed Michael back-to-back; Michael to cover their one down to six, the Chechen, seven up to their twelve. Michael braced the butt of his spear in the earth like ancient infantry readying against cavalry. Aimed its point at the envisioned level of the boar's broad and tangled breast. The hoped-for heart.

"You get it on your spear. That's just the beginning."

Michael: "Yeah. He'll kill himself to—"

Skvoznyak hit Michael straight from the brambles with the force of a car, scattering the remaining dogs, tossing Michael with a hammer blow from the side of his gargantuan head into the muddy slope of the knoll.

Spear gone.

AK47 ripped from his back.

Michael pressed to his knees, concussed. Mixed up in sequence of thought.

Skvoznyak impales on the Chechen's spear point—

Skvoznyak turns from hitting Michael—

Skvoznyak hits Michael/the world spins/red-light and stars—

The Chechen howls. "Your three!"

Skvoznyak hits him, but Michael's spear is not lost; it holds firm between himself and the beast—

Nothing impaled. No penetration.

—Skvoznyak: whirling, coming back. The Chechen pivoting. Valiantly/vainly attempting to train his broad, well-honed this morning—

(Sparks fly from the grinder in the dark of the dacha's vehicle shed)

—spearpoint between himself, on his knees, and the unstoppable/unkillable beast—

How do I see it impaled? When is/was that?

The stars blurred Michael's vision. Mist thick; his rattled brain revealed the intolerable stench as mist-glow and flare.

Saw silver: flat, leaf-shaped.

Saw Skvoznyak: squealing impaled—

Time restiches.

Me: hit—from out of the bramble. I fly. I smash.

The Chechen: Skvoznyak glances him. The spear's shaft breaks between man and raging beast.

The Chechen's hands tangle in his AK's strap.

Skvoznyak wheels. In for the kill.

The spear: mine: in hand; the impaling: mine: by my hand; I straddle the Chechen. Take the full force of the old immortal boar onto my iron.

Skvoznyak rakes his huge and deadly head for Michael's chest. Fabric shreds. Down flies. Michael scrabbles backwards over the Chechen's chest. Over his head.

Foxtail Farm. A childhood wind storm. Michael in Doris's lap, T.H. White's The Once and Future King. *I sound out words under my mother's encouraging eyes, under her warm voice:*

"'Love is a trick played on us by the forces of evolution. Plea-sh-ure,'" she sounds along with me, "'is the bait.'"

My small face turns up to hers. "'Bait.' Like cheese in a mousetrap." Mom nods. Points to the next line.

Bristle-coated red, gray, brown snarling/snapping laikas lock jaws: Skvoznyak's neck, Skvoznyak's shoulder, Skvoznyak's leg.

We read: "'There is only power.'"

Michael's hands give length, backing down the spear.

We read: "'Power is of the individual mind, but the mind's power is not enough.'"

Michael's knees, his back leveraging, burying the butt-end into the elemental earth from which man, beast, metal all once came.

Doris stops reading. I finish alone: "'Power of the body decides everything in the end, and only Might is Right.'"

The lugs catch. Michael watches the boar's sharp, split and heavy hooves churn air. Carpus dewclaws quiver as tusks slash straight for Michael's throat only to lose a thinking guidance mid-swing. Michael released his spear. Fell back now, over and behind the Chechen.

Skvoznyak collapsed. Lay on its side. Its other side rose and fell, rose lower/fell deeper life faded.

Michael rocked to his seat. Wrapped himself with his arms in tattered sleeves. Watched the Chechen stumble upright. Watched the titan make four staggered steps to collect his shotgun; check its single load; two strides back. He pushed the barrel through the fur at the base of the animal's skull. Hesitated. Offered the gun to Michael.

Michael shook his head. The Chechen blasted the slug into the animal's brain.

2.

THE BOAR'S ENTRAILS HIT the snow steaming. The dogs tore into them. Their bodies flashed in the cast of wind-whipped flames outside the ring of the bonfire. Darkness came early to Les Dikiy, the Forest Wild. Michael and the Chechen, scraped, battered, bruised and muscle-strained sustained no serious wounds. The local vet, who urged the Chechen to put down Grítsa, acquiesced to Lulu's bodyguard. Anesthetized the hound, stuffed her innards, sewed her belly and the Chechen sat in a folding beach chaise, stroking his dog; whispered to it in Chechen. Their eyes held each other for two hours until the animal died.

The butcher, Tikhon Balakin, was a flurry of orders, stroke of meat ax, and flash of carving blade; in with his workers, dressed the beast, and a deer (bow-shot by Chuprikov, the fancy candlestick man) and, the snow lynx stand-shot with Finnish sniper rifle by Levka Rodyaevand the artisan baker who extolled to everyone who would pretend to listen the new anti-aging discoveries associated with lynx liver.

Tenderloin and ribs went to the bonfire. Cuts of shoulder, loin, legs, belly: packed in ice chest divided between the hunters. The head would be frozen until the Great Feast of Christmas, celebrated in the Skhodnya village former People's Recreation Hall on January the seventh.

"You will join us, Mikhail Nikolaevich? Seat of honor. The skull and tusks are yours," he said.

"Sounds like a dance I won't want to miss." Michael showed Father Vadim eyes that spoke otherwise. *My dance is done, Father. I leave as Kaladoskop commands.*

Wives, girlfriends, some children, motored to the camp inside a converted military ZZGT all-terrain/amphibious transport. Five strange old men on cross country skis pulling a skid, somehow having known, had tended the campfire all afternoon. They brought the spit. Brought homebrew beer in six small kegs. The vodka, a dozen bottles packed in egg crates. The banker Kravtsov—changed from hunting outfit into reindeer boots, Siberian mink long coat, sable Cossack hat—with spiked tea from the samovar, sidled close to Michael who quietly ached and watched the boar's unmaking. Unbecoming to unbeing.

"It was beautiful in it own unsightly way. Full of life. Embraced its violent dance and yet, a stranger appears—unexpected, unaccounted—and that strangely beautiful creature dies violently when perhaps the sow shouldn't have."

Strangely beautiful creature: sow: a Lulu threat.

Michael ignored him with his eyes. "He was a boar. In English, b-o-a-r, not b-o-r-e. Not a furry little bitch."

Kravtsov. Fake laugh. Bladed words. "Lulu—as I'm sure you're wondering—is with my wife. They will arrive presently. She predicted this. Lulu. They say her grandmother, from whatever village her bloodline flows, was a witch. Her father married her mother because she had second-sight." A furry-shouldered shrug. "And you cannot imagine how impressed everyone is with your bloody achievement. Lulu will need comfort from you when she arrives."

Michael snapped eyes. Now it was the banker who watched the butchers. Didn't look. Continued. "She may have told you about her daughter. She usually visits her for Western Christmas. But that won't happen this winter. Understandably, she is saddened by this. Will rely on your comfort." Snapped gaze. Locked eyes. "What this means—and this is very important to prevent surprises—" a jerk of his chin at the boar carcass—"You will remain at *Chasovnya Opasnaya* through December twenty-fifth, then the two of you will be our guests at my dacha until after New Years."

Chasovnya Opasnaya. Chapel Perilous. Three graves behind a ruined chapel. I watch ice dendrites—perfect snowflakes like child cut-outs, like hard Christmas sugar, melt on the curve of Lulu's pale pink lip.

"I swear—I pledge to you—I will come back to you."

"No. You could come with us. But once you've saved me, given me my Alina, we will vanish. Where she and I go, no one will find us."

"Why can't I have both?"

Michael mumbled. "I see. Appreciate the invitation."

The banker spiked his tea. Offered Michael the flask. "Medovukha. Honey spirits."

Michael knew he must drink. Exchanged a smile. Exchanged a nod. The banker leaned in against his shoulder. "I worked alongside Maxim before his stupendous ascension. Lulu was his light. They loved. But not the way she loves you. I say this to you not as a representative of Maxim's former colleagues, not as a host they require look out for you and their Gazprom/Nord Stream 2 interests that must not include a certain Yurenev."

The Enchanted Forest. I bounce the red balloon in the air. The sun bounces off its bright surface. Reflected: Silas. Weak. Pathetic. Impotent.

The balloon man: Yurenev—Kolya—kissing my mother.

(My father.)

Doris kisses him back.

The banker: "I tell you Lulu loves you fully. One human utterly joined to another. Adjustments could be made. A pledge of loyalty from an American who is, perhaps, more than a systems consultant. Her life would not be a prison if you were to give her heart."

Lulu strokes Michael's face with her mitten. "You found my heart. Yes?"

Michael: "I didn't need much convincing but listening to you—*hearing* you—I swear on all that his holy: I will do as you say and give Lulu the truest heart overflowing with the greatest love."

Kravtsov patted his cheek with bear-furred gloves. "A hunter *and* a poet. You must be Russian." He laughed and wandered off. When Michael looked back at the boar, nothing remained of Skvoznyak.

TRUE TO KRAVTSOV'S WORD, Lulu arrived at nightfall with that banker's wife, the pair leathered and furred—all glamorous and mythical—trundling into camp in the open back of a logging truck hung with sleigh bells and packed with furniture. Rugs. With piles of furs. Lulu's snow hair—first time Michael had seen her wear it entirely unbraided/unpinned/uncoiffed—teased wild and free and blowing. This vision of her riding and queenly, her face turning to him blazing with love and joy would be the last memory he would have the last breath, the last day of his life. A day in future past. A day unknown, but Lulu dreamt. But this night Michael lived. Alive: all of it and everyone in it. More folk from the town came in caravan to work and to celebrate; they lit candelabra, hung chandeliers from pines and powered these from the ZZGT's extra generator; Lulu joined Michael, and they came together perfectly fit like lock and key or the two sides of a seashell closing on a precious pearl. Music. Laughter. Vodka and beer and champagne. Heaped platters of grilled meat. Silence came with the presentation of Skvoznyak's heart.

Thinly sliced, marinated all afternoon in oil, in red wine, garlic, spices, and in herbs, skewered and grilled until deep-sizzled like bacon Michael and Lulu fed it to each other from ashy sticks. Everyone cheered, everyone toasted, everyone shouted for them to kiss and it would be hard to tell the difference between this moment and the wedding they would never have. The musicians arrived. The folk songs played. The old men who'd known today would be *that* day, the day the forest died, had old wives who knew they would need to dance; and they had also known to come. Wore the old dresses. Pulled their men to the dance floor which was the forest floor and had always been the forest floor and recreated the old dances as if inventing them this strange night.

Lulu pulled Michael to the edge of the fire, closest to the snowy forest. Snuggled with him across a divan piled with fox and beaver, rabbit and mink blankets. Hummed to the song the musicians played. Whispered in his ear. "Sing it to me. So I can be certain."

Lulu's song; the Cossack Lullaby Michael worked on every day.

He sang gently. "*Softly, pretty baby, sleeping* / Bayushki-bayu, / *Quiet moon bright watch is keeping* / *On your crib for you.* / *I shall tell you tales past number.* / *Sing you ditties too.* / *Close your tender eyes in slumber,* / Bayushki-bayu."

Lulu. "Do I mystify you?" A surreptitious dart of eye drew Michael's gaze to the dark edge of the forest over their shoulder. A man stood alone. Out of sight to everyone but the two of them. "Are you frightened yet?"

Michael smiled. Sang. "*Terek on his stones is fretting* / *With a troubled roar;* / *Wild Chechen, his dagger whetting,* / *Crawls along the shore.*"

The man's features—what little appeared between hat and thick wool scarf—resembled Michael well. His dress matched Michael exactly.

"*But your father knows war's riot,* / *Knows what he must do.* / *Sleep, my darling, sleep in quiet,* / Bayushki-bayu."

Later, everyone watched Michael carry Lulu in his arms to where her Chechen waited with his snow cat. Later, Kravtsov's oligarch foot soldiers in place around Lulu's dacha watched Michael carry her inside. Observed them into the bedroom where the shades were drawn and metal shutters lowered by motor. They would watch and report through the twenty-fifth of December that Lulu and Michael were glimpsed many times through windows or ducking outside for the sauna, but mainly remained indoors, rarely dressed, presumed to be constantly making love.

Michael Kingston saw none of this. When he finished the second verse of the song, Lulu rose from the sofa, wandered, singing among the party, encouraging the people of Skhodnya, her friends and her enemies to watch her become possessed of the song upon the forest floor. Her arms—widespread and taut—Lulu twirled serene and mad and hypnotic. Hands supple. Fingers drooping. Undulating. Leaves at the ends of lissome birch boughs in slow, soft, summer breeze. Her chin tilted upward.

"*You'll find in time that's ever nearing, / what soldiering has won. / You'll mount your horse and not be fearing / to brandish high your gun.*"

Michael traded places with his doppelganger from the woods. He faded back, deep into the darkness on the trail of footprints. Lingered. Listened.

"*And what I stitch in silk may be / the saddle cloth for you.*"

Lulu's fingers. Delicate. Drooping.

Undulating like leaves in summer's breeze.

A small and leafy town. You know it's out there.

Wish your whole life for its pleasant, dreamy, warm-misted streets.

A town no one has ever found.

"*Sleep, my dear, beloved baby, /* Bayushki-bayu."

Until you have.

A harsh whisper. “Mikhail Nikolaevich.” Lulu’s lunatic bodyguard. “This way. Hurry. Germans never wait, and the Swiss timekeepers are worse.” He slapped a motorcycle helmet into Michael’s stomach. “We have to make the chopper before first light, lover boy.”

This moment.

This now.

Lulu.

Sunday, December Twenty-third

1.

HAL'S ENCRYPTED TEXT IN ROT13 read: *Bcrengvbaf pbaarpg: PVCQQE PEBJA. Ab riraqvr bs gernfba. Arrq rkgenpgvba. V'z cebprrqvat gb eaqriragmh cbvag sbe 24 Qrpnhera 2012.*

On his IronKey flash token. Ready for the PRC-343 transmitter inside the false bottom of the scorched fuel drum at the burn pit. Translation—when it hit Drexler's console—*Operations connect: CINDER CROWN. No evidence of treason. Need extraction. I'm proceeding to rendezvous point for 24 December 2012.*

He hauled his refuse cart through the wire. Hit the path to the burn pit. He'd burst last call into the atmosphere. Thumb the self-destruct. Toss the transmitter into the pit. Pop smoke and un-ass outta there. So long, "Corporal Cooper". So long Camp Abu Omar.

He'd come to prove or disprove his father. Prove/disprove for the slovenly Morton Drexler who nursed professional rejection and lifelong inadequacy, a Silas Kingston/Colonel Finn Houton conspiracy to treason. Treason connected/covered under the operational designation: KALEIDOSCOPE. He'd found KALEIDOSCOPE all right. No one was hiding that here and Houton and his lieutenants, his staff, his military advisers: no one: viewed it through any other lens than those of deceit, deception, betrayal. Going on here—? The intentional sacrifice of assets under false orders.

Assets who weren't American. Weren't even allies.

Former enemy combatants who existed more than expendable. They were usefully—on KALEIDOSCOPE/CIA authority "useful" backstopped—expendable. One hundred fifty Sunni Iranian Jundallah. Terrorists in the State Department book. Gearing up, loading, shipping out for three days now. Camp was breaking down. Orders coming for the regular Army advisers. Pay coming for the private contractors. New contracts offered—his, presented personally by Houton, tucked in the breast pocket of his Desert Combat Tunic.

The pillar of smoke that never ceased climbed into the rose-colored twilight. Bent on hot wind, it beckoned Hal from its rocky bowl. Another Christmas in the desert. Near holy land. The evening star twinkled.

Maybe the same the Wise Men followed.

In the chaos of deployment, Hal had taken his greatest risk. Broke into Houton's trailer/office. Seen/phone-photo'd the operation briefing memo.

TOP SECRET / SI / OTRAC-CODEWORD

U.S. Department of Commerce (OTRAC)

Office of Treaty Regulation and Administrative Compliance

Project: KALEIDOSCOPE

Operation: CINDER CROWN

The objective straightforward: *To destabilize hostile energy corridor competitors through limited, non-attributable strategic ignition points inside designated proxy territories, using indigenous assets plausibly disavowable to U.S. interests.*

Operational background clear (for those it was meant for; of little meaning to Hal): *Recent Sino-Russian economic convergence poses a threat to Trans-Caspian energy routing independence. Direct confrontation is inadvisable given Eurasian soft alliances. Energy flow, not military force, will dictate Eurasia's next hegemony. Proxy ignition within Iran will force reallocation of Russian defensive energy resources, while simultaneously destabilizing Sino-Iranian backchannel negotiations concerning Arctic sea-lane mineral rights.*

EXPECTED OUTCOME: Iranian regime forced into heavy-handed crackdowns. Russian Federation pressured into open defensive posture to stabilize Iranian oil output. European energy confidence in Russian supply chains undermined. Enhanced U.S. leverage at Baku Oil negotiations.

SECONDARY OUTCOME: Displacement of Chinese Wànhuātōng assets from Iranian Revolutionary Guard Corps communication channels.

A final *"Eyes Only" written by his father (AdSec OTRAC): CINDER CROWN's operational doctrine draws on historical models of sacrificial ignition: strategic provocation of controlled burn-off of rival ambitions before full conflagration. Final success measure is not regime collapse but redirection of hegemonic resources.*

Already, the desperate men of Camp Abu Omar were entering Iran via covert desert crossings. Christmas morning they would begin simultaneous coordinated attacks on the Ahvaz Refinery; South Pars pipeline valve stations; Abadan oil terminal.

Hal hurled bags and boxes into the fire. Got his smoke thick. Got it black. Went to the fuel drum. Opened the false panel.

Empty.

"You'd be looking for this?"

Finn Houton sat like some fucking genie on a wind-ragged stone outcropping. The Dulles boys—Bors and Vale—carried HK MP5s. Didn't aim them. Didn't need to. Houton wiggled Hal's PRC-343 burst transmitter.

"Huh, 'Cooper'?" Finn cocked his arm. Lobbed Hal's burst transmitter into the pit.

Hal stared. His sidearm wasn't going to do anything for him. Drew it—two finger. Tossed it between them. Houton appreciated the gesture. Warmed to a smile. Scrutinized Hal. Some kind of internal debate. Shook his head.

"I don't get you. I don't. Who spies on the spies? Warzone—you ain't law enforcement. My authority supersedes DoD—DIA—but you ain't no Corporal Cooper. Want to tell me your name while we're still in the easy part?"

"Hal Kingston."

"Honesty. That's refreshing. Like a drink of water in the desert." Houton tossed Hal a water bottle. "Might be awhile until you'll be having more." Made a drink motion. "I'd take it all."

Hal drank.

"I'm guessing your pops didn't send you. He's good about keeping me in the loop."

"No. I was here to investigate him."

"And me?"

"Doesn't matter. What you're up to here is way above my pay-grade. A personal fucking waste of time for me."

Houton stood. Towered on the rock. "I guess here's the part I give you a chocolate bar and let you go."

"Don't need the chocolate."

"I would, too. I'm fond of Silas. He saved my ass way back when. Everything I've made for myself has a Kingston stamp on it." He fished a letter from his pocket. Unfolded it. Unfolded reading glasses. "It's from you dad. Guess you'll appreciate it before Bors and Vale take you back to that playroom you've done some exercise in with the bad boys."

He read. "*'This operation will not save them. I never meant it to. Not the men you trained, not the country they will bleed in, not the system that will spend them.* CINDER CROWN *is sacrificial ignition: not designed to win a thing. Only to burn enough political stability that* KALEIDOSCOPE *Baku/Caspian Oil Conference objectives become achievable. If you must explain it to anyone later, explain it like this:* We did not light the fire. We only chose the wind. *I have long believed in quiet adjustments, the patient turnings of the glass. But patience is a kind of arrogance, too. And kings who sit too long at their tables forget the kingdom rots beneath them. There will be no victory written from* CINDER CROWN. *Only one more illusion ash-drifted across the battlefield. Hold steady. We do not seek war. We offer them the fire they crave.*' I'll give him this: Silas Kingston has always been an inspirational son of a bitch."

A silent/invisible cue. Bors shouldered his weapon. Covered Vale, who—"You got a knife. Toss it."

Hal complied.

"Hands on head. Fingers interlaced."

Hal complied. Vale went around behind. Zip restraints out. Yanked Hal's hands behind his back. Zip restraints on.

Houton: "Like I said, I owe your daddy a hell of a lot. But he's been bought out. And hegemonies change. I hate to do this, but we're all up in a *Who* song. New bosses are coming, baby. They'll want to talk to you and they won't want you comfortable."

Fifteen minutes later. The evening star, that Bethlehem beacon, high overhead was the last thing Hal saw as his head jerked, face snapped upward on the boot delivered to his back. He sprawled onto his face on the Goat Shed floor.

Bors and Vale came in behind him.

Hal was going to miss Christmas.

2.

WHAT WAS THE DEAL with lawyers? Her lawyers. Gwen was paying them and—although they returned her retainer and worked on a contingency entitling them to 33.3% of her award, be it against Silas or the US government. Or both. Which it damn well should be. Her suffering, not theirs and now they—*her* lawyers—were making her suffer more. Shouldn't she be entitled to a claim of 66.7% of the 33.3% she was paying them because they were the major instigators of shit-she-had-to-tolerate today? Two days before Christmas. And it's fucking Sunday!

Tolerate this.

She pointed her middle finger behind her buttocks her hands low and back while the Indian or Pakistani or what's-the-difference? tickled her cleavage with her cheap-flash manicured fingers.

"I'm sorry if this is weird. But Tony with our security is better at doing this, but you're a woman..." Ms. Gupta, nervous, fumbled with the miniature microphone up through Gwen's bra.

"Hun, I've felt it just like that before with longer nails." Gwen hadn't, but winked anyway, enjoying the paralegal's discomfort. "So do *you* have Christmas plans?"

"Well. Yes. Of course. It's Christmas."

Gwen wide-eyed her. Pissed her off.

"Ms. Kingston. I am both Hindu and Christian."

"Oh. I'm making *you* uncomfortable."

"Gwen." Senator Ossani on the edge of the conference room desk. "No one gets your sense of humor. If you had gotten your father-in-law to answer the one simple question I needed—"

"Simple doesn't work well with complicated old assholes."

"And now—" Senator Ossini pushed in. Pushed aside Ms. Gupta. Shoved the mic where she wanted it. "Button up and listen."

Gwen buttoned. Ms. Gupta hurried out. Mr. Pinchbeck—head of security for Marsh, Gertz, and Ossani—explained how the wire would work. Voice-activated. Switch it on in the bathroom before going to the dinner table. Belted to the small of her back; wear a dress you can pull up; use the mirror to watch how you do it— "After dinner just remember to switch it off again. I don't want to hear anything else you got going later, huh?"

"Rude."

Mr. Pinchbeck. "Whatever."

Gwen adjusted her bra. The microphone, small as she'd ever seen, magnified its sensation. Distracted the hell out of her. "Ugh."

"You'll get used to it." Pinchbeck again. "Just make sure you don't unstick it between changing tonight and tomorrow. You can do that?"

"I *can* do that. Sir."

"Good. I'm out too. Merry Christmas, Senator." He left.

Gwen gives the Senator a helpless look, like— *These people these days*. Said, “If this is illegal, I’m just not sure why I should be doing it.”

“Anything we get from the recording will not be used in any direct manner. It will only be used to point me in directions you’ve been unable to provide. At dinner tomorrow night: keep after him with questions about Michael. About Hal. About Lynn.”

“It’s going to piss him off.”

“No. Not if you do it from a loving place. Those people are your family. You love them, you are concerned about them. Always put it that way, you’ll get your other sister-in-law on your side.”

“Miss Saccharine Melody...” under her breath.

They spent another thirty minutes rehearsing questions for Gwen to ask. It got touchy again after that as the senator had Gwen go into the bathroom, remove it all and put it all back in and then it was lady Ossani running her finger beneath her bra.

Wow. I would die for that manicure.

“I got it, Senator. I’m sorry I’m so difficult. I want to do everything right and I’m nervous and I’m angry and I don’t want to be and it’s Christmas.” Buttoned up. Again. “I’ll do it right.”

A soft hand on her shoulder. Guided Gwen to the door. “I know you will, dear. We got this.” A wink. An out-you-go through the door. “We’re the last people here, Sunday before Christmas Eve. Garage will open automatically, you won’t need to pay.”

THE ELEVATOR. Door slid open. Face-to-faced another Asian. Clutched a briefcase.

Not the hard-to-tell/embarrass me brown-kind but Chinese or something. Knock-out suit. Great looking man. If I were one, I'd whistle at him.

She gave her hottest smile. He averted his eyes in that Made-in-China way. He stepped out of the box—briefcase two-handed to chest; silly/slight little head bow—Gwen *tootle-looed* stepped in. Rode down. Wasn't until she checked her lipstick in the review she realized her problem.

Fricking Silas with that Madonna crack. Don't think I won't be wearing a beautiful corset tomorrow night. Especially if I'm required to speak from a loving *place.*

She unbuttoned her blouse. Flipped the top edge of her bra. The mic had a tiny bit of velcro hook-y stuff that attached to the patch of fuzz they'd all had so much trouble getting in the right spot.

I could probably do it.

Would the sticky last if I transfer it to the corset?

(Uh. It's so beautiful I can't wait!)

Maybe they have another little piece.

IF NOT FOR HER OWN POINT OF VIEW, little nice could be said of Gwen. When acting genuine (when it wasn't acting, but *genuine* Gwen) her combo of vapidity and narcissism created a sort of emptiness vacuum within her. This condition was natural. DNA. To live like you're falling down a bottomless well—a psychic sensation since her earliest childhood too intense self-awareness—she learned the simplicity of sensation, of desire, slowed the fall better then trust and love. It made her obnoxious and sad to love. To live inside her would be to sensate what it was to constantly force a smile over a tearful lump in your throat that never goes away or tells you why you have to feel like crying all the fucking time. So you fed desire and called it something else—anything else—and you try to be nice.

*But everything that let me be me, let me be nice-to-them—sooo every-*one *not* -thing—*I've lost.*

She cursed. She'd be walking back in with moist eyes. But the law offices were dark. Gwen cursed that bad luck: must have missed the Senator—her going down, Gwen up—in the elevators. Something made her try the door.

And it opened and that was the thing; there are always trade-offs in nature. Missing crucial complex personality components, Gwen existed more fully than most in animal instinct. That thing inside her that drove her to creature comforts, was just that: creature. She heard voices within the suite, but didn't call out. Crept on in darkness. Stalked the hushed conversation in darkness.

Sunday night. Building empty. Firm empty. Alone. Senator Ossani had left her office blinds open. The Asian man and the Senator were inside. Spread across the senator's desk were everything Gwen recognized from her case file. The Senator running documents through her copier; the Asian man putting them inside his empty briefcase.

This is crazy. Bad. Wrong.

Why?

(Silas would know.)

Without thinking twice, Gwen opened the camera on her iPhone. Made sure the flash was off. Clipped-off a flurry of shots.

Silas would *know. (And I could—*

She'd held them back from the elevator to now, but the taps in her eyes opened.

—I could win them all back.)

Monday, December Twenty-fourth – Christmas Eve

1.

THREE DAYS TIGHT-TAILING SILAS paid off when Fergus clocked him entering the abandoned Enchanted Forest amusement park. A check of the dead drop behind the brick in the tumbledown castle revealed Silas Kingston had taken the old Sov's encrypted letter. That was 11:30pm, the seventeenth. Fergus Ebay'd his way into possession of the correct edition of the White novel—the code key—that Silas would use to decipher it. It arrived midday the nineteenth. Silas's advantage: he knew the agreed upon chapter/page/paragraph start point to make his decryption. Nonetheless, Fergus spent three mind-numbingly useless days with his own matching copy of *The Once and Future King* and attempted to match repetitive three-number patterns from his photographs of the letter cipher, that he might discover the *and*'s or *the*'s and link alphanumerically to the very same page. He knew it was next to impossible—alright, smack-dab-bullseye center of impossible—but after so many years hunting Silas Kingston, after so much institutional doubt and mockery, career failure over what always had been thought a fool's quest, well, what a Christmas plum cracking the code would be?

A supercomputer could do it, and MI6, with the book and some time to create/refine/lock-in the algorithm, would basically do what Fergus attempted by hand. It would take that supercomputer 72 hours. Fergus's attempt only proved—to the ghosts of Garde-Joyeuse (and to Silas, remote-viewing the Scotsman's full-tilt madness through hidden camera)—that Fergus was an obsessive fool. And fools chasing hubris were always dangerous.

Fergus reported his find to headquarters on the twenty-third. They agreed, reluctantly, that best security would be hand-exchange of the photo intel and the code-key book.

In morning darkness, Christmas Eve, Silas Kingston observed Fergus leaving Garde-Joyeuse and, satisfied the fool had bit the cheese in the trap, wouldn't think again about him until after the Christmas holiday. No way of knowing this and, for the first time in over a decade, drunk on the idea of employing tradecraft in a target nation's capital, he ran an extensive Surveillance Detection Route.

A bus to a taxi to the MARC (Maryland Area Regional Commuter) train. Boarded the Penn Line North to Washington Union Station. Perfect tradecraft took time and getting to the Penn Line in New Carrollton took over three hours. The excitement of the clandestine officer on the move wore off in two. Waiting on the train in New Carrollton, Fergus cracked the label on a half-pint of Dewars. Polished it off by his arrival in Union Station where he enjoyed the pleasant warmth, the fuzzed edge it added to his experience of the bright chrome, sparkling glass, brushed-steel, fresh-painted, scrubbed and transcendent shimmering hub of the sanitized/securitized/consumerized energy, activity, *Jingle Bell Rock* blaring train station.

Found the Pret-A-Manger right where it should be. Bought the sandwich as instructed (bogged the whole thing); into the twine-handled paper bag, Fergus put the brown-wrapped White book and the thumb drive with the high-def photo blow-ups beneath the wax paper and the napkins. Paused at the 18-foot tall Norwegian pine Christmas tree—all bright white lights and hand-blown/hand-painted ornaments—the engraved plaque noted the tree was gifted annually to the station by Norway. Scanned the crowd. People moving with purpose, Christmas fitting person/place/thing a perfect accessory that set festively without intrusion or interference with the devices everyone buried their noses in. Trusted the silent and precise LED Arrival/Departure board implicitly. Clock told him time to kill. So, Fregus began his second SDR with a stop for a pint of Guinness in the perfectly re-created Irish pub, The Dublin Double.

Hoofed it onto the snowy sidewalks into sheets of blowing sleet. Ducked back inside—*Jingle Bell Rock*, again, and good he liked that one—tossed a what-the-hell couple shots of Jamison's.

Fired inside, he locomoted through the weather to the Ellipse. This year (same as forty before) the old National Tree had recently perished. This time, knocked out by a hurricane. Found its replacement in a forty-foot Colorado blue spruce. Red, green, and white lights, and the perennial fifty small state trees on the Pathway of Peace.

No stage. No performers. People—some—bundled up and hurrying past without notice. Snowblind in their devices.

The National creche, removed in 1973, was replaced with a Pageant of Peace "Living" Nativity and Fergus found the bench he'd been instructed onto facing a braying jackass in the back of a horse trailer with Mary and Joseph and the Wise Men huddled miserably in a tent by a weak propane heater.

"I'm Smith. You have something for me?"

Fergus purposefully not looking at the fancy-overcoated embassy wonk who lumped beside him. Fergus adjusted his down parka. Revealed the Pret-A-Manger bag.

Smith enveloped it with his coat. "Better be bloody worth it. Christmas Eve."

"Queen'll bloody thinks it is."

They sat for a moment, fresh looks for surveillance both of them knew wasn't there. Fergus said: "What've you got for me?"

Fergus's rough conviction bothered the political officer. He stood, the Pret-A-Manger bag hidden. Secure. "How 'bout bugger off, you soak."

And the embassy spy vanished into the weather, muttering about the Queen, not knowing that Fergus was correct about Her Majesty. More than Fergus would ever comprehend.

2.

AN AZERBAIJAN EMBASSY CHRISTMAS pageant. Extraterritorial trial proceedings in the interest of national sovereignty. A collegium panel of three judges flown in from Baku, robed behind a long table at one end of the embassy's formal reception room. A facing team of prosecutors—also flown in from Baku—behind their table. Lynn. Russell Aiken seated to her left, a translator behind, her attorney, Ms. Nermin Jalilova, at her right. This room, as the lead prosecutor laced his opening statement with irony, would have been the venue where Lynn Kingston, invited onto Azerbaijan soil, would have dined in the company of her victim, Roman Sayadov the night she chose instead to take his life in most cruel brutal fashion.

Whatever else went on—the presentation of evidence, Ms. Jalilova's moves to strike each piece as uncorroborated, withheld from discovery, inadmissible, that were shot down one after the other (more bullets into the corpse and memory of Roman; kill-shots to the truth)—Lynn ignored. The proceedings designed and carried out as theater, the verdict manufactured and predetermined, held no interest for her.

She spent the short trial soul-centered on Leigh. Her nieces and her nephews. Her siblings, her mother. Melody. Even her father she was, in the deepest part of her, desperate to love. Rusty would whisper to her every now and then, but she ignored him; Lynn's feelings for Aiken held only serenity. Satisfaction and trust that no more words were needed between them. After this, after she was gone: Russell Aiken would have, if he chose, the very best of what they were, how they connected, and who they had been. Carried into eternity.

There was no miracle in this sham trial. The miracle—in a life that had no others Lynn could recall—was a terrific/vibrant/lovely-of-heart, of soul, of face and disposition girl of ten. It was more than enough for Lynn Kingston. In fact, it was bountiful.

The verdict was rendered at 12:30 pm. Guilty of all charges.

The sentence was delivered: death by military execution.

A week was allowed for Ms. Jalilova to return to Baku and file an appeal.

"I'll travel with her, Lynn. This is far from over." Aiken squeezed her hand.

Lynn acted as though she didn't hear; her hand offered no response.

Returned to her storeroom cell, her cot, she slept through the rest of Christmas in sadness that somehow was content.

3.

BOONE KELSO JERKED AND blew enough dudes to stay alive his whole stretch at Fountain Correctional Facility. He still knew how to hit the men (old/young black/white; didn't make no difference) no-tell-straight as he was—the rest stops and truck stops, the malls and the metro station johns—enough to make more than he needed to pay for the no names/no questions, by-the-week motel-apartment he'd been holed up in West Baltimore since he slipped into Maryland, start of December. Made enough cash to buy what was needed for what Boone Kelso would achieve bringing Christmas out to Foxtail Farm this holy night. Made enough for six cans of his turp plus a bottle of 30 ppm-thujone absinthe from a distillery in Waldorf that, all these years, still back-doored it if you knew how to ask. Made sure to bring in enough dough on top to rent—by-the-day or night—the Subaru wagon from the waitress-read-crackhead who crashed next door.

The day was getting away from him. Christmas Eve and he needed the car. Still had a stop to make before he joined the family celebration. But his neighbor lady was crashed out after a three-day straight-up smoke fest and no amount of pounding returned any sound from beyond her door. He had her keys. She wasn't going home for the holiday. Boone Kelso pushed two twenties under her door with note he'd return her junker with gas Christmas Day in case she wanted to go see her kids. Knew she wasn't going anywhere. She'd grab the forty, skip the note, call her guy and burn the pipe another two days. All the time he needed. What he had to do.

Snow fell but it was light. Edvard Munch oil on canvas: *New Snow on the Avenue* dreamy. Lifted the broken hatchback. Propped it open with the 9-iron golf club his crack neighbor kept in the back. Stuffed in the big painter's drop cloth he'd stolen out of a house painting van last week. Had the Kingston family Christmas present in its Ziploc bag he'd dug up in Arkansas after ditching the court-strapped anklet in Alabama. Old brass—Melody's brass—saved. New brass loaded. Had something to pick up for the young Doris he'd met in the woods. Couldn't shake that vision out of his head—

One last portrait. Save the girl, damn the ghost.

His sweet gift would convince her more eloquently than words/logic he'd tried last time with Silas.

"Everything I do is for love! Doris is unfaithful to you. Has always been unfaithful."

"She told you this?"

"Her soul screams it. I painted it. It's what you're witnessing looking at it but are too stupid to recognize!"

A gift that would protect his new Doris once Boone Kelso opened the present for Silas and bitch-Melody and whoever else wanted a shot of mistletoe.

Engine had a tough time starting in the cold but it caught. He let it warm as he concocted a full turpentine/absinthe dose in the empty gold turpentine can he was using as a flask. Revved the engine. Sounded better. Found his cheese cloth and strained a hit down his throat. His vision pulsed. Glowed. His snow scene went from the somber blues and grays of Munch, its isolation, contemplation—world in the stillness of lies—to Kandinsky's immediate capture of true snow: Pink, yellow, blue and black: oil on cardboard: *Winter Landscape*. Yeah, that looks just right.

Boone Kelso pulled out of the refuse-strewn motel lot. Didn't notice the Chevy Captiva Sport—weather mucked, but 2012, and a model only sold to rental fleets—that swung out a U-turn behind him, fell back, four cars between, and followed.

4.

THE AIR WARMED WITH a peekaboo morning sun between snow flurries; above freezing by noon, the sun retired, dark clouds marched in from the river. Encamped overhead. Oozed drizzle. Summoned fog, thick brown and greasy wherever it licked. Streaked. Clung. A day that every other year her boys and their cousins woke bright with anticipation, fought over the last Advent calendar window and started the *Why does this day take soooo long* vamp, the warmth of this Christmas Eve morning fattened the air inside the upstairs hallways and rooms and sat on beds and pinned the children with smothering pillows of sleep. Beaumont refused to go out to do his business since ten days ago, Charlotte had refused the dog their snowy rambles. Melody still didn't know why.

Beaumont whined from the porch. Melody came from the kitchen. For the fourth time, pushed open the screech-screen door. The dog stared, sniffed, whale-eyed Melody and trudged back to his bed beneath Doris's portrait.

"You'll have to go sometime!" Melody called after. Went back to the kitchen. Finished the orange rolls and bacon—both done in the oven—put them on the counter beneath the old furnace vent. Get the smell into the house's lungs. That was 10:30ish. Before 11:00, bounding footsteps pounded the stairs, Beaumont yipped and yapped, and her kitchen filled with the sound of scuffing chairs, cutlery, little food convos, and the final morning argument: whose turn to finish the Advent Calendar.

Now, after noon, breakfast cleared, kitchen cleaned, Paige-glowing/Melody-knowing, the pair worked together on Melody's Bûche De Noël.

"It takes ten hours?"

"If you want to do the best you can. It does."

"But we don't have ten hours."

"What do you think I've been doing in here the last two nights?"

"Didn't we all watch *Love Actually*?"

"Only the part where he learns Portuguese. I like my Christmas miracle with subtitles. Just to be sure." Melody pulled eggs out of the refrigerator. "I did the ganache last night and the sugared cranberries and rosemary, and the merengue mushrooms the night before."

"You're eating it all!" Little Silas from the porch where he and his brother and Leigh strung cranberry and popcorn garlands.

Melody didn't need to see them. "Share the popcorn ball, Jack!" To Paige as Melody began separating eggs: "You can mix the cake flour and cocoa, and these other things here—" she pulled two folded sheets of steno paper from her apron pocket. "I wrote my entire recipe for you this morning. You can keep it. Follow this part." She showed Paige where, and they set to work together, quietly and more like sisters than aunt and niece, and

Paige thought back to summer when she'd felt her future coming fast against her. The feeling had only increased. But looking at Melody's careful handwriting, how she'd taken the time to add green and red ink to draw holly leaves and berries at the end of the title, *Paige and Clive's Timeless Yule Cake,* and the feeling she'd had in July that she had not allowed herself time to appreciate what the future, hurtled into, would force her to leave behind—*that* was gone. She knew now because all that was behind her and Kingston, that grew inside her womb and gathered whole in new life would walk, smiling back at her, innocent, in the eyes of her child. It was like Merlyn, a way of purely living life backwards in forward motion.

"Chop-chop, Paige, it's still going to take four or five hours and we'll be prepping dinner as we go."

Paige looked at Melody and saw her as if Paige were Melody looking at her. "Time is sadness. Did you know that? Do you know what that means? I mean, is there anything good about that?"

Melody wiped her hands.

On the porch, Leigh belted *Hard Candy Christmas* with Dolly Parton.

Melody hugged Paige as Clive partially emerged in the kitchen hallway. Stopped in the doorway, unobserved.

Melody said, "Like something growing over time, if you care for it, give it the love it needs, I think sadness can be a real healthy seed for appreciation. Compassion. You know, for the good things and people in your life. Over time, sadness, cared for properly, heals parts of you that need healing and gives that extra little push of appreciation, life's unaccounted changes."

"Yeah. Right. Exactly what I thought." Paige rolled her eyes, obvious, and Melody swiped a little streak of wet flour from her cheek.

Clive *Merry Christmas Eve*'d them and busied himself with Paige's recipe. "You put cognac in this thing?"

"This year. It was Silas's suggestion."

The old man, having entered, stuck his head in the refrigerator. "Shouldn't this roast be getting to room temperature? Get the cake factory finished. And this needs to be medium rare—that was Vivi's request."

Paige brightened. "She'll do a service?"

"The woman's a priest. I'm not sure why else she'd be here, but if we feed her right she'll do the midnight show."

Paige, Clive, Melody touched each other with glances; Vivianne Tremelin had been seen coming and going at Foxtail Farm, late nights/pre-dawns summer through fall and not only Sundays to the chapel.

"Time to inspect my dragoons. Can't do the ornaments until the garlands are up. And Clive: when it's time for the whipped cream and liquor—" Silas tossed him his keys—"You'll go down to the cellar and get a new bottle of Timeless."

Clive felt time stop. "Just me?"

"If there are two Clive's under Melody's roof feel free to bring the other one."

The cake-making continued with Paige and Melody. Silas marshalled the children and calling Clive to join them, carried the garlands into the common room to decorate the tree.

Paige went onto the porch. Would pick some music. She jumped as a figure loomed from the fog. Reached for the screen door.

"Earth to Paige!" Morgan Eiger, her bewitching best friend, shuffled inside wearing a bright pink parka with a fur-rimmed hood. "What's with Miss Jumpy? And Merry Christmas back atcha-not-said." She carried a Neimann's bag brimming with wrapped gifts. She set to lining them up on a sofa. "Each one has nametags."

"Coming through!" Charlotte hustled in from the dining room gathered the popcorn bowl, the cranberry bag. Singsong: "Didn't make enough, Papa's getting grumbly, and Grandma Doris looks like she going to start laughing at us." Looking around, "Paige: you seen the yarn—Beaumont? You bad dog!"

Paige up beside her friend: "You startled me."

"I bet I did. You haven't seen me or called me or texted in like a month. I finally came here—it's like, this gross oily fog: it's just plopped right on your guys' place. Weird. And you know what else is weird?" Finished with the gifts, she turned, and Paige right there, they did cheek kisses. "The other day, I didn't come in 'cause I didn't want to go in the gate because I was creeped. There was this old dude, creepy-as-fuck, trying to climb your wall. I laid into my horn and he flipped me off, and I told him to go fuck himself, and that I was going to call the cops, and he'd get shot if he went over that wall. And he took off. Anyway, you haven't seen this dude?"

Paige shook her head. Whispered. "I don't have a present for you, but I know how you like the tea, and I got some to spill for you that's going to blow your mind. Come up to my room for a minute."

Wide-eyed delight. Morgan grabbed Paige's arm and pulled her toward the French doors to the dining room. Paige looked back to the kitchen. Melody stood, rigid in the doorway.

Distant: "Go on. I heard." Her eyes were on Charlotte. Color gone from her cheeks, cranberries dribbled from the bag all over the floor.

"Aunt Melody?" Charlotte trembled.

RANDY'S RAZZAMATAZZ DELIGHT – Total Liquidation! – Everything Must Go! A front window with hooker wigs. With plastic high heels. Pink chicken feather boas. And the cheapest quality lingerie you could purchase anywhere on the planet, faded from months/years of sunlight. A headless see-through dummy with a neon green afro on the neck stump, a Red Cross hat on top of that. It was—worse quality than the lingerie—a nurse get-up: cheapest quality in the universe. Pinned to the front a handwritten sign. "We Have Adult Halloween Costumes!" Out of his car, shoulders hunched in the cold, hands buried in his pockets, DA Calvin Kirby slow-walked past. Peered between crumble-edged panels of the rotting peg board displays. Third hooker shop Boone Kelso had gone into. First two, he'd come out empty-handed. This one, making a purchase. Some kind of outfit in a cellophane sleeve. Couldn't see what it was, but Boone Kelso wasn't finished. Pointed out a pair of long crimson gloves inside the counter. Added to the bag. Pointed out a small plastic headband with a red feather and a pink plastic jewel. Added to the bag.

Calvin Kirby jogged back to his Captiva as the clerk rang up Boone Kelso's purchases.

BEAUMONT'S VEINS ran with the blood of Piscataway wolf-dogs and his fog-beaded fur, down from the top of his head to his shoulder bristled every step of their wet walk to the holly grove.

"How do you know who he is? He said he knew Papa. And Grandma Doris."

"He did know them. I know how scary he looks, but he was once a famous artist. He had a family—a wife and daughter about Leigh's age. He painted your grandmother's portrait, so he did kind of know them. Once."

"How do you know that?"

Before Hal left he'd showed Melody his .38 snub nose revolver. A grab's-length from behind the pillows of their bed. Behind the mattress. A fitting rigged on the headboard; while Charlotte had leashed up Beaumont, Melody checked the cartridges in the pistol, the safety, tucked the gun in her jacket pocket. "It's just one of those things I've learned, living here. Is this the tree?"

Melody stepped in. Drizzle made the bark slick. Fog clung to the trunk like thick scum. The letters Boone Kelso carved, blackened from seeped/dead sap glared. Accused. Threatened.

One woman's light, one man's dark / Bound beneath the holly bark.

Berries red, Beaumont dead, / If a single word is said.

Melody read them silently. Met Charlotte's fearful gaze.

"I can see why—"

Loud: the sound of Melody's phone. A text. Charlotte yelped.

Beaumont growled. Melody quickly unhooked his leash clip. He circled the grove. Melody scooted Charlotte behind her. Reached into her pocket. Beaumont lifted his leg. Melody withdrew her phone.

"Will see all of you tonight. Presents for everyone."

Her device *dinged* again. A string of crown emojis.

Melody laughed. "That sure surprised us. It's Paige, we need to finish our cake. Thanks for showing me this. And don't worry too much about it. This guy is old and weird and likes to scare people, but he's not coming back. He's...just a weird old man."

"Should we tell Papa?"

"Get Beaumont."

Charlotte leashed the dog.

Melody switched the phone for the pistol inside her pocket. "We will. But let me, okay?"

"Okay. And I'm sorry I didn't tell anyone."

"Ah. It would scare me. But you knew it was a game. That's brave."

Melody kept behind Charlotte and the Claypoole hound the whole way back, her head on a swivel. But the fog was merciless. It trapped them in their own small circle and would not let go.

BEAUMONT WAITED until inside the mud room, leash off, paws braced, to give a full-body shake. Charlotte followed him back into the main part of the house, Melody's advice she make sure the hound had water trailing behind. "And tell Paige I'll be right back down with her."

Melody's parka went on its peg over the chest of car blankets.

"Ma'am, something just holds you back from doing the right thing."

Upstairs, her bedroom—

"The years churn and my calls and my letters keep going unanswered."

—behind the pillows, down between the mattress and the headboard: the pistol went back into its holster. She was ready to do what she should have done the first time he called, all those times he wrote.

"Guy like Boone Kelso, what all he did, and knowing you know what-all whatever it is you do, might not think twice about doing it again."

What better Christmas gift to my family than their safety; time I speak my truth.

Melody went through her desk. Her nightstand. The sewing room; she dug through her sewing basket. She'd torn apart every business card Calvin Kirby ever sent her. Thrown each one away. She went back. Sat on the edge of the bed. Hands shook. She hadn't been this scared since she pulled the trigger. Since her mother.

Her eyes went to the bedside clock. It was after three in the afternoon. Dinner was in the oven. She and Paige needed to make the whip cream filling for the Bûche De Noël—

Need to send Clive down for the Timeless.

The clock again. 3:18 pm. Her mind jumped. A memory.

4:14 am.

When I keep waking in the morning. Every time I shock awake from nightmares:

Killing my mother.

Haunted/taunted—my demon father.

4:14.

She slid open the nightstand drawer. Her Bible. Reached for the book. Riffled the pages. They split on a bookmark. A business card—backside up—as an underline.

"For if you keep silent at this time, relief and deliverance will rise for the Jews from another place... And who knows whether you have not come to the kingdom for such a time as this?"

She pulled the card. Before she turned it, remembered and knew. Carried the book since she was sixteen. Had the card since eighteen when she'd walked in, in Richmond, and chickened out the first time and Calvin Kirby said: *"Esther 4:14."*

Calvin Kirby, Esq; DA
Office of the District Attorney, Richmond, Virginia

Office phone. Email. And circled in blue ink: his cellular phone number.

5.

GOING ON FIVE O'CLOCK. Going fifty-five, southbound, Maryland Route 4. And the sun was going down, hurrying through drizzle clouds, to trade places with the cheese-faced smiler in the evening sky. The fog slithered between trunks of the dense snowy woods. Up the dead grass verge. Dervish-danced across the rural two-lane blacktop. The fog made the going tense, treacherous since the 301 interchange at Marlboro Meadows. Closer they got to St. Mary's County—the fog worsened. Still, it made Boone Kelso in the Subaru clunker a whole lot easier to tail and Calvin Kirby in his Captiva rental: whole lot harder to see.

Just south of Port Republic, Calvin Kirby's phone lit up. He slowed to take the call. Vague recognition of the number, couldn't place it for the couple seconds it took to answer and say, "Hello," but between his greeting and her first words, Kirby knew Melody Kingston had finally come to him. He added to the point-of-no-return silence a little encouragement. "Melody. Merry Christmas Eve and I'm awfully glad you're doing this."

"I know you know why I'm calling. I think you have for a long time."

"I need to hear you say it, ma'am. Not for any legal reason, any onto-the-record can't take it back, just for that private moment of honesty that will define our relationship, settling everything before, with a light shining out of the black place that we can both see by."

"A place of blackness. Only real way to say it. That past/present black wrecking ball you told me about? Swings forever."

Headlights from opposing traffic burst through the fog. Glared-up the viscous fog on his windshield. He naturally slowed. Boone Kelso's taillights dimmed in front of him.

"Tell me, Melody. You and me'll put a grip on that chain and slow that ball way-way down. You'd be surprised."

"My dad was beating my mother, Roberta Kelso, to death. He always beat her, but this was the finish. I was only ten, but I knew it. She knew. I took his gun to shoot him. Stop him. I shot and killed—" He heard the choke in her voice.

Kirby's speed slowed a bit more as, concentrating, made her the focus of his present. Waited for her to continue.

Boone Kelso's taillights grew smaller as his consistent speed increased the distance between them. Kirby watched them disappear into the enveloping fog.

Kirby kept rolling. Careful and waiting.

Melody said, composed and clear: "Sir, I shot and killed my own mother."

"I'm so sorry that happened to you. Sometimes our fear of the living force innocent ghosts to torment us."

"She's haunted me every moment of my life."

"Has she? Naw. That's your daddy's hand-puppet scaring you with shadows, dear. Her real ghost—whose always smiled on you—you've made her more happy tonight than...well, all the Christmas trees and presents, just about ever."

"That's kind of you to say so. Thank you, Mr. Kirby."

"So, why you choosing right now? 'Cause he ruined yours and my Thanksgiving, and this's a tit-for-holiday-tat?"

"Because he's coming here tonight. And I know he's bringing the gun. It's his only hold over me and my family. It's in Ziploc bag and it's got my fingerprints."

It was Kirby's turn to pause. "Okay. I know. He's driving a Subaru wagon. An old one, rusted silver paint job. He's headed down the Calvert County peninsula right now and I won't let him out of my sight. I won't let anything happen to you. Now or once I have him. So enjoy your Christmas—just don't open the gate for anyone other than an official police car. And I will keep in touch and you can call me anytime you want."

"Okay. And I'm sorry. For what I did."

"Mrs. Kingston, I'm going to need to ask you never to even think that again. The State of Virginia—and heaven's own authority—says you've nothing to be sorry for."

They traded goodbyes and Merry Christmas and disconnected.

Kirby sped up. Even from inside the disorienting fog, he could do the speed/distance/time calculus to quickly figure out, as he had cut speed to focus on Melody's call, Boone Kelso had used the opportunity to pull ahead. Meant he was onto him. DA Kirby increased his speed into the curve that led into the short, straight narrowing of road as Route 4 approached the bridge of St. Leonard Creek.

Calvin Kirby wasn't stupid. He saw the skid pattern coming off the icy bridge. Saw the snow muck tire splatter across the guardrail battered and twisted like old armor from numerous battle where it withstood the crash of motored steel from ice, from recklessness, drunk folk or high or Boone Kelso's case: every damn one of them. But Richmond DA Calvin Kirby was not a stupid man. He'd followed Boone Kelso all day through this shit, needed an extra hand if he wanted to tally up the curves and icy bridges they'd crossed over. Drinking—sure, he'd watched Boone do that—but no weaving, nothing reckless; Boone Kelso slowed every time they'd crossed a creek or hollow or overpass bridge.

This was staged.

Kirby slowed. Pulled over. Bridge's end. Front tires in the snow/earth/rock tire furrows. Headlights illumined the Subaru. Nose into the bracken and trees. No body hunched over the steering wheel; no Boone Kelso in sight.

PAIGE PUT THE ROAST into the oven. Couldn't wait for Melody to come down to finish the cake. Sent Clive for the Timeless while she whipped up the cream and now, Clive stood, key in hand at the cellar door, clutched by tendril sticky fingers of the strange brown fog; clutched by a dread that Silas sent him alone to find something entirely more than contraband cognac.

Key in the lock. Bolt turned: *clack.* Each footstep down the stairs weren't steps. They were confessions; each creak, each warped board groaning under time. Under pressure. Under weight they no longer cared to carry.

Every breath inside this dry and dusty tomb of fermented fruit and spent/seeped blood stank of the rot of inheritance. Was this—this Foxtail Farm—a legacy that he and Paige would emburden of their child and keep the rot rotting and the blood beneath the stones set in the floor, seeped between their seams into the hungry earth that in a land like this can never dry sufficiently enough to kill it—

That flicker on the ultrasound. That fast little pulse of beating life.

—would this become through their child's blood a perpetuance of corruption?

Last time, they'd played at *Notorious.* This time, the pit of his stomach, played something beyond his grasp and played it for keeps.

Clive stood at the shelf where the Timeless waited.

Madame Dieudonne: a clifftop cut-out against the blue-sky sunshine above diamond-dripping, sparkling sea. My Tortola. She'd made one of these French cakes one Christmas.

Hazelnut liqueur.

Why don't I grab that—what's-it-stuff—Frangelico? The bottle dressed up like the harmless Jesuit—or was it Dominican—priest?

He looked down the aisle.

The secret door to the Place of Blackness. Closed. Hidden. Forbidden. May as well have been gone from its hinges as he saw the glint of instruments of terror beyond it. The warm, close darkness of the worst secret of all.

He pulled down the Hennessy presentation case. Clutched the neck of the next bottle. A new bottle. It didn't fit properly into its slot and—

Don't take the obvious bet.

But what if the obvious bet's the real game?

Clive lifted the bait bottle. His fingers rubbed old dusty leather.

Don't notice. Leave it the fuck alone.

Clive placed the Baccarat bottle on the next shelf down. Lifted from its slot a small and scuffed leather-bound book. A code book written in Russian.

KIRBY WATCHED KELSO'S CAR—devoid of movement, void of life—five full minutes before he hit his hazards and stepped out into the cold. Cell phone; no weapon. Drizzle. Curling/licking fog. Greasy on the blacktop beneath his feet as, cautious, he stepped from the road. Didn't see any movement in the facing wood. Thankfully, Kelso's headlight were also on so if he was lurking, he wasn't too close.

Didn't mean Kriby dared move any closer. Closed his fist around his mobile device and kind of bounced it into the open palm of his other hand. Kind of a game of rock, papers, scissors with himself. Kept one eye on Kelso's vehicle. Looked at the phone.

Call it in now—staties, locals, medics—Boone Kelso gets hauled back to Alabama on the parole violation.

No murder charge.

No Richmond justice.

The true case will vanish into the red tape swamp of bullshit bureaucracy. Like it did the last time.

I walk over there now... Keep a careful eye. Just see if I can see the Ziploc, the gun. Call that in—a murder weapon—everything breaks my way.

Melody's way.

Roberta's way.

A look back over his shoulder. A car slowed. A window down. "You alright? Need any help?"

Half over his shoulder. One eye on the woods. "We're okay, friend. Just an icy slip. You have a nice Christmas!"

The car rolled on. Kirby activated his phone flashlight. Neared the back of the Subaru.

Another glance back. An eye to the foggy woods. Shone his light into Boone Kelso's car. Spent an extra second on the painter's tarp. No Boone Kelso beneath it. No Boone Keslo inside or out.

Glance up to the road. Drizzle. Fog. Empty.

Glance into the woods. Big drips from leaves and branches. Fog unmoving. Brown between trees.

Kirby swung out a little away from the vehicle as he moved to the driver's compartment. Door half-open. He crouched. Quick look back, quick look woods: nothing/nobody. Aimed his light across the seats, empty footwells, rising, driver's seat empty, rising angling his light onto the passenger seat.

Red sequins wink and sparkle back from the cellophane bag. Something lumped beneath the costume bag.

A step closer. Road look. Woods look. No Boone Kelso. Close enough to the driver's door to pull it wide. Get the light in. Get a better look.

Red sequins in a bag labelled: *1920s Flapper Slut. Size: Small.* A card taped to it: *Merry Merry Merry Doris.* A sketch of Charlotte. Innocent/young. Wearing the portrait dress.

Something in dirty plastic lumped beneath it.

Look to road/look to the woods/look deeper into the car.

Deep enough to reach...strain...reach farther. Kirby hit the perverse costume from the seat.

A pistol in a Ziploc bag.

A rush from the woods.

Kirby pushed off the driver's seat. Pulled out of the door.

Boone Keslo launched his entire mass into the car door. Slamming/folding Richmond DA Calvin Kirby backwards—half-sitting—into the seat.

Kelso lunged up from hands and knees. Kirby out of car, out from the door, two running steps—he's going for the bridge, the road, his car.

The 9-iron thrust between his feet stops/drops him face down. In the three seconds it took Calvin Kirby to push himself halfway up, the 9-iron was already beating his skull.

Hammer, hammer, hammer—snow snow-coned red—Kelso like a happy elf hammering away at his North Pole toy bench.

6.

THE KALEIDOSCOPE TURNS FORWARD where, in Christmas to come, a Christmas without a Yule log without its pyre, Paige would scroll photographs on whatever device that might yet be, and she would say, fond and sweet, "This is a good one of her. That's my Mommy."

And everyone agreed that night, when Gwen arrived, she carried with her a glow. Not happiness necessarily but a Christmas hopefulness, a confidence to step into something unknown and unfamiliar to her nature with faith.

"Gwen. You look graceful. Hand me your phone, Paige. Ladies, kids. Clive, you stand in the back with Silas. Hold on—" Reverand Vivi moved a chair from Doris's table. "I want to get everything you've done with this beautifully set dinner, Melody."

"Compliment Paige. She did most of it this year."

"I didn't."

Silas. "Take the picture."

Gwen. A little tug at her waist at the hidden button seam of her faux-coat dress. Red and green plaid, false pockets, flattening and flattering and svelte. But for the button, nothing else was hidden.

That was my *Mommy.*

She drank little, slathered Melody and Paige with compliments, and when Jack, or maybe it was Little Silas, teased Leigh over nonsense, Paige watched Gwen crouch beside Leigh and stroke her hair and whisper in her ear, "I'll tell you a little secret—" and did. And though Paige never learned what that secret was, she knew the big Leigh secret. Knew that secret probably tormented the worst parts of Gwen, and felt pride for her mother for leaning so far away from that aspect of her character and leaning into love. Leigh wrapped her arms around Gwen's neck, pressed her cheeks to Gwen's and said, "I've missed you, Mom. A lot."

Because it was Christmas, Charlotte and Leigh, Jack and Little Silas were allowed at the grown-up table where Leigh helped the twins on either side of her, cutting their meat, buttering their rolls, giving them extra jam.

Almost opposite in mood to Gwen, Melody radiated manic energy. Paige noticed her hands tremble with the roast tray. Noticed when Melody thought that no one would, she checked her cell phone. More than once.

Maybe Uncle Hal is supposed to call in.

Paige had more on her mind to worry about than that. And frankly, out of everyone in her family, Melody never needed worrying.

"You think I'll be able to do this?" Paige to Clive as soon as they'd pulled their chairs into the round edge of Doris's table.

He nodded her attention to the convex mirror hung beside the French doors.

Doris reflected in her portrait, the curved angle such that her expression clearly smiled; her hands offered Paige her flowers.

Vivi asked the blessing. Added special prayer and thanksgiving and protection for Michael, Lynn, and Hal, and as one, the family said, "Amen."

Conversation bright, they all skated the silver and gold surface of Christmas and America, and childhood dreams, and comedies, and Melody spoke, Paige thought, profoundly about Modern Hope and Ancient Hope. It caught the Reverand Tremelin a bit off guard.

"I like how you're thinking, Melody. But remember, all of it was prophesized in the Old Testament. Isaiah 53, most scholars believe prophesies Jesus' entire life, death, and resurrection. Jews would certainly know exactly what they were hoping for."

Melody thought about it a moment. "Maybe. But somehow the main twelve, surprised in the garden of Gethsemane, his own mother and Mary Magdalene wrecked and frightened by his execution and hoping to claim his body from the tomb—all hope lost—all his followers in Jerusalem, that whole crew must've forgotten their Isaiah. First Easter and all."

That cast a pall. Not at all like Melody. Until Silas laughed. Turned his laugh into a "Ho-ho-ho!" He bore down with his toothsome smile direct line of fire on Clive. "You've been fairly quiet all night, what say you as heir to the testament of Modern Christmas as written by the great Charles Dickens?"

Clive smiled back, teeth just as bright, like a couple of Claypoole hunting dogs about to test supremacy. Paige could do without that. Took her knife, turned her glass into a ringing bell.

"Oh, good," Gwen said. "I have an announcement. Something ginormous-important, Silas—" She paused for dramatic effect; an olive branch, a secret piece of intelligence, a willingness to bow before him and take her own crown of—

"Paige?" Silas bore on. "You rang the gong."

"Yes. Everyone raise a glass. To me and Clive—"

Gwen's golden vision of her Ossani/Chinese crowning secret dashed against her worst instincts and jealousies, and her insecurities and brittle pride refracted apart, sharp-edged as glass chips scattering beneath a turning lens. Thorns were all Silas handed out at this table.

"Paige! You are too young to get married!" Gwen snapped. "Clive you're already getting the full Kingston free-ride here—love your nobility, but honestly, babe, this—"

"Gwen." Clive: soft, even kind, obviously forgiving. "We're not getting married."

Gwen collapsed in her seat. Relief washed over her. Water over a fire. Washing the ash across the floor.

There's still time. I can pivot. Say something small. Gracious. Let them have whatever their stupid little announcement is.

The room exhaled with her. The house itself. Paige would always remember from that photograph of Gwen, the added whistle across the chimney top. They all heard it; the sound Papa and Aunt Linny claimed was Grandma Doris.

Gwen noted the little ripple of relieved laughter (at her expense). Just for a moment, all of it turned back to her control.

I'll regain the floor. My due respect can still come.

"What are you getting, Paige?" Charlotte almost knew.

Silas knew now. In that instant of knowledge, every dream and wish, every fear and nightmare, every false move or trapped step or bold error rose before his eyes like golden doors pulled open. He cut meat. Chewed thoughtfully. Chuckled to himself. "Guess I ho-ho-hoo'd too early. Mazel tov as Isaiah would say." He leaned across the table toward the children: "How's it feel to be aunts and uncles?"

Melody hugged Paige, widened her arm for Clive. Reverand Vivi kissed Silas's cheek. Gwen stared at all of them. No one was paying her the least bit of attention. The corners of her eyes burned. She'd been mad before, angry not to have her earned moment, her public family sacrifice of the fortune owed her by being a Kingston. That was over a silly wedding announcement—that wasn't even happening, but this? This changed everything. Calmly she stood.

Now they look. Good. Hear my voice.

"As your mother, I will not permit you ruining your life. You will fix this. And later, when you are ready and with the right guy—not this jobless, Caribbean parrot-head, man-slut—you will thank me."

Their eyes. All of them. I've gone too far.

"I've not been drinking. Either. That's how serious I am."

She shut her eyes and fired off two big tears, bracing for Silas's attack.

He stood up from Doris's table. "Gwen. This is Christmas, literally a night that celebrates birth." He handed Gwen her wine glass. Lifted his own. "Yours is the fear Melody spoke of. But fear is the mirror we hold to love. And you're not ready to see what's in yours."

They'll listen. They always listen. If I say it with love, they'll see I'm right.

Silas at his gentlest. His place of Doris. "Gwen? Will you raise a glass with me to Paige and Clive, their child to be; to Christmas?"

Gwen's eyelids lifted. She appeared taller than any had noticed before. Stronger. Calmer. "Paige: will you listen to me? Trust me?"

"Mom: don't go where you can't come back from. I love you and I'm begging you, Mom. Choose your words." Unlike her mother, mostly like Melody whose shoulder she felt against her own. Paige did not feel the pressure of tears.

"I'm going to take you to Planned Parenthood. You are going to thank me later, probably for the rest of your life—once you choose to step out of your childishness—or—" She toasted without any of them, all of them. Big drink. "I'll make my goodbye. To all of you. Now."

I'm not built for any of this. If it must end. Here it ends.

"Bye, Mom," Paige finished her. Kingston cruel.

Charlotte: "What's Mom saying? Mom, are you going to be here tomorrow?"

Leigh: "Mommy?!"

Gwen was finished. The glow she carried earlier: entirely gone. She left Doris's table. She left her family. Reverand Vivianne chased her, but Gwen was done with

Foxtail Farm—wished it ash—and vanishing into the fog, left that life behind.

THE TRADITION OF THE YULE LOG burning at Foxtail Farm went back to Christmas 1742, established by Silvanus Kingston III. It burned twelve days from Christmas morning until Three Kings Day when the Magi, who followed the Star of Bethlehem, delivered their holy gifts to the newborn Jesus. It wasn't until Silas's father—Harry Kingston—that the Kingston log was lit one night earlier to burn for thirteen days; Harry didn't care much for Kings, a bunch of messy avian gifts, or the tomfoolery of milk maids and leaping lords in tights as a Reformation intelligence operation to teach the Catholic catechism as a secret code. Harry liked American Christmas. And American Christmas kicked off Christmas Eve with the tree and a first round of presents.

Harry could recontextualize like the best. Twelve days equaled twelve apostles. You subtract one for Judas. Eleven. Add one back for Matthias. Then comes Paul. He's thirteen and, Harry argued, leaning into his Episcopalian denomination, Paul's primacy over the Catholic's Peter. (Harry didn't like Popes any more than kings.) So, number thirteen was the most important; *"I'm adding a thirteenth day to the log and Silas can open the present of his choice Christmas Eve because I say so."* Amelia, his wife, was on board without the silly biblical gymnastics, but secretly delighted in working her husband out.

"Thirteen is an unlucky number, dear."

"Say witches and fortunetellers!"

"Says King James of his Bible."

"America and Americans live to reject British kings!"

At Christmas, especially, Silas remembered his parents and with fond amusement. After Gwen's dramatic exit, his smile and force-of-will good cheer led the family to the common room; stuffing the newspaper, wedging in the kindling, he gave Clive the lighter to ignite the blaze.

Thirteen is an unlucky number. Everyone knows it.

But Silas liked the creative anarchy of his father. He liked that King James *did* make thirteen biblically unlucky pointing out "as gospel" that thirteen in the Bible emphasized rebellion and apostasy. Silas sat squarely with the patriots and their distaste for British monarchy for rebellion and, damn it, apostasy, and he would be happy to point out—if anyone bothered to ask him—Jesus was a Jew. To the Jews, thirteen is the numerical representation of infinite mercy. *Hashem*: the Thirteen Attribute of Mercy. Plus, and he'd never tell anyone this: the children—his kids once ago, now his grandchildren—

"My lambs! Just look at you!" Doris echoes.

—felt the extra-special of being Kingston and getting Thirteen Days of Christmas while everyone else and their Drummers Drumming only got twelve.

Clive frustrated over the log not catching and Paige received her first gift when Papa didn't mock him, but reached in past the budding flames to clear some ash—

"Papa!" Melody. "Not your hand. Please. It's fire. Use the poker."

"I'm always careful." He answered her but his eyes met Clive's. Held.

He showed Clive where to stuff more pine twigs. The fire blazed.

He carried the colonial serving table used in this family tradition at least two hundred years, up to the stairway landing. The curved wall that faced Doris's portrait. He smiled at her as Melody brought in the Bûche De Noël centered on James Jesus Angleton's wedding gift of the scrying glass. Placed it on the mahogany serving table. Heirloom. Inlaid surface of geometric patterns, star-shaped lily flowers, bloodwood and redheart and maple in contrasting shades of the spectrum from pink to darkest crimson. Dragon-claws clenched round globes for table feet. This year, without Michael, without Lynn, and without Hal, Paige and Clive took charge of the grandchildren. Helped them light their brands from the large, flaming log sticking out of the common room fireplace. Charlotte, Leigh, Little Silas and Jack—as excited as they were serious—held their burning brands in file at the common room door and Paige mimicked her father's cry of many years (Michael's spirit closed in around her; she knew if she looked deeply in the Doris mirrors surrounding, looked hard enough and with heart, she would glimpse Daddy there): "Lights! Cameras! Action!"

Angleton whispers in Silas's ear: "Action!"

Silas fires the pistol.

Internal gears unwind a spring; staccato sprocket; ticka-ticka *tickle of light and shadow store upon celluloid inside.*

Silas shut off all the lights inside Foxtail Farm plantation house.

"I think we are in rats' alley where the dead men lost their bones."

Candlelight flickered from the dining room. Doris's round table. Small flames danced out the common room doorway where Paige held the door half-closed.

Melody's phone lit up, too. Inside her apron pocket. It vibrated with a silent call. The energy that is fire was the pent up white-burning electricity in her every cell, alternating a current all night inside her of dread and expectation. A peek.

Calvin Kirby's number glowed on her screen.

Expectation washed her with relief, fire became warm inside her. Hope. Natural, not electrical; ancient not modern. She let the call go to voicemail. Clapped her hands. Pressed them, balled into fists against her smile. Silas saw this and was glad.

Clive slipped through the door.

Silas sang, hearing Doris sing silently with him, hearing his father, whose voice had been robust and always sounded ready for humor. Heard the voice of his grandparents, dimly. *"The boar's head in hand bear I—"*

My mother, Amelia: "Harry, you do know that is as British and kings and queensy a song as you could possibly sing!"

Harry Kingston: "Bah, humbug, Lady. I've always liked a few of them."

"Dickens and Scrooge."

"Churchill and King Arthur!"

"Bedecked with bays and rosemary, / And I pray you, my masters, be merry, / Quot estis in convivio."

Paige, lighting the way with her own burning pine knot, shepherded the children out of the common room and through the front hall. The mirrors caught them all. Doris posed/poised like a queen. The infinity illusion of facing glass made them appear an army of firebringers marching forth. One by one they filed, lamb-like, up the stairs to the portrait landing. Each lit their candle in the Yule log cake. Melody blew out each brand in turn. Ash floated on the house's breath. Each child carried their gray-tipped stick down to join Silas. Clive stood next to him and filmed on his phone.

The old man leaned in. "You found the Timeless to your liking?"

"I found what you sent me for. Want to be a chum and tell me what to do with that?"

A sharp edge on Silas's laugh.

"That's about what I expected."

But Silas added this: "A wife. An unborn child. It started there for me."

Fire's illuminations stretched up the portrait canvas. Higher until it painted the edge of char where Doris took the plunge.

Paige added the last flame to the largest candle. Watched Melody as the fire transferred wood to wick. Melody's smile tightened and Paige told herself it was "Hal nerves" and not the over-the-shouldering at the quiet shadow she hadn't shook since she and Charlotte had come back inside with Beaumont.

Reverend Vivianne, also filming from the dining room door, exclaimed, "My goodness. Silas, you Kingstons are all quite dramatic." The shadows from the landing rail fell long across the floorboards. The firelight stretched higher now, licking the walls. "Aren't you afraid not to have a fire extinguisher on hand?"

"House is afraid of fire."

Melody surreptitiously checked her phone. Missed call, no voicemail. Her gut tightened. Calvin Kirby wasn't the type to skip a message.

Beaumont yowled.

Cake candles blazed.

Melody tucked away her phone. Carried the cake on the sorcerer's mirror; its twenty-four circular reverse convex optics drew light from the entire house. Threw it around to magical effect. Everyone followed her back into the dining room. Took their seats at Doris's table and devoured the desert ritualized as a path to good luck and prosperity.

Melody's phone vibrated in her apron pocket. A second to check. No voicemail. A text from Calvin Kirby's number:

Lawyer's out. Just you n me n them now. Give young Doris a smooch. Merry Christmas, girl.

Epilogue

At Lyceum Marrow, Oberaufseherin Frau Irmgard Kohler, served as senior matron of Haus Eichelberg, the Middle Cycle girls' dormitory. She'd felt horrid delivering the news to fourteen-year-old Alina Voronina, bitter news that her flamboyant, careless mother, couldn't find the time for her Christmas Eve visit. A heartless Russian gangster's widow. Those oligarchs. Those people. An albino, too. Ick. Too many of their children at Marrow already, too many thick-necked bodyguards skulking across the border in Stein am Rhein.

Alina was a strange child. Bred in Moscow but behaved like she'd been shaken from the pages of a Russian fairytale. In manner and comportment, the Voronina girl chose—and conspicuously so—to keep apart from others. Girls and boys alike. Scholastically, she achieved what was required. Nothing more. Physically capable, she excelled in general athletics. Refused to compete on any team. Chose equestrian studies as her necessary sport but, Frau Kohler suspected, more to understand the horses than to bend them. Conquer them.

Alina Voronina was a provisional placement; Frau Kohler expected the girl would vanish in a year or two—none of the female gangster offspring needed to complete their education, bred for other uses. And since Alina remained quiet, solitary, and never caused trouble, she was already half-faded from Frau Kohler's mind when Alina took her Christmas Eve dinner, lonely and alone.

Received permission to miss the Haus Eichelberg mixer with the holdover Middle Cycle boys from Haus Falkenstein. Retired early to her room. And no one thought twice; she had trained them not to.

At eleven o'clock, the accident happened.

The boilers in both dormitory houses failed. Scalding water flooded showers, hallways, bedrooms, stairwells—all at once. Herr Asendorf triggered the alarms to evacuate all stay-behind students to the Middle Cycle gymnasium. Frau Kohler called their HVAC contractor. The line was disconnected.

Panicked, she searched online. A new plumbing company—satellite office, based in Schaffhausen, across the Swiss border. Reputable. Well-regarded.

The emergency technician answered at once. Almost as if he'd been waiting. Understood the situation completely. Sounded confident. Sounded prepared. Promised a rapid solution.

Frau Kohler sighed relief. Hung up. Sat back and—since it was only once a year—threw back three quick shots of Rumple Minze.

Fog rolls off the Rhine.

Hiss of tires.

Gleam of wet stone.

Twin beams of halogen light dazzle plowed/tended snowbanks. The Cistercian priory looms, grand and airless, a place where even the stones forgot how to breathe.

Under the pale gleam of the Christmas Star, Michael Kingston drove the white Mercedes Sprinter through the gates of the Lyceum Marrow. His headlights swept the school's crest picking out the carved words—

Ad Ossa Fidelis. Faithful to the Bone.

The motto stretched in warped shadow across the frost-slick stones. Disappeared as the van rolled into the dark of Christmas morning.

About The Author

Award-winning novelist Michael Frost Beckner began a Hollywood career as writing assistant to Academy Award winner Barry Levinson on "Good Morning, Vietnam" and "Rain Man". In 1989, Beckner's script for "Sniper" launched a military-thriller franchise now in production on its eleventh sequel. Three consecutive record-breaking spec script sales and three films later, Tony Scott directed Beckner's original screenplay "Spy Game." An international hit that paired Robert Redford and Brad Pitt as CIA partners and rivals, it is now a classic in the espionage genre.

The pilot for Beckner's CIA-based television drama "The Agency" for CBS, predicted Osama bin Laden's terror attack and the War on Terror four months before 9/11. In that series alone, Beckner would go on to predict three more international terror events.

Having penned close to 100 original screenplays, adaptations, and teleplays in the employ of every major film studio, television network, and cable outlet, he is a Hollywood institution.

As a commentator on American espionage, Beckner has appeared on CNN, Fox News, CBS News, TF1 in France, and as a featured guest of Bill Maher on HBO.

www.ingramcontent.com/pod-product-compliance
Lightning Source LLC
Chambersburg PA
CBHW050528110726
47899CB00005B/1638
* 9 7 9 8 9 9 2 9 9 3 2 2 6 *